HER
FROZEN
HEART

BOOKS BY STACY GREEN

HER
FROZEN
HEART

STACY GREEN

bookouture

Published by Bookouture in 2022

An imprint of Storyfire Ltd.
Carmelite House
50 Victoria Embankment
London EC4Y 0DZ

www.bookouture.com

ISBN: 978-1-80314-696-6
eBook ISBN: 978-1-80314-695-9

I do not wish women to have power over men; but over themselves.

MARY SHELLEY

Dedicated to women everywhere. We dissent.

Whoever fights monsters should see to it that in the process he does not become a monster. And if you gaze long enough into an abyss, the abyss will gaze back at you.

FRIEDRICH NIETZSCHE

PROLOGUE
BLACK FRIDAY

Kesha struggled against the twine around her wrists. Her efforts only tightened the knot. The twine had shredded her skin. Good. The more DNA she left in this miserable piece of hell the better.

"You're only making it worse." The man lounged in the doorway of the dingy room, shirtless. Her fingernails had left angry, red scratches down his chest. She prayed enough skin had been collected for the cops to find the man who'd kidnapped her.

"I told you if you didn't fight, I'd let you go when the time was right." He stepped toward the bed. Kesha drew her legs to her chest, fighting sobs. She knew he was lying. He wouldn't let her go after the things he'd done to her.

And deep down, she wasn't sure she wanted to live after the hours and hours of hell he'd put her through. When he wasn't attacking her, he'd drugged her. Black plastic covered the lone window in the room. Between the lack of sunlight and the drugs, Kesha had no idea how long she'd been here.

He sat down on the edge of the bed and trailed his fingers over her naked skin. She recoiled, ashamed of her sweaty, injured body. Dried blood caked her inner thighs. Pain rippled through her lower abdomen.

"If you're going to do that to me again, just kill me now," she choked out.

He stopped caressing her. "All in due time."

"My name is Kesha." She fought to speak over the ache in her throat. "I'm only seventeen. I don't have siblings. My parents..." The words caught in her throat. She'd never see her parents again. She'd never have a girls' day with her mom or watch football with her dad. Her parents would never recover from Kesha's death.

The man smiled. "Are you trying to humanize yourself so I won't kill you?"

Kesha couldn't answer. His hand had started roaming again.

"Don't feel bad," he said. "It's a survival instinct. It might work on a normal person, but not me."

She couldn't stop the tears from rolling down her face. "Why not?"

"Because I'm far from a normal human being. I'm evolved. I understand life and death on a level most don't. Animals hunt for prey. Humans used to do the same until they got lazy and started raising animals to murder. Now man hunts wild animals for sport." He leaned closer, his lips grazing her skin. "Why shouldn't I do the same?"

ONE

FRIDAY, DECEMBER 24

"It's snowing again. We already have ten inches on the ground, and this stuff is almost like sleet." Rory set a pile of mail on the counter and leaned over Nikki's shoulder. "Is that gingerbread cookie batter? I should taste it and make sure—"

She blocked his reach with her elbow. He'd already eaten enough sweets over the past few days to put a normal person into a sugar coma. "Back off. These are for Santa and your parents."

"What about those rum balls?" he asked.

"You can have a few, but not many. They're Mark's favorite. Lacey wanted to make them for him."

Lacey climbed back on the stool she'd put next to Nikki. "I just hope nobody gets drunk eating the cookies," she said with serious eyes. "Because when Mommy drinks rum, she gets goofy."

"Yes, she does." Rory patted Nikki's rear end. "Among other things."

Her cheeks burned at his husky tone. "Stop it."

He laughed. "Which cookies are for Santa, Lace?"

"The plain round ones. I put sprinkles on some." Her happy smile faded. "I don't know if I should put out milk or soda."

"I thought Santa preferred milk," Rory said.

Nikki kissed the top of her daughter's head. "Tyler always encouraged her to leave soda, because Santa probably got tired of milk."

"I see," Rory said. "Well, if your dad said so, then it's probably true. And I bet Santa looks forward to your house every year just for the soda."

"Maybe," Lacey said. "If he comes."

"What do you mean, if he comes?" Nikki asked. "You've been a pretty good girl this year, haven't you?"

She shrugged. "I guess, but everything's different now. Santa might not be able to find me."

"Of course he will," Nikki said. "We already talked about this, sweetie. Santa knows everything."

"And just in case he somehow forgot where you were, I sent him a letter a while ago with this address and told him he needed to stop here to see Lacey Hunt." Rory beamed at her.

Nikki could see the torment in Lacey's eyes. She wanted to be happy and excited for Santa, and she was, but when thoughts of her father crept in, so did the guilt. Lacey had told her last week that she felt bad celebrating Christmas without Tyler, especially since he wouldn't have any more Christmases.

After they'd cried together, Nikki had gone into her photos folder on the computer and showed Lacey her favorite pictures from every Christmas since Lacey had been born. Even after they'd divorced, Nikki and Tyler had spent Christmas together with Lacey. Tyler thrived during the season—he loved looking for the perfect gifts, and he always knew exactly what would make Lacey wild on Christmas morning.

"Your daddy would be heartbroken to know you weren't enjoying Christmas," Nikki had told her.

"Even if Rory's here and he isn't?" Lacey had asked.

"Yes," Nikki had answered firmly. "He would be relieved to know we had someone like Rory to be here since he can't be. You understand no one will ever replace Daddy, right? Rory doesn't want to do that, and he doesn't expect you to feel that way. He just wants you to be happy and safe."

Now, Rory gently picked Lacey up off the stool and set her on the counter so they were at eye level. "I know this is a really tough time for you, Bug. It's okay to be excited about Christmas and sad about your dad at the same time."

Lacey rubbed her teary eyes. "I miss him so much."

Nikki's heart broke as she gathered the little girl into a tight hug. "Me too, but Daddy's still here with us. He's watching over you."

Lacey shrugged. "You really believe that?"

"Yes," Nikki said. "You remember that my parents died when I was sixteen, right?"

"Murdered, like Daddy."

Nikki's mother used to tell her that God never gave people any more than they could handle, but six-year-old kids shouldn't even know what murder was, let alone grieve their loved one because of the actions of a callous psychopath. Were murder and abhorrent cruelty really part of God's so-called will?

"Every Christmas after that was tough, but the first one without them was brutal. My aunt said I should I ask my parents to show me they were still here, watching over me, by giving me a sign. But not just any sign, a specific one that would mean something to my parents and me. I thought it was crazy, but I tried it anyway."

"What did you ask them to show you?" Lacey asked.

Nikki grinned. "A blue jay, because Mom thought they were a beautiful nuisance, and Dad loved how tough they were. And you know what, within a couple of days, a blue jay started nesting in the tree next to my aunt's house."

"Really?" Lacey asked, wide-eyed.

Nikki nodded. "Remember how your dad loved cardinals? He called them redbirds, because that's what his grandma called them."

Lacey nodded excitedly. "Should I ask Daddy to bring me some cardinals?"

"To show you he's always with you," Nikki said. "Make sure you include that part."

"Should I do it now?"

"If you want to," Nikki said.

Rory moved out of the way, and Lacey hopped down to the stool and then to the floor. "I'm going to get my boots and coat."

"Start in the backyard." Rory's eyes were on Nikki. "I still need to shovel the front, and the step is really slick."

"Okey dokey." Lacey hurried off.

When she was out of earshot, Rory pulled Nikki close. "I happen to know there are at least two pairs of cardinals nesting in the big evergreen in the backyard," he whispered in her ear.

"Me too." Nikki leaned against his strong chest. "I feel a little guilty for making that up, but I want her to be able to enjoy tomorrow."

He kissed her cheek. "Some lies are worth telling. She'll see the birds and feel better."

Lacey's boots thumped down the hall. "I'm going to the backyard."

"Be careful," Rory said. "The snow's getting heavy and make sure you put on your boots and hat... actually, I'll just go with you. Unless you don't want me to, which is totally fine."

Lacey looked at Nikki and rolled her eyes. "Boys ask too many questions. Come on, Rory. We can play in the snow and look for the birds."

Nikki pressed her lips together to keep from laughing. Rory cared so much about her daughter, and nothing warmed Nikki's heart more than hearing the two of them giggling and playing in the next room. While the cookies baked, she quickly put together her hash brown casserole to bring to dinner at the Todds', keeping an eye on the kitchen window so she could see Rory and Lacey in the backyard. He fell flat in the snow, and Lacey rushed to cover him.

She flipped through the mail, surprised to see a letter for her since she still got most of her mail at her house in St. Paul. Her heart faltered when she saw the return address.

Oak Park Heights prison, Minnesota's only Level Five maximum security prison, current home of the cop who'd murdered George Floyd a year ago, along with the man who'd murdered Nikki's parents and the Frost killer responsible for the deaths of six women and Tyler Hunt.

Nikki stared at the envelope as though the handwriting would tell her the identity, but she didn't have a clue. Should she open it or throw it away?

"If you toss it, you'll just be digging it out of the trash in the middle of the night," she said to the empty kitchen. Since all forms of communication were searched before leaving or going into the prison, the envelope had been opened and resealed, making it easy for her to tear it open now.

Her eyes went straight to the bottom of the one-page letter to see who it was from.

OLIVER, your half-brother

With shaking hands, she quickly read the letter, which consisted of a few paragraphs about prison life and a reminder that she still had a living family member and that he wished she would come visit.

"Rat bastard." Nikki shredded the letter into bits and tossed it in the garbage, along with the envelope. She'd dealt with enough serial killers and all-around vile people that Oliver's manipulative tactics didn't surprise her. He must have known she wouldn't consider visiting or even acknowledging him as a biological relative, and he'd sent the letter to get under her skin and remind her of his permanent impact on her life.

Anger coursed through her, but Nikki managed to control her breathing before her rage bubbled over. She wouldn't give Oliver the satisfaction of ruining the day.

Nikki grabbed three of the rum balls and stuffed all of them into her mouth. She'd made three dozen, so there were plenty left for Mark to enjoy. Right now, getting drunk off rum cookies sounded like the perfect way to spend her afternoon.

Nikki's phone rattled on the counter, and her heart dropped when she saw Sheriff Miller's name on the screen. He wouldn't call on Christmas Eve unless something bad had happened.

"Happy holidays, Kent." Nikki kept her tone light and crossed her fingers he wasn't about to ask her for help with something terrible.

"Same to you, Nikki. Listen, I know it's Christmas Eve, but I've got a situation out at Big Marine Lake. A bad one."

"Drowning?" Nikki asked. The ice fishermen were out of their minds, as far as she was concerned, especially the ones bold enough to drive their heavy trucks out on the lake.

"An ice fisher caught human remains," Miller said. "He recognized her as Kesha Williams. Still waiting to confirm that."

Kesha had disappeared from the Mall of America last month, and the Bloomington police had made very little headway in the investigation. Nikki had thought about calling and offering her team's assistance, but her partner Liam's absence meant she was even more overloaded. Nikki had decided the police would call if they needed her help.

Now she felt sick to her stomach with regret.

"The ice fisherman recognized her face?" Nikki knew cold water greatly slowed decomposition, but surely Kesha hadn't been dead very long if the fisher was able to recognize her. "Have you seen her yet?"

"The divers are headed out on the water now," Miller said.

"We're short-staffed right now. Reynolds and I are at the scene. I hate to ask given the holiday—"

Nikki had already covered her casserole and turned off the oven. "It's okay. Big Marine Lake, you said?"

"At the North Access Point," Miller said. "DNR forest wardens are helping us keep the area blocked off. I'm trying to keep the news out of the media, at least until we can get an official ID. Her family lives ninety minutes away, but I've got their local PD on standby in case we're able to confirm it's Kesha."

"I'll be there as soon as I can."

Nikki went to the back door and called for Rory, who was in a serious snowball fight with Lacey. After the first big snow of the year, he and Lacey had gone to the store and purchased two snowball shooters. Nikki was surprised they hadn't broken from heavy use yet.

Rory called time out and jogged to the house. "Her aim's getting better." His grin faltered when he saw Nikki's expression. "Someone's been murdered, haven't they?" Without waiting for an answer, Rory told Lacey he'd be right back out and followed Nikki to the bedroom. She quickly shed her Scottie Dog fleece pants and T-shirt for jeans, thick socks, and an oversize cashmere sweater. Between it and her winter coat, Nikki should be fine in the cold for a while.

"It's supposed to snow for a few more hours," Rory said. "It's thick and heavy too."

"I've got hat, gloves, all of that in the jeep," Nikki told him. Her winter hiking boots were the best choice for walking on ice, and even then, Nikki would be lucky not to fall on her face. "Someone caught human remains on Big Marine Lake and identified them as that high school student who disappeared from the Mall of America on Black Friday. No official ID, though, so that's between us for now."

Big Marine Lake was about twenty minutes from Stillwater, in the northern part of Washington County. It was one of the largest lakes in the county, near the tiny community of Marine on St. Croix. The lake was popular year-round, but its location at the Big Marine Park Reserve, a large nature area, gave the lake an isolated feel.

"Jesus," Rory said. "Is that the one—"

"That I could have offered assistance with and didn't? How'd you guess?"

"Babe." Rory trailed behind her as she gathered her things. "That's not your fault. You didn't have the manpower." He wasn't wrong. Nikki's team was a small, elite unit within the major crimes division of the Minnesota FBI office, utilizing her training and experience as a profiler on the area's most complicated cases. If Nikki's team accepted every case that came across her desk, none of them would ever sleep.

"I still should have offered," Nikki said. "It may not have made a difference, but we'll never know, will we?" She yanked a brush through her dark waves, trying to ignore the deluge of crushing blame currently washing over her. Every good cop struggled with guilt over decisions in their career, but Nikki knew what it felt like to be on the other side. Her first experience with death had been her parents' murders, and over the years, the blame and guilt Nikki carried from that night infiltrated every murder she worked. That's probably why she remembered the names of every murder victim she'd encountered since her first day on the job.

"Big Marine Lake." Rory stood in the doorway, looking worried. "I built a couple of houses there several years ago. I bet the road out there won't be cleared. Our road isn't great right now. But the main highway should be fine." Rory lived in the house he'd grown up in, its rural property adjacent to the farm Nikki had lived on until her parents died. The road used to be all gravel, but the county had finally put down concrete this past summer. "The roads around the lake probably won't be very good."

"My jeep can handle it." Nikki glanced out the window where Lacey had been playing in the snow and keeping an eye out for cardinals. "I'm going to tell her the sheriff needs my help because he doesn't have enough people, but I'll back in time for our Christmas Eve dinner at your folks'."

Rory looked doubtful. "I'm all for fudging details but do you really think you'll be back? Normally a case like this means you're working around the clock."

"It's Christmas Eve afternoon," Nikki said. "The FBI office is closed, and Courtney's team has the day off since Christmas falls on a Saturday this year. She'll come in on Sunday, but I don't know about her team. The medical examiner's office is probably operating with minimal staff too. Whatever the situation is at the lake, our options are limited right now."

Nikki remembered her mentor at Quantico scolding her when she'd wanted to work a case on Christmas Day. "The victim is dead, the family informed, and we're working on the case file. Even workaholic profilers need to take the holiday off, Nicole," he'd told her.

"I'll keep you posted on when I'll be home." She'd already made the hash brown casserole, and the pre-cooked ham wouldn't need more than an hour or so in the oven. "You might have to heat up the casserole, though, and take it to your parents'."

"Don't worry about it," Rory said. "I can take care of it."

The back door slammed open as Lacey rushed into the kitchen. "Mommy, I saw a cardinal! A fat, red one. He looked straight at me and sang his song. I asked Daddy to show me he was still here, and he did. He is watching over us."

Relief washed through Nikki. "That's wonderful, Bug. I knew he'd find a way to show you."

Lacey's grin faltered. "Why are you getting ready to leave?"

"Sheriff Miller needs my help finishing up paperwork,"

Nikki lied. "Everyone in his office has left, so I told him I'd come help."

"When will you be home?"

"As soon as I can," Nikki said.

Doubt lingered in Lacey's eyes. "Promise?"

"Promise."

TWO

Nikki cursed and turned the windshield wipers on high. Fat snowflakes poured from the sky, and the pickup truck in front of her churned up even more off the road. What should have been a twenty-minute drive had turned into thirty, and she still had a few miles to go.

She glanced in her rearview mirror and spotted a dirty, white SUV coming up fast behind her. Nikki gripped the steering wheel as the SUV cut over into the left lane and sped up, easily passing her and the truck in front of Nikki, despite the looming curve. "Idiots," she muttered to herself. "God forbid they worry about anyone else on the road."

Nikki turned the radio to a local affiliate for Minnesota Public Radio and one of the few stations that played something other than top-forty music. The station also provided frequent weather updates during winter storms.

"In breaking news, a body believed to be the remains of Kesha Williams, missing since late November, has been discovered at Big Marine Lake in Washington County. The sheriff's office and Department of Natural Resources have closed the area off, and divers have been spotted on site."

"What the hell?" Nikki couldn't believe the information had leaked so quickly. "How does the media have that information already?" Miller had told her that only he and Reynolds, along with select members of the dive team, were aware of the remains, along with the DNR who'd been working on site.

She slowed and turned right onto an even more narrow two-lane road that bordered the northwest side of the big nature reserve. Nikki thought she could see the lake through the bare trees, but the blowing snow made it impossible to see how many cars were in the parking area. She nearly missed the turn, but she'd been driving so slowly the jeep barely fishtailed as she righted the wheel.

"Are you kidding me?" she shouted to the empty jeep.

News vehicles filled the small gravel parking area at the north entrance of Big Marine Lake. Local network affiliates had sent reporters, who, along with their camera people, had taken up position near the mouth of the lake, all vying for the best visual. As soon as her tires hit the icy lot, every head swiveled in her direction, and like seagulls desperate for their next bit of free food, they headed toward her.

Cursing, she cut right and squeezed into an opening between Miller's SUV and the dive team's van. Between the poor condition of the skinny, winding road leading to the parking lot and her apprehension over what she was about to encounter, her nerves were a jumbled mess.

Nikki grabbed her things and got out of the jeep before the media could surround her. She double-checked that her phone and latex gloves were in her coat pocket and then held up her hands at the encroaching throng.

"No comment, guys."

"But Agent Hunt—" A young reporter emerged from the same white SUV that had whipped by Nikki minutes earlier.

"I just got here," she snapped. "It's Christmas. Stop looking for the big story and enjoy your holiday. And stop driving like an idiot." Nikki brushed past all of them. As pushy as the reporters and their camera people could be, they'd worked in the area long enough to know not to challenge Nikki—yet, anyway.

Free of the crowd, she headed toward the lake access. Feet shuffled behind her, and Nikki imagined the group moving together behind her in unison like a determined pack of hunting dogs.

Several camera-mounted tripods, each from a different station, had been placed to the right of the ramp that led into the water. Fortunately, a DNR truck along with two Minnesota Department of Natural Resources deputies blocked direct access to the lake.

"Agent Hunt's the only one who gets past this point." The female DNR officer nodded at Nikki. "They're waiting for you. We'll deal with these guys."

A football field away, crime scene tape surrounded the white tent that had been set up over the dive area. At least there wouldn't be any footage of the remains being retrieved from the depths of the lake.

"Thanks," Nikki said, trying to hide her nerves. This time of year, most people parked in the lot and took smaller ATVs or walked out to their ice shack, but the dive team had taken a couple of amphibious vehicles to the recovery area.

Frost had used a similar vehicle when he killed Nikki's childhood friend and left her body up north for the rangers to find. He'd also planned to use it to escape with Nikki and Lacey after he'd kidnapped her daughter and killed Tyler. Nikki would have drowned that day if it weren't for Liam's girlfriend, Caitlin, and ever since, she'd been nervous around water. She still had nightmares about sinking into the deep lake, unable to save herself or Lacey. A few inches of ice made water even more terrifying.

Out on the ice, Miller waved his arms and motioned for her

to join them, his bright orange winter hat a beacon in the snow. Nikki wished that Liam were here. His calming presence would make things a lot easier, but he was still recovering from post-concussive syndrome and limited to desk duty. Nikki made sure she had her cell phone, notebook and pen tucked into her coat pockets. She grabbed the life jacket the DNR officer offered and made sure it was secure. Heart pounding, she started out on the ice, penguin-style as snow whirled around her.

Just put one foot in front of the other, she told herself. *Plenty of people heavier than you have walked out on this ice and been fine. Worst-case scenario, you fall on your ass and it'll be on the evening news.*

Nikki's left foot slid, and she stuck out her arms to keep her balance. Miller walked confidently towards her, his wool hat pulled down to his eyes.

"Please tell me you have a spare set of ice cleats," Nikki said. Miller's family were into everything outdoors, and the back of his SUV was always loaded with seasonal necessities.

Miller held up a pair of slip-on ice cleats. "They're medium."

"My feet are size eight, so that should work. Thanks." Nikki held onto Miller's arm as she shimmied the cleats onto the bottom of her boots. She'd never worn cleats before, but Nikki could tell the short spikes gripped the ice a lot better than her regular boots. She let go of Miller and carefully fell into step next to him. "Where are they at on recovery?"

Dives were usually planned in advance, especially in sub-zero temperatures, but in Nikki's experience, protocol was often broken for missing kids. The task might be miserable, but in cases involving children, every available diver wanted to recover the victim ASAP for the family.

"They just finished bringing her up," Miller said grimly. "Her hands and feet have been cut off. The rest of her body was in a black bag, but the weights that had been fixed to her legs somehow slipped out of it, so the body had started to come off the bottom of the lake. That's how the ice fisher—his name's Stanton—managed to get her to the surface."

Miller pointed to the crooked line of small shacks along the northeastern side of the lake. "Most people come out here for pan fish like crappie or blue gill, which is why the shacks are set up in a shallower area. Victim was left a little further out, at a depth of around thirty feet. Only reason the ice fisher found her was because he wanted to fish for bass. He went another ten to fifteen feet out onto the ice and saw an already used spot and decided to try it."

Nikki squinted against the cold wind rushing in from the north. "In my experience, killers usually go for the deepest parts of the lake, which means Kesha must have been left after the ice came in. Not to mention you said Stanton recognized her? Is that even possible?"

Miller's dark skin was an ashy color that Nikki had learned to associate with the very worst of moments. "I saw her. Her face is in good condition, and she has a tattoo of a frog on her hip. It's Kesha."

"He just happened to pick the spot she'd been left in, weighted down?" Nikki asked. "What do we know about Stanton?"

"He claims he chose that spot because it was obvious the ice had been cut recently and would be easier to access. According to the DNR, the first time the ice measured more than six inches was less than two weeks ago," Miller said.

"It's been a month since Kesha was taken," Nikki said. She could only imagine what Kesha had endured in the interim, unless she'd been killed quickly and hidden somewhere else until the killer could put her body into the lake. "What a nightmare. Where's Stanton now?"

"He's waiting in the main building to talk to us, on the south side of the lake." Miller worried the corner of his mouth. "Stanton's strategy for finding a spot makes sense to me, but something about Stanton is off. You know someone started a GoFundMe a couple of weeks ago to raise money for information on Kesha's whereabouts? As of yesterday afternoon, it was up to twenty-five thousand dollars."

"Interesting timing, then," Nikki said. "Is Stanton the one who told the media it was Kesha?"

Miller looked shocked. "They already have her name? I saw them piling into the parking area, but I figured someone had heard we'd found remains on a police scanner or something."

Nikki nodded. "I heard it on The Current on the drive out."

"I haven't even come in off the ice since they pulled her out of the water," Miller said. "Meaning only you, myself, and the divers know her identity." He paced on the ice without so much as a wobble. "Deputy Reynolds is with Stanton, and he was told not to contact anyone other than to let his family know he was all right until we informed next of kin." Miller's voice dripped with anger. "I hope to God the local police get to her parents before they hear it on the news. I just spoke to the local police about twenty minutes ago, and they were leaving to inform the family."

The white tent blocking the reporters' prying eyes was big enough to hold a hundred people, at least. Four divers in wetsuits emerged from the tent and climbed into the amphibious craft.

"They're heading back to the south entrance to change," Miller said. "It's closed and we're not allowing media into that area at all. We'll take her body out that way too."

Nikki felt for the divers. They saw more horrific things than the average cop, but she suspected today's events would weigh heavily on them for a long time. She hoped they would all take advantage of the mental health resources offered by the department.

There was a welcome center at the south entrance of the lake, which provided heat and bathrooms, along with a large play area. It was a longer ride, but at least the divers wouldn't have to deal with the shouting media horde.

"Good," Nikki said. "She deserves some dignity."

They ducked beneath the yellow tape and went inside the swaying tent where the remains had been placed in a body bag. A stocky man with a clipboard knelt next to the open bag, making notes. His mouth pinched into a straight line, his jaw jutting out. His hand trembled as he wrote.

"Lieutenant Huff, this is Special Agent Nikki Hunt with the FBI," Miller said. "Huff is the dive team leader. We're fortunate he was available today."

Huff glanced up at them with moisture in his eyes. "She's my daughter's age."

"I'm sorry," Nikki said. She'd worked enough terrible scenes to know that no words would make Huff feel better. The only solace for cops was knowing that someone else truly understood the mark something like this left on a person. "Thank you for helping with the recovery."

Huff cleared his throat. "It's the job."

Nikki moved closer, bracing herself for the bloated, slippery-skin look that water bodies usually had even though Miller had told her Kesha's body was recognizable. "Jesus, you weren't lying about her condition."

Kesha's dark skin had lost some of its pigment and gone slack, especially around her eyes, but Miller had been right. It was obviously her. Her eyes were still open, the soft tissue damaged from underwater scavengers. The poor girl was fully nude. Nikki's throat tightened with emotion. For some reason, the idea of Kesha being so exposed to the elements bothered her as much as anything.

"Medical examiner's probably not going to be able to establish an accurate time of death." Miller knelt down on the other side of the remains and Nikki followed suit. She snapped on latex gloves and gingerly touched Kesha's forearm, her stomach turning at the mangled stump of the girl's right arm.

"We haven't found her hands and feet yet," Miller said grimly.

"I personally searched for them, working my way out from her body for several feet. Doesn't look like her hands and feet were left with the rest of her body. I can't say if they're in the lake, but they aren't near the rest of her," Huff said.

"No sign of ligature marks on her arms, but I'd expect those to be on her wrists." She examined the wound site. "These don't look like hesitation marks to me, but the medical examiner will have to confirm that." Cutting through human flesh and bone required a lot more strength and determination than people realized. No hesitation marks usually meant they were dealing with a cold, experienced killer. "Do we have copies of her case file?"

"I already contacted the Bloomington police," Miller said. "They're happy for us to take the case out of their hands. The detective doesn't even want to be involved in telling the family."

"Normally I would go into the precinct and drag their ass out, but I have no interest in working with people like that," Nikki said. "We're better off on our own."

"I agree," Miller said. "Is Liam off desk duty yet?"

Nikki shook her head. "He's still dealing with post-concussive symptoms, and he's been a real bear about it. He can still help with background checks and anything that can be done on a computer. When did the ice fully come in?" Nikki asked Miller. Fall had been unseasonably warm, but mid-November had turned frigid.

"According to the DNR, the lake was confirmed iced-in on December ninth," he responded. "They never post the date in real time, and they don't measure ice-thickness, but the lake started to get busy the following week."

Nikki knew there were dozens of sites and blogs dedicated to the various lakes, and serious fishermen shared information, especially during ice seasons. "How easy would it be for someone to come in here at night?"

"They'd have to leave their vehicle on the road and carry everything," Miller answered. "During the winter, the public gates are locked, and this place is pretty buttoned up, even the smaller, unmarked dock areas. Not impossible, but there are houses close enough to see lights at night."

"Chances are he came out here during the day and pretended he was fishing like the others," Nikki said. "Which means he's confident as hell. That usually comes from experience."

"That's what I was thinking," Miller agreed. "We need to find her hands and feet, but the divers won't get back in the water without confirmation there are more remains in the lake."

Which would be impossible to get without bringing a lot of expensive equipment out, Nikki thought. "We need a cadaver dog. They can smell remains in water and through ice." Nikki checked her watch. "Unfortunately, it's two p.m. on Christmas Eve. We probably won't get anyone out here until the day after the holiday at best."

Any other time of year and Nikki would be able to pull enough strings to have a dog out by morning, but the holiday made everything difficult.

"You guys care if I take her on in?" Huff asked. "They're ready for her over at the shelter."

"I took plenty of photos already," Miller said.

"Of course, go ahead," Nikki told the lieutenant. "I hope you're able to salvage your holiday after all this."

Huff grunted his thanks and turned on the craft's engine. Nikki peeked out of the tent, and sure enough, the reporters had heard the noise and started moving closer to the shore. Huff backed out of the covered area and turned the ice boat sharply to the left, heading to the opposite shore. The press must not have realized that was the plan, because a couple of reporters yelled their displeasure, while others rushed to pack up and try to make it to the other landing.

"Courtney will need the bag her remains were in," Nikki said. Her forensic team lead was a wizard at her job, but water changed everything about a crime scene. Courtney wouldn't have a lot of opportunity to work her magic.

"Deputy Reynolds will have them at the office later today," Miller said. "Assuming someone is available to receive?"

"The office is closed," Nikki said. "Keep them locked up at the sheriff's station, and we'll get them to Courtney when she comes back to work the day after Christmas."

They started shuffling toward the shore; Nikki's cheeks stung from the cold wind. "What about the tent?"

"DNR's," Miller said. "They'll take it down. It's always so strange to just walk away from a scene like this."

"Water is a bitch," Nikki said. "Did you check the shoreline and parking lot for anything the killer might have accidentally dropped?"

He nodded. "Bagged some cigarette butts and a vape cartridge. We'll send to the lab for prints, but the lake's been pretty busy since the ice came in. Could belong to anyone."

"Kesha disappeared from the Mall of America, right?" Nikki asked.

"She and her boyfriend Dion went shopping the weekend after Thanksgiving," Miller said. "According to the Bloomington detective, Kesha left Dion at the food court while she hit a couple of stores. Mall security videos show her walking alone a couple of times, and she did purchase some things from Victoria's Secret. That's the last confirmed time she was seen alive."

Nikki tried to ignore the rush of anxiety at the mention of

the mall and its security. She and Rory had taken Lacey last spring, losing sight of her after one of the rides in the amusement park area. Frost had followed them and given Lacey a rose for Nikki—his first of many torments aimed at her. "The mall has its own police force, and they're pretty well equipped with security. I'll go there first thing Monday morning."

Since Christmas was on a Saturday this year, it would be even harder to get anything done over the weekend.

They'd reached the shore, and the reporters who hadn't raced to the other side of the lake were starting to converge on them.

"No comment. We aren't answering any questions right now." Miller waved off the reporters and then pointed to the curvy, blonde woman in designer sunglasses and parka standing near Nikki's jeep. "Well, this is kind of like déjà vu."

Last January, Caitlin Newport had shown up at Nikki's first scene back in her hometown on a mission to free Mark Todd. Since then, she'd become Liam's girlfriend and Nikki considered her a friend. She was also a shrewd reporter who could easily become a thorn in their sides.

Caitlin leaned against her truck and waved. "Hey, guys."

"I thought you were doing media consulting now," Miller said when they'd reached the cars.

"I am," Caitlin said, her cheeks uncharacteristically red. "But this is quite the scene. I thought I'd come out and check on things."

"Please." Nikki rolled her eyes. "Liam sent you, didn't he?"

Caitlin grinned sheepishly. "Just to observe."

"That's what I'm doing," Nikki said. "We have it covered here."

"I know, but it makes him feel like he's contributing." Caitlin pulled her coat hood up against the wind.

"Tell him I'm going to contribute my foot up his rear if he

pulls a stunt like that again," Nikki said. "He knows I can't share information with you."

"Not on record—" Caitlin said.

"Not legally," Miller cut in. "You aren't a cop. No offense."

One of the reporters they'd rebuffed earlier had crept up. "Hey, man, does Newport get the exclusive because she's in bed —literally—with the FBI?"

Caitlin swiveled, the heel of her boot digging into the iced-over pea gravel, her eyes flashing. Nikki grabbed her arm before Caitlin could get any further.

"She's not here about the story," Nikki said curtly. "This is a private matter, so back off." She dug her fingers into Caitlin's elbow, practically dragging her toward the truck.

"All right," Caitlin grouched, pulling her arm away. "Listen, you need to know the chatter is that the Bloomington Police Department blew off the case because Kesha's black. And it doesn't matter if it's true or not because of all the issues the Minneapolis police have caused the last couple of years. I heard a couple camera guys saying the reason Miller brought you in is because he doesn't want to get lumped in with them."

Nikki rolled her eyes. "Even though he's also black? Come on."

"I know," Caitlin said. "But that's the narrative that's already brewing. The gray area doesn't matter. I'm just giving you a heads-up, Nik. We live in a volatile, angry society, with one side doing everything they can to prevent change, and the other side desperate to force it through, even if the truth has to be fudged along the way. Normally I'd be okay with that since I'm not a racist bigot, but you're my friend, so I'm telling you the spotlight is going to be excruciatingly hot on this one."

"Thanks for the warning," Nikki said. "I'll call my boss as soon as I get a chance so he can hopefully get ahead of it."

Miller cleared his throat. "I just got a text from Reynolds.

He wants us to look at something over at the other end of the lake. Follow me?"

Nikki nodded. "Lead the way. Caitlin, don't follow."

"I won't," she said. "But please call Liam the first chance you get and update him. It will do a lot for his mental state."

"So will following the doctor's orders," Nikki said dryly. "But I will brief him as soon as I get the chance. You guys still coming to Rory's parents' for dinner?"

Liam's family lived out of state, and he'd never been close to any of them. He normally worked as many holidays as possible. Caitlin's teenaged son lived with her former in-laws, and Nikki knew Liam would rather be working than spend all Christmas Day sitting around pretending to enjoy a family ritual that had never interested him. Nikki usually managed to get him over for Christmas Eve dinner because Liam loved food more than just about anything else.

Caitlin nodded. "You think you'll make it over there by five thirty?"

"I promised Lacey that I would." Nikki crossed her fingers she didn't have to break that promise.

Like most parks, the Big Marine Contact Station consisted of a mid-sized log building, with a metal roof that shifted in the wind gusts. The playground and a sandy beach area near the building were closed for the season, while the motorized boat launch remained open during the winter. Miller's deputies had cleared the area to ensure privacy when Kesha's body arrived. Lt. Huff had already docked the ice boat, and he was helping a middle-aged man in snow boots and furry cap with ear flaps transfer the remains to the transport vehicle from the medical investigator's office.

"Most of the death investigators are off, just like the medical examiner," Miller said as Nikki exited the jeep. "When we called for transport, the service said only part-time employees were available today and tomorrow, with no autopsies or tox testing being done until the day after Christmas."

"I know it's unavoidable," Nikki said. "But I hate being this behind already."

The stout man from the M.E.'s office shut the vehicle's loading door, double-checking that it was secure. "Sheriff Miller, since this is your scene, I need you to sign off before I take the body to the morgue."

Miller took the clipboard and quickly signed. "Happy holidays. Before you leave, can we get another look at the black trash bag her remains are in? I want to compare them to some others we found."

The investigator looked at Miller in confusion. "You mean the body bag?"

"No, I mean what her remains were in when she was put into the lake."

"Yeah, that's a body bag, not a trash bag. I guess it would be hard to tell since it's all water-logged and ripped, but it's the kind of body bag we use in major disasters. Guess the divers didn't realize it."

"You're certain?" Nikki asked.

"Ma'am, I've worked more major disasters than I can count. Have your people do their testing, but I'm positive that's exactly what your victim is in, not a trash bag."

"Thanks for the help," Nikki said.

"Happy holidays." He climbed into the van and drove out of the lot, leaving Nikki and Miller confused.

"I've seen those disaster bags before," Miller said. "They do feel about the same as a strong yard bag. What kind of killer has those on hand?"

"The kind who plans," Nikki said. "Where's Stanton's truck?"

Miller pointed to an old, white 1976 Chevy Scottsdale held

together by rust. A blue tarp that must have been covering the bed flapped in the wind.

"What was your initial impression of him?" Nikki asked.

"He'd been smoking pot," Miller said. "Recently, because it just hung in the air over him. He's shaken up and a little jittery, but anyone would be in the situation. That's why I didn't say anything about the weed when I arrived."

They walked over to the truck, both snapping on latex gloves. Thanks to the wind, the tarp had nearly come completely loose, and it was easy to peer over the side and get a good look into the truck.

Stanton had covered the rusting bed with a large piece of plywood and from the looks of it, the wood had been there for a while. It was stained nearly black, and Nikki could detect the scent of engine oil and grease. Her dad used to smell like that when he came in from the fields.

"What are you smiling about?" Miller asked.

"Just thinking about my dad. He was always working on equipment because he never bought anything new, and his work clothes were always stained with grease and oil. Some days Mom would make him strip to his underwear before he even came into the house."

"It's good to see you smile about your parents," he said.

"It feels good." Nikki wasn't sure how to explain it, but the once-fragile scab barely covering the wound of her parents' murders had actually started to heal. She couldn't remember the last time she'd thought of them without wanting to cry.

"This could be blood." Miller pointed to the corner of the truck bed not covered by the plywood. "Or half a dozen other things, but we'll have to get it tested."

Nikki stood on her tiptoes to get a better look. The red stains looked fairly fresh, and there were several smears along the interior wall of the truck bed. The rest of the truck bed was full of odds and end tools and junk, along with three partially full jugs of Drano and a box of thin, generic, black plastic trash bags.

"Those are dollar-store trash bags," Nikki said.

"Drano speeds up decomposition," Miller said. "If this turns out to be blood..."

"I agree it doesn't look great, but I've also seen plenty of old trucks with similar stuff rolling around in the bed," Nikki said. She pulled on the lid of a steel toolbox sitting up against the truck cab, but it didn't budge. "I'd like to see what's inside this thing."

"Let's ask Stanton to show it to us."

"Assuming he doesn't agree, I'm not sure we have enough probable cause to seize the truck," Nikki said. "We don't know for certain that it is blood, and black trash bags and Drano are common household items." She went to the driver's side door and looked through the dirty glass. The truck's interior had seen better days, but the tan leather was in better shape than Nikki had expected. Fast-food wrappers littered the dash along with a layer of dirt.

"Looks like a bag of weed and a pipe on the floor." Minnesota had decriminalized marijuana a few years ago, which meant police only fined a person carrying up to a certain amount. Nikki couldn't tell if the baggie contained more than that, but smoking and driving was still very much illegal.

"Between that and the circumstantial stuff, I'm going to submit for an electronic warrant. You can head in and start talking to Stanton. I'll see if I can get this thing rolling." Miller headed back to his SUV where the mounted computer made submitting the warrant through e-Charging relatively simple. "I know it's Christmas Eve, but"—he checked his watch—"hopefully at least one judge is planning on staying after three p.m. today."

"It's also Friday," Nikki reminded him. "So, fingers crossed.

Either way, I'll take my time questioning him. Hopefully that will be enough time to get the warrant approved."

Nikki bent her head against the wind gusting off the lake and speed-walked to the contact station's door. Like most park structures in the state, the building was made of wood and resembled a log cabin, with a small office for the park ranger and two restrooms. The black flecks in the common areas' white tile reminded Nikki of the doctor's office when she was a kid. As a kid, she always counted the specks while waiting for the doctor to finally come into the exam room.

Reynolds met Nikki at the door. "Good to see you again, Agent Hunt, even though the circumstances suck as usual." He glanced over his shoulder. "He's stuck to the story he told us when we initially arrived. He's currently unemployed after his auto shop went bankrupt. Wife's a nurse, he's got three kids under ten."

"Word's already out that it's Kesha," Nikki said quietly. "The reward was up to twenty-five thousand dollars yesterday, so we have to at least consider the possibility he's somehow involved and that he came back to get her and claim the reward. Miller's submitting for an e-warrant. How's he been acting?"

"Like you'd expect considering what he found," Reynolds answered.

Nikki went over to the other man, who had been twisting a knit cap and staring at the floor, his ash-blond hair standing on end. The smell of pot clung to his clothes. "Danny Stanton?"

Stanton jammed the cap into his coat pocket, stood up and looked at her. "Yes, ma'am. You're the FBI lady?"

"Agent Nikki Hunt," she answered, motioning for him to sit back down. "I know you've already spoken with Sheriff Miller and Deputy Reynolds, but thank you for waiting on me. I know this must be awful for you." Nikki sat down in the chair across from Stanton, retrieving her notebook and pen from her bag.

Reynolds leaned against the wall behind Stanton, his eyes on the door.

Stanton's fair skin looked as white as the ice they'd just come in from. "Do you think she was alive when she went into the water?"

"From the looks of it, no," Nikki answered.

"Good," Stanton said. "I keep thinking about how scared she would have been. Drowning is terrifying."

"It is," Nikki said, fighting the sudden pressure on her chest. "I'm sorry but I'm probably going to ask you a lot of the same questions the sheriff asked."

"Figured," Stanton said. "If you don't mind, can we get started? I've got three kids, and Christmas Eve is always a big deal. I know it sounds selfish—"

"Not at all," Nikki assured him. "What time did you get to the lake this morning?"

"A little after ten." Stanton rubbed his trembling hands together. "There were a couple of other guys fishing, but they left not long after I got on the ice."

It had been a long time since Nikki had gone ice fishing with her father, but she remembered the ice had been hard to get through, even with an ice drill. "How did you come to pick that spot?"

Stanton dragged a hand through his hair. "Well, my ice drill is old, so I like to look for places that have already been cut through. Even if they've started to freeze again, the ice usually isn't as thick. So, I was walking around and noticed the ice had been cut recently. It was the perfect, minimum-effort spot. I knew bass were deeper out anyway, and that's what I like to eat."

Nikki nodded. "According to the DNR employees, the ice is about seven inches right now. How thick was this spot?" She'd have to do a little research, but Nikki assumed it would take at least a few days for the ice-hole to re-freeze to that depth.

"Shoot," Stanton said. "Maybe a couple of inches? Took maybe ten seconds to break through."

"Can you walk me through what happened once you started fishing? And how long would it normally take?" she asked.

"Well, I've only ice fished a few times, and like I said, my drill's pretty old. If the ice hadn't already been cut and was around seven inches, it would still only take around a minute."

"Sounds right," Reynolds said. "A newer drill can pull that off in under thirty seconds, but I checked his out. It's definitely got some age to it."

Nikki jotted that down in her notes.

Stanton nodded. He reached into the front pocket of his coat and pulled out a lighter. He laughed awkwardly. "Sorry, forgot where I was." He put the lighter back in his pocket, his heels bouncing against the tile floor. "I'm impatient, so I probably dropped the line down a couple of times, and the hook got stuck on something. I figured weeds or maybe a log, you know? I wrestled the line for a few minutes, but I finally just cut it and put on a new jig. I changed my depth a little, so I didn't lose another hook and jig." Stanton shifted in the leather chair. "A little while went by, and I sort of drifted off. It was so peaceful out there."

He hesitated for a moment. "I have a medical marijuana card, so I decided to smoke a little. I was going to be there for a while, so I'd be fine to drive home."

Nikki picked up on his defensiveness. "We're not worried about the pot, although I disagree about the driving. Go on."

"I'm sitting there, relaxing and barely paying attention to my pole, but then something hit the line. I tried to bring it in, but I realized the line was wrapped around it. So I knelt down next to the hole." He stopped, staring past Nikki, his mouth quivering. "I reached down into the water, thinking I might be able to grab whatever it was, but it was way bigger than the ice hole."

"How did you end up seeing her face?" Nikki asked.

"I didn't know what I had, so there I am, gloves soaked and my hands numb, trying to shimmy this thing around enough to at least figure out what it was." He stopped talking and looked down at his hands. "For a second, I thought I'd smoked some bad shit, but nope. It was human hair, stuck on black skin. I knew it was a body then. Whatever she'd been put in had torn enough that I was able to see her face." Stanton had turned a sickly shade of green. "I was so shocked, I don't think I moved for several seconds. Then I went back to the truck and called the police."

"Your phone was in the truck?" Nikki asked. "That's kind of risky considering the location and weather."

"Not really," he said. "If I fell through, the phone isn't going to help. And I didn't want it buzzing every five minutes with a text from my wife. I just wanted peace and quiet, you know?"

"Did the bag sink when you left?" Nikki asked.

"My line was wrapped around her," Stanton answered. "I realized that I hadn't done anything to secure her when I was on the phone with 9-1-1 and came back out to see if she was gone. The line had her pretty good, but I used some twine I had in the truck to help secure her so she didn't float off. Then I sat down to wait for the police, with that poor girl floating like a dead fish."

Nikki felt queasy, trying not to think of what it felt like to sink into the freezing water. "I'm glad you had the twine in your truck," Nikki said.

Stanton snorted. "My wife says I never throw anything away. For once it paid off."

Nikki debated asking him about the reward money, but decided to wait. "Speaking of your truck, Sheriff Miller and I noticed there was something that looked like blood in the bed. I have to ask you about that."

Stanton stopped fidgeting. "Why were you looking in the back of my truck? I didn't give anyone permission."

"The tarp was loose in the wind," Reynolds said. "You've got a lot of Drano too."

"My shop's sink was constantly clogging," he said.

"Your auto repair shop had to close?" Nikki asked.

Stanton nodded. "This economy sucks."

Nikki checked her notes to make sure she had the date right. "Were you working the weekend after Thanksgiving?"

"What does that matter?"

Nikki smiled, trying to set him at ease. She didn't want Stanton to clam up and stop talking. "It's just procedure. With homicides, we always have to clear the person who found the body."

"You think I did it?"

"I'm not saying that." She kept her tone pleasant. "But I have to follow procedure."

"I wasn't working because I had to close the shop down a couple of weeks before that," he said. "I couldn't compete with the bigger shops. They can get away with charging less." He leaned back in the chair and crossed his arms over his chest. "I was stuck home taking care of the kids."

"Your wife was working at the time, then?"

"She's a nurse, so yeah. Picking up extra hours with the shop going under and all of that," he said. "Look, what do I need to do to get out of here?"

"Would you mind letting us look in the toolbox in the back of your truck?"

His eyes widened. "Yes, I would. I've done nothing wrong."

"I understand, and we don't mean to offend you, but a teenaged girl was brutally murdered. I'd really like to cross you off the suspect list before we go any further."

A muscle in Stanton's cheek twitched. "What happens if I say no?"

"You have the right to do that," she said. "But since the substance on the bottom of the truck bed looks like blood and you have a box of black trash bags similar to the kind her remains were placed in, not to mention the Drano, we need to look more closely at the truck."

"The hell you do." Stanton glared at her. "I know my rights."

"Your bag of weed and pipe are on the driver's side floor, in plain sight," Nikki said. "That's enough for us to search."

Stanton put his head in his hands. "I already admitted to the weed, man."

"I'm aware the legislature passed a law allowing medical marijuana in flower form this year, but most people who use for medical prefer pills or oil," Nikki said. "Gives them relief a lot faster."

"It's also a lot more expensive," Stanton said. "You really going to arrest me on Christmas Eve for that?"

Nikki seized her chance to earn his trust. "We can legally search the truck with drug paraphernalia in plain sight, especially since you admitted to smoking. Normally we'd already be doing that after we saw the drugs, but given the circumstances, we wanted to speak with you first. Is the red substance in the truck bed blood?"

"It's deer blood," Stanton said. "You can do a rapid test to prove that it's animal blood, right? I saw that on TV."

"Most of what you see on TV is wrong when it comes to actual police investigations," Nikki said. "Although that kind of test is being developed, it's not ready for the field."

"The blood looks recent," Reynolds said. "Like it hasn't had time to fully freeze yet. When did you shoot the deer?"

"Yesterday," Stanton said, sighing. "Brought it home and

skinned it in my garage and was too lazy to clean the truck, okay?"

Nikki wasn't a hunter, but she knew the deer season was over for most weapons. "I assume you're using something other than a muzzleloader?"

"Rifle," Stanton said. "I know it's illegal, but I'm out of work, and we eat the meat. I didn't kill him for the rack."

Nikki wasn't sure she believed him yet, but the scenario he painted was definitely plausible. "We have evidence techni- cians on the way to take a sample of the blood and anything we find in the vehicle. What's in the toolbox?"

"Old tools and junk. The rifle," he said. "But I have a permit for it. That's in the truck too."

"Is the toolbox locked?" Nikki asked.

Stanton crossed his arms over his chest, his teeth digging into his lower lip. Nikki decided to try another tactic. "No one wants to drag this out, Mr. Stanton. It's a pain in the ass for all of us. What's important is finding out who killed Kesha, but we have got to clear you first. We're going to search the toolbox and the inside of the truck. Is there anything we might find that we need to be careful of, like a knife or a needle?"

"I don't do drugs," Stanton said.

Miller appeared in the doorway, bringing a blast of cold air with him. "Got it."

Stanton looked between Miller and Nikki. "Got what?"

"The warrant to search your truck based on everything I just told you," Nikki said. "We just need to clear you so we can move forward with the investigation. Sheriff, he says the blood is deer blood and admitted to illegally hunting yesterday. I told him we'll have to collect a sample and confirm the blood type."

"Is the toolbox locked?" Miller repeated.

"Lock's broken." Stanton's shoulders sagged in defeat.

Nikki glanced at Miller. "Why don't you and Reynolds go search, and I'll hang out here."

Miller checked his phone. "We'll try to be quick, Mr. Stanton."

"Am I in trouble for the pipe and the deer?" he asked.

Miller shook his head. "As long as we don't find anything else, I'm willing to let that slide since it's Christmas and you've already had a hell of an ordeal."

Stanton looked relieved. "Thanks, man."

Miller and Reynolds headed outside. Nikki found a couple of dollar bills in her purse and bought two bottles of water out of the vending machine. She handed one to Stanton.

"Thanks." He twisted off the cap and drank greedily.

"You're welcome." Nikki still hadn't gotten a good read on Stanton yet. Her gut told her he was probably a victim of lousy luck, but she needed to be sure.

"Mr. Stanton—"

"Call me Danny," he said. "That way I can pretend I'm not an old man."

Nikki laughed. "You look around my age, and I don't think I'm old. Most days," she added.

"I'll be forty next month." He picked at the water bottle's label. "Thought I'd have more to show for myself by now."

"I'm sorry you're going through hard times financially." She knew mechanics made good money, and if Stanton had his own garage, he must have decent skills. "Have you tried other auto body places? I know it's not the same as owning your own business, but it's still money."

"I'm working part-time for one starting next week," he said. "Hoping to eventually get full-time hours. But who knows?" He looked out the big window at the lake. "Today was supposed to be relaxing."

"Is this the first time you've been on the ice this year?" Nikki asked, keeping her tone conversational.

"Yep," Stanton said. "I only go a couple times a year because I'm not a huge fan of freezing my ass off for hours."

"Me neither," Nikki said. "I'm always amazed at the guys who bring their ice sheds out and set them up. My dad used to leave his all winter."

"Can't do that now. Not if you have anything you don't want stolen inside." He tore a long strip of label off. "Can I ask you a question about that girl?"

Nikki nodded. "I can't promise I'll be able to answer, but go ahead."

"I've been watching a lot of true crime documentaries." He flushed. "I guess that probably doesn't help my case for being innocent."

"I'd rather talk to people about true crime documentaries than TV police procedurals," she said. "Especially the ones about profiling that make us look like mind-reading magicians."

Stanton grinned. "You guys don't have a private plane and fly all over the country to solve terrible murders?"

"Not even the Behavioral Analysis Unit at Quantico does that," Nikki said. "At least, not how it's depicted. What's your question about Kesha?"

"Right, I get sidetracked. When I was waiting for the police and she was just there, in the water, I saw some of her face. That's how I knew who it was, poor kid. But she looked kind of like she was sleeping. She wasn't all gross like they say bodies found in water are. Does that mean she hadn't been in the lake very long?"

Nikki studied him, trying to decide if he was feeling her out to get a sense of how much she suspected him or if he was genuinely interested. "The medical examiner will have to tell us that." Nikki never shared details with anyone not directly involved in the case, but she wanted to see if Stanton reacted to her theory. "My first impression is that someone put her down there after the ice came in. Maybe even during the day, under the cover of an ice shack."

Stanton's eyes widened. "Christ, I hadn't thought of that. Who is that demented and ballsy?"

"Someone sick and desperate," she answered.

Stanton chugged the water. "Shit like this makes me wish Minnesota had the death penalty."

"The evidence techs are taking a sample of the blood and fingerprinting the inside of your truck and looking for any trace evidence that might belong to Kesha," Nikki told him. "They should be done before too long."

"Won't find anything," Stanton said sullenly. "Mind if I call my wife again and let her know I'm still giving my statement?"

"Sure, but please don't tell her anything about the victim's identity." Nikki decided to test him. "There's a large reward for Kesha's disappearance, but we want to make sure the family is notified by the police before word gets out to the press."

Stanton reddened. "Well, I already told her it was the girl on the posters."

Nikki leaned forward. "Did you send her any photos, Danny? We don't want those to be seen by the family."

"Absolutely not," he said. "But my wife knew about the reward. I told her to keep quiet." He took his phone out of his coat pocket and put in the number.

Nikki debated staying seated, but the building was small enough she could give him a little privacy and still hear most of the conversation.

"Yeah, they aren't done with me yet," Stanton said. Nikki could hear yelling coming from the phone. His wife wasn't happy with the delay.

Miller returned, bringing in a fresh blast of cold, lake air, a pointed look on his face. Leaving Danny to argue with his wife, Nikki joined Miller near the front door. "Pot residue on the pipe that appears fresh, and some weed left in the bag, but Reynolds confirmed he's got a medical permit. The toolbox is a different story. He's got motor oil and other tools I'd expect a mechanic to have, but we also found two eight-inch fillet knives, and a sharp axe—all of which appear to have blood on them. I've got evidence techs collecting samples of blood from the back, hair in the front seat, and all three of the bloody weapons. My gut tells me he's probably telling the truth about the deer, but with the media already all over this, I've got to make sure we don't miss anything." Miller shoved his hands in his pockets, rocking back on his heels. "Kesha's family called the Bloomington detective, who in turn called my office to give us hell for informing the media." He glared at Danny. "Please tell me he didn't send his wife photos of Kesha's body."

"He didn't, thank God." Nikki glanced back at Danny. He was silent, his head hanging down, while his wife talked loudly on the other end of the phone. "Assuming he's telling the truth, I don't want to vilify the person who found Kesha without being certain."

It was a PR nightmare, but Nikki was accustomed to those. She didn't want to screw up Danny's life if he was innocent. "Well, he admitted to being high. Even with a medical permit, he's obviously not supposed to be getting high and driving. We can impound the truck so Courtney can make sure no evidence was missed. I'll see if she's willing to leave her parents' place early—I doubt it will be a problem. She dreads the family get-togethers."

Nikki's phone vibrated in her hand. She glanced at the caller ID and rolled her eyes. "Well hello, Liam. Did Caitlin report back to you yet?"

"Yep," Liam answered without missing a beat. "She said a guy named Danny Stanton found the body. She also told me about the reward. Obviously, we need to check Stanton out. What's his address?"

"You're not officially back on duty until Monday," Nikki reminded him.

"Everything I can do Monday, I can do from home since I

can't go in the damn field yet," Liam said crossly. "Nik, I'm going stir-crazy sitting here. We're spending tomorrow with Caitlin's family, and she's out getting last-minute stuff. That's the only reason I had her stop by. I wasn't sure Miller would have called you yet, but I had a gut feeling. She saw your jeep and stopped. Please bring me up to speed. I need the freaking distraction."

Nikki sighed. "Fine, but don't even think about trying to work somewhere other than your desk. Concussion issues are serious."

"I'm aware of that," he said tersely.

"Fine." Nikki told him what little they knew.

"How long was she dead before she went into the water?" Liam asked.

"We don't know," Nikki said. "Medical examiner has to look at her and even then—"

"What's Stanton's address? I'll pull it up on Google Maps and see what the area looks like. He might have storage buildings or a work shed."

Nikki checked the notes Miller had given her and gave Liam the information, glancing over her shoulder to make sure Stanton was still on the phone with his wife. "That's the western side of the county, and it's definitely rural."

"I've got it," Liam said. "These satellite photos were taken within the last year. Looks like a ranch-style house, detached garage. Doesn't look like there are any other buildings on the property but that doesn't mean he couldn't have added some since the photos were taken."

"Miller didn't find anything in Stanton's truck that directly ties him to Kesha, but we did find blood in the bed and on some weapons, but he also admitted to illegally killing a deer. We're talking about impounding the truck—"

"Yeah, well, Caitlin found out that Stanton's wife called the family about the reward not long after Stanton told her about the body," Liam interrupted. "That doesn't sit well with me."

"Me neither, but it doesn't mean he's involved. Their financial situation isn't great," Nikki said.

"Well, what can I do?" he asked. "And please don't say nothing, Nik. I'm going insane sitting here doing nothing."

"Since you've got access to the FBI databases, go ahead and run a full background check on Stanton." She glanced back at him and realized Stanton had ended his call. "I'll touch base with you later."

Nikki and Miller walked back over to Stanton. He looked up at them sheepishly. "I guess I should have told you I didn't clean my stuff after skinning the deer."

"We have to test the blood," Nikki said. "This a high-profile murder case, so we have to take those things in as evidence along with anything else found in the truck."

"But not the truck itself, right?"

"We need to seize the truck," Nikki said. "There are too many circumstantial things to ignore, but more importantly, you're still high. We can't let you drive anywhere. Your medical card doesn't mean you can get high and drive."

"Normally, I'd write you a ticket and send the truck to impound," Miller said. "But like Agent Hunt said, we just have to do our due diligence. And if we seize the truck to go through it looking for evidence in this case, you won't have to pay impound fees to get it out. I'll make sure of that."

Danny dragged his hands over his face. "When will I get it back?"

"As soon as possible, but that likely won't be until sometime next week," Nikki said. "Assuming we don't find something that does put Kesha in your truck, like her blood or hair."

"You won't," he said. "I never saw her until today. At least, not in person. Just on the news. God, my wife's going to be pissed."

"Is she able to come get you?"

"Oh, she's already on her way to talk to you." He looked embarrassed. "Hopefully she'll let me ride home with her when she finds out about the truck. I better call and tell her now."

Nikki nodded. "Sheriff Miller and I will be outside." She shrugged her coat on and followed Miller out into the freezing weather. "God, it's still snowing?" She dug her knit cap out of her pocket and pulled it on.

"It's supposed to peter out soon," Miller said.

"Where are the evidence techs?" Nikki asked. She spotted Reynolds in his patrol car, labeling the evidence bags.

"There weren't any available to come out," Miller told her. "But it's more intimidating if he thinks there are. Reynolds called the tow truck, and it should be here soon. He's going to handle logging the evidence. We need to find her hands and feet. There could be DNA under fingernails that might help us nail this bastard."

Nikki chewed her bottom lip, trying to figure out their best move. She scanned the lake, her stomach knotting. "More divers are out of the question until at least after the New Year, and the earliest we can get search volunteers out is the day after Christmas. I can put in a request for a cadaver dog to search for her hands and feet, but again, the holiday is going to mess everything up."

"Let me make some calls," Miller said. "One of the K9 handlers owes me a favor, and I know he's around. I can't promise I'll have an answer before Saturday, but I'll try."

"Check in with me when you get a chance," Nikki told him. "We won't be able to follow up with the Mall of America security until the day after Christmas, but if you're able to get a dog, I might be able to cobble together volunteers for Saturday."

Liam wasn't technically allowed in the field, but he could help with a search if he felt up to it. Since he was dying to get out of the house, Nikki was confident she could count on him to help.

An aging gray minivan peeled into the parking lot, coming to a stop next to Stanton's truck. The dark-haired woman in the driver's seat glared at them through the dirty windshield. She shoved the minivan's door open and got out, immediately lighting a cigarette. "Who's in charge here?"

Nikki hid a smile as Miller put himself between the woman and Stanton's truck. "Sheriff Kent Miller. This is Agent Hunt with the FBI. I take it you're Mrs. Stanton?"

Flour dotted her Vikings sweatshirt. "Sheri Stanton. Why can't my husband take his truck home?"

Miller explained the situation, but Sheri didn't appear to be as understanding as her husband. "He's done nothing wrong."

"The blood in the truck bed, and the blood on the knives and axe in the toolbox are things we can't ignore. Mr. Stanton says all of the blood is deer blood, but we can't know that definitively until it's tested."

"He should be treated like a hero since he's brought this family closure," Sheri said. "That's what I was told when I called in about the GoFundMe reward. They were very appreciative."

Nikki tried to bite her tongue and failed. "You contacted whoever set up the reward before we released any information to the public. Do you realize that means her parents probably found out that way instead of being informed in person by an officer?"

Sheri didn't seem to care. "What's the difference? Bad news is bad news. For all we know, they wouldn't have found out until after Christmas. At least now—"

"They know their child was found discarded in a freezing lake," Nikki cut her off. She'd had enough of the woman's lack of empathy. "I suggest you collect your husband and go home.

The truck has to be processed by my forensic people. You'll hear from us after the holidays."

Sheri's pale cheeks turned bright red. "You'll hear from my attorney before that."

"Let me make something clear to you, Mrs. Stanton," Sheriff Miller said. "Your husband is lucky we aren't bringing him in for getting high and operating a vehicle or giving him a ticket for poaching since he admitted to it. I'm even going to make sure he's not charged an impound fee, providing the blood all turns out to be animal."

"This is just ridiculous," Sheri snapped.

"It's procedure," Nikki said through clenched teeth. "But feel free to call your attorney and be charged for something he can't legally do anything about. Mr. Stanton is inside."

Sheri looked like she wanted to claw Nikki's eyes out, but she brushed past them and marched into the contact center, yelling for her husband.

"No wonder he wanted out of the house on Christmas Eve," Nikki muttered.

"Right," Miller agreed.

A fresh gust of wind blew cold snow into their faces. Nikki tucked her chin into her coat collar. "We need to talk to the Bloomington detective and the family."

Miller nodded. "The DNR will help keep the area secure. I checked with BPD, and the detective is off for Christmas, but I've got his contact information. We can call him and the family from the sheriff's station. Reynolds is going to wait for the truck to be towed back."

"I'll follow you there." Nikki's mind barreled ahead as she walked to the jeep. In addition to BPD and the family, they needed copies of the case files so they could talk to all of the witnesses. They needed to request CCTV footage from the county's traffic cams nearest the lake along with the Mall of America's security videos. They were already so far behind

Kesha's killer, and the autopsy results would definitely be affected by the cold water, which made figuring out Kesha's time of death difficult, if not impossible.

That's not what had her stomach turning, though. She'd been in law enforcement long enough that working a case was often like muscle memory. Every murder had its own unique circumstances, but at the beginning of an investigation, certain bases always had to be covered and Nikki could run those in her sleep at this point. As sickening as the crime might be, Nikki could compartmentalize those emotions—at least until it was time to talk to the victim's family. That experience never failed to leave a mark on Nikki's soul, but she knew today was going to be even worse.

So much for Christmas being the happiest time of the year.

THREE

On the drive to the sheriff's office, Nikki called Courtney and broke the news. As she'd expected, Courtney was eager to get back to the city and help with the case. "I'll make sure I'm at the lab by tomorrow evening. What's priority?"

"The blood from the back of Stanton's truck along with the weapons we found in his toolbox. He said it's all deer blood, and I believe him, but I need to rule him out. Those have already been bagged for evidence, but the truck itself is a different story." She explained the decision to impound the truck. "We may not be able to get the truck to the lab until Sunday, but the electronic warrant allows us to search the inside for any biological evidence tied to Kesha. I'm going to call Blanchard in a little bit and see how quickly she can get to the autopsy."

Blanchard had a reputation as a hard-nosed, no-nonsense medical examiner, but Nikki had earned her respect in the last year. She was banking on that to keep her from getting reamed for calling on a holiday.

"She'll handle the tox tests, I'm sure," Courtney said. "If there's anything with the body she needs me to test, let her know to send ASAP and I'll do it myself."

"You sound way too excited to cut your holiday short and work a murder," Nikki said. "Things going that badly?"

Courtney snickered. "Just the usual judgment from my self-righteous family. It's okay to spend time in jail for drugs, but apparently, being a lesbian and a forensic examiner means I will never find love or happiness in my life."

"Good grief," Nikki said. "Too bad you're not in a serious relationship right now. You could have brought her home to the family and really caused a stir."

"I know, right? How's Lacey doing?"

"Better than I expected, honestly. I'm still a little worried about her spending a week with Tyler's parents, but she says that she's excited." Her ex-husband's parents had always blamed Nikki for the divorce and resented the time she spent at her job, and Tyler's murder had spurred them to threaten a custody battle for Lacey, blaming Nikki for his death and for Lacey not wanting to visit them. Fortunately, they'd been receptive to the mediation Nikki's attorney offered, and after speaking with Lacey's therapist, agreed to take a different approach. Lacey's reticence had nothing to do with her grandparents. She just struggled to spend time with them because they reminded her of her father. At the therapist's suggestion, Tyler's parents had been brought into a couple of therapy sessions with Lacey. The open dialogue had helped everyone, and Lacey was excited to go to Florida with them and spend a week on the beach. "I just hope she doesn't realize it was a mistake once she's on the plane."

"She won't," Courtney said reassuringly. "And if she does, you've got people who can step in and help out."

"I know," Nikki said, turning into the big parking area at the Washington County Government Center. "Try to have a good holiday and enjoy your mom's cooking."

"There is that," Courtney said. "And same to you. I know you already know this, but it's okay to be happy on Christmas, even when everything else is shit. That's my version of Christmas spirit, anyway."

"Thanks, Court." Nikki parked in the same row as Miller. Normally she'd have to park way in the back, by the exit, but the holiday exodus meant half the lot was empty. "Be careful driving home tomorrow."

"I'll call you when I get in," Courtney said. "Mom made enough to feed several families, so hopefully I'll still be able to fit through the lab door."

"Good luck with that," Nikki said. "I'm going to check in with Hernandez, so I'll talk with you tomorrow. Drive safe."

As Special Agent in Charge of the Minneapolis Field Office, Hernandez usually took a hands-off approach, but with all the media attention bearing down on them, Nikki knew he'd appreciate her checking in.

"Nikki." Hernandez sounded surprised to hear from her. "You calling on Christmas Eve seems like a really bad omen."

"I'm sorry to say you're right, boss. We have a situation in Washington County." She briefed Hernandez on what little they knew so far. "Thanks to Stanton's wife, the media knew the victim was Kesha Williams by the time I arrived on scene. Local channels and a couple of national affiliates are camped out at the north entrance to Big Marine Lake. There's already chatter about how the Bloomington Police Department dropped the ball on her case because she's black."

"Christ," Hernandez said. "Even if it's not true, we have to control the narrative."

"Honestly, at this point, we don't know enough to really do that," Nikki said.

"We can make it clear that we are putting Kesha Williams at the top of our priority list."

"She's at the top of mine."

"That appearance needs to be given to the media too," Hernandez said. "My bosses have made it clear they don't want any of the racial bias in the city leaking into our investigations. I know you won't do that, but we need to make sure the press understands we're doing everything we can to prevent it."

"I'm going to let you handle that, sir." Nikki got out of the jeep, cradling her phone against her shoulder. "I'll check in with you later."

Nikki signed into the sheriff's office at the front desk, the young, unfamiliar officer at the county sheriff's entrance barely greeting her with a grunt and a nod. The officer looked more like a high school student than a young cop, but seniority always won the holiday battle. As she walked past the cubicles towards the conference room, the nearly empty bullpen was silent, save for the deputy with the back corner desk.

She found Miller in Conference Room B, his laptop already open. "My office is a mess right now," he told her. "Hope this is okay."

She took the chair next to him. "Conference room B is kind of our tradition," she said, referring to the previous cases they'd worked together. "Might as well continue it. Has the family been informed?"

Miller nodded. "In the most disastrous way possible, just like we expected. By the time the local police got to the Williamses' home, Stanton's wife had already contacted them and told them what her husband found. All hell sort of broke loose after that, so the police brought the family into the station and set up a video call that's supposed to begin shortly. I'm just waiting for them to pick up."

Nikki pushed away the protein shake she'd just opened. "How could anyone be so obtuse? Whose contact number was on the reward information?"

"Kesha's aunt, who's staying at the house during the holiday. So, there was no buffer. She got the call and turned right around and told the parents."

"Those poor people." The Williamses lived in Northfield, a

small town about an hour from the Twin Cities, famous for Jesse James and the Younger Gang's bank robbery in 1876. Nikki had a vague memory of an elementary school field trip to the First National Bank historic site in Northfield. The old building had been restored to its 1876 appearance, and walking inside made Nikki feel like she'd stepped back in time. One of the people giving the tour had claimed to be the descendant of one of the town members that fought back against the infamous gang. Nikki had always loved history, and it was easy to imagine the gang racing off down Division Street on their horses, with a posse of angry townspeople on their trail. That night, Nikki had told her parents she was going to be a historian like the people in the museum. Her father thought it was a great idea, but her mother had gone on and on about how little money historians made. Thinking back, she realized that had been the first spark of divide between Nikki and her mother.

The video call flashed on. Three chairs had been set up in what looked like a smaller, dingier version of the room Nikki and Miller currently occupied. A short, white woman with thick, graying hair occupied the chair on the right. "Sheriff Miller, I presume?"

"Correct, and this is Special Agent Nikki Hunt with the FBI. Thanks for setting this up for us. It's Captain Farley, right?"

The woman nodded. "The Williams family are waiting to be brought in."

"Before you do that, can we ask you a few questions?" Nikki asked.

"Of course. I assume you want to know everything possible about the Williamses and Kesha's boyfriend?" As the North-field police chief, Farley had been tasked with bringing Kesha's parents into the police station.

"That would be great."

Farley removed her tortoiseshell glasses and sighed. "This is a close-knit community, much like Stillwater and Washington County," she said. "Everyone has been reeling from the disappearance. We worked in conjunction with the Bloomington PD for the first couple of weeks, but we haven't been able to turn up any evidence that points to a perpetrator, including her boyfriend."

Nikki caught the edge in her voice. "Do you not like him as a suspect?"

"I don't like their single-mindedness," she said. "The boyfriend has a bit of a past, his story regarding the sequence of events changed a bit, but nothing extensive in my opinion. More importantly, he's on video for much of the day, including when he sought out the security officer."

"What were the inconsistencies in his story?" Nikki asked.

"He had trouble remembering exactly when they finished eating and said he stayed on the bench until he sought out security, but he forgot to mention his fifteen-minute bathroom break," Farley said.

"Security videos back his story up?" Miller asked.

"He spent about five in the bathroom, the other ten unaccounted for on the mall security cameras. He said he was looking for a vending machine that had something other than Coke." Farley shrugged. "He originally told mall security about going to the bathroom, but he omitted it when the police showed up. The guard said Dion was upset, panicky, and kept talking to himself. That and his past were enough for the BPD to put on blinders."

"What sort of past does he have?" Miller asked.

Chief Farley shook her head. "A few years ago, Dion was on his way down the wrong path, running with the wrong kids. He got in some serious trouble when he was fourteen, fifteen, but he turned things around."

"What sort of serious trouble?" Nikki asked, already thinking about the headache of dealing with juvenile records.

"Breaking and entering, accessory to robbery. He was given probation and hasn't been in trouble since." Chief Farley leaned back in her chair, rubbing her temples. "Yet the Bloomington PD barely looked at any other options, as if a black woman can only be killed at the hands of her black boyfriend." Farley rolled her eyes. "I've seen the mall security footage. She went to some other stores while he waited, and she never came back. He could have left the mall, but instead he's the one who reported her. He's been followed by the police, his financial records checked, his parents' home searched. I'm confident he had nothing to do with her murder, and so are her parents."

Nikki's anxiety ticked up with every word. They were not only weeks behind the killer, but the initial investigation appeared to have been handled badly from the beginning. She skimmed the few notes she'd had time to jot down about the case. "The boyfriend's name is Dion, right?"

Farley nodded. "He's helped search and done everything asked of him. I swear the Bloomington PD treated us like small-town idiots any time we dared suggest they refocus the investigation. I hope that won't be the case with you two."

"Absolutely not," Nikki said. "Do you have any leads or theories they didn't follow?"

Farley sighed and shook her head. "Unfortunately, no. Kesha was a good student, she'd earned a couple of partial scholarships. Her father's an engineer, Mom's a schoolteacher. They moved up here from Kentucky when Kesha was around seven because she was bullied for being mixed race."

"A decade ago," Miller said in disgust. "Some places are just stuck in time."

"And not a good one," Farley agreed. "Parents both well-respected members of the community. Kesha was too. She worked part-time, volunteered. She hadn't told anyone about feeling unsafe in her relationship or in any other aspect of her life. From our point of view, she was just taken at random."

"Whoever took her had a plan and executed it perfectly," Nikki said. "They'd have left some kind of evidence or information behind if they hadn't planned this meticulously. But you're right, she very well may have been chosen at random." Which would make the case even harder to solve. Victimology was always essential in solving cases. Random selection took that tool away.

"If you don't have any more questions, I'll bring in her parents," Farley said.

"How much have they been told?" Miller asked. "I'm sure you know we want to keep as many details locked down as possible."

"An ice fisher caught her body and brought it up," Farley said. "He recognized her face. His wife called him a hero when she contacted the aunt. According to her, he risked his life to recover the remains."

Nikki couldn't hide her disgust. "Not quite."

"Is he a suspect?" Farley asked.

"Everyone is until we clear them," Nikki said. "If you're ready, please have them join us."

Farley stood and walked out of frame. Nikki heard a door open and voices. Seconds later, Kesha's shell-shocked parents sat down in front of the computer, with Chief Farley next to Mrs. Williams. "Crystal and Seth Williams, Special Agent Nikki Hunt with the FBI and Sheriff Miller," Chief Farley said.

"First off, let me say I am incredibly sorry for your loss, and for the way you were informed," Miller said.

"That woman who called my sister said her face was recognizable." Crystal spoke first. "Is that true?"

"Yes," Miller said, his tone gentle.

"We want to see her."

"She's been taken to the medical examiner's office," Nikki said. "I don't know that anyone is answering the phone this afternoon, but I'm going to speak with the medical examiner later today. I will make sure she has your number so she can set that up for you."

"When can we lay her to rest?" Seth asked.

"We aren't able to give you that information yet, I'm sorry," Nikki said. "Is Dion with you?" She already knew the answer, but Nikki wanted to see their reaction when she asked about Kesha's boyfriend.

"No," Crystal said. "We stopped by his house and told him and cried together for a bit. He wanted to come, but Seth and I thought it was better if we spoke to you privately first. But we don't think he had anything to do with this. If the Bloomington detectives had listened, our baby might still be alive."

"I haven't had a chance to go through all of their case notes," Miller said. "But at first glance, it does appear the only suspect they seriously considered was Dion."

"Even though he's on the security video the whole time," Seth said. "Sitting on his phone while Kesha was supposed to be shopping."

"Out of curiosity, was this the first time the two of them had taken a trip together like this?"

"No," Crystal said. "They've known each other since middle school and had been together for eighteen months or so. We never allowed overnight trips, but Dion was responsible. She was always home on time."

"And she never mentioned thinking about breaking up with him or issues in their relationship?" Nikki asked.

"She'd decided to go to Mankato State, and Dion's still got a year left at community college before he can transfer. They squabbled a bit about that, but she told me Dion understood her decision." She wiped her nose with a tissue. "Please tell me you aren't going to spend all of your time just looking at him again."

"Of course not," Nikki said. "Your impressions of him are crucial. That said, did Kesha ever mention being around anyone who made her nervous? Maybe she felt like someone was watching her or following her?"

Both parents shook their heads.

"Can you think of anyone she might have known who lives in Washington County?" Miller asked.

"We were trying to figure that out on the drive here," Seth said. "I can't think of anyone. We have access to her social media accounts. She's friends with a few people who live in the area, but she's also friends with people in Florida who she's never met in person, you know?"

"We made a list for you, though," Crystal said.

"Thanks, that's helpful. Would you mind emailing me the names?" Nikki gave them her FBI email address. "We'll make sure we check them out, although I'm going to be honest with you—Kesha may or may not have known her killer, but it's unlikely someone her age could have done this. Even if she was taken by a stranger, this killer knew he was going to abduct someone that day, and he'd prepared for it. That's not usually something we see with younger people, or in domestic situations. I'm not ruling anything out, but I want you to understand that we are likely dealing with an experienced predator, and with the media already converging, there will be 'experts' on the news. Hopefully they don't mention the idea of a serial predator, but if they do, expect even more chaos."

"I've advised them not to talk to any media," Farley said. "Let the family attorney handle it."

"That's good advice," Nikki said. "I would try to ignore the media as much as possible, because all of it's going to be speculation on their part. Unless we deem it necessary, Sheriff Miller and I will not discuss the case with any sort of media."

Normally Nikki didn't spend so much time talking about the press with a victim's family, but Stanton's wife had made that difficult. Her actions had taken control of the narrative away from law enforcement, and the only way to regain it was to lock everything down.

"Do you think she suffered?" Crystal invariably asked the question every family member wanted answered. "Please be honest. I don't believe in sugar-coating things."

"It's impossible for us to know that right now, and the medical examiner may not be able to tell, either. The water tends to make things like that much harder to figure out." Nikki wasn't about to tell Kesha's parents that in all likelihood, Kesha was at minimum verbally assaulted and more likely endured much more, even if she was killed shortly after her abduction. Dismembering a body wasn't an easy task, and in Nikki's experience the sort of person capable of the clean cuts she'd seen on Kesha's extremities had a cruel streak that had to be satisfied before he took her life.

The call with Kesha's parents lasted almost an hour, with Nikki and Miller asking the same questions the couple had likely been asked a thousand times already. They were adamant that Dion wouldn't have hurt Kesha and asked Nikki to let him have Christmas Eve before they interrogated him. Both said Dion wasn't an outdoor type of kid, and Mr. Williams had recalled a conversation last year with him about the perils of ice fishing.

"That boy didn't walk out on that ice, I promise you," Mr. Williams had said before the call ended. "Don't waste more time on him."

Normally, Nikki wasted no time interviewing suspects, but given the holiday and the parents' insistence, she decided to wait until tomorrow afternoon to call Dion.

She checked her watch. It was nearly four p.m., and Nikki

had promised Lacey that she would be at the Todds' in time for dinner at 5:30 p.m.

"What's the BPD detective's name again?" she asked Miller as the video call came through.

"Wiley."

Nikki sipped coffee while Miller made the introductions. She noticed the detective appeared to be calling from a home office. He was also not far from retiring, and Nikki suspected he was eager to pass this case on.

"Detective Wiley, thanks for talking with us today."

"No problem," Wiley said. "I just looked at the photos you sent on the secure server, Sheriff Miller. It's definitely Kesha Williams. I would have preferred to tell the parents myself."

Nikki bit her tongue and let Miller field the lie. When Wiley had initially been informed about Kesha's body, he'd instructed Miller to talk to the family. Now that he knew they'd found out in the worst of ways, he was eager to deflect blame.

"We had intended to hold her identity until local police were able to inform her parents, but unfortunately, the news media had other ideas." Miller sounded friendly, but Nikki picked up on the edge in his tone. That was the only fib he was going to let the detective get away with.

"Her dad chewed most of my ass out," Wiley said. "Please make it clear this screw-up wasn't mine, nor did it have anything to do with her skin color."

"We will," Nikki said, not bothering to hide the edge in her voice. "Did you send over the file?"

"Emailed it to both of you," Wiley said.

"Did you have any suspects?" Miller asked.

"Initially, the boyfriend. He said he'd waited for her the whole time, but then changed his story when the mall police got him on camera doing differently."

"What was he doing?" Miller asked.

"He said that he stayed in the same spot except getting up to go to the bathroom, and then he came back. Security cameras show he browsed a kiosk and paid cash at a vending machine during that time. The vending machine was in the direction Kesha had walked in, but Dion not only forgot about getting up, in his version, he walks a couple of minutes back to where Kesha left him instead of just going to find her. Why backtrack?"

"Because that's where they were supposed to meet," Nikki said. "With all the people in the mall that day, it would have been easy for them to miss each other walking. His decision makes sense to me."

Wiley looked unimpressed. "Because the mall was so busy, there's at least fifteen minutes he's unaccounted for."

"You think that in those fifteen minutes, he did something to her, hid her, came back and then contacted mall security because she wasn't answering her phone?" Miller's jaw was tight, his voice steely. Nikki couldn't imagine what it would be like to be a black cop in situations like this, especially in the current climate, so she waited to hear the detective's reaction.

"I'm saying he wasn't truthful, and we had no one else," Wiley retorted.

Nikki unlocked her tablet and opened Wiley's email. She scanned the documents. "You interviewed her family and boyfriend, and a couple of other friends. What about witnesses at the mall?"

"We talked to the employees at every store Kesha was known to shop at. No one noticed anything unusual. We followed every possible lead, which, to be honest, weren't many. Kesha was a senior in high school. Honor student, honor band, and she played soccer. She worked part-time at the local YMCA. Never reported any issues or concerns. By all accounts, she was happy and getting ready for college. She planned to attend Mankato State in the fall."

"And now you've eliminated her boyfriend as a suspect?" Miller asked.

Wiley shrugged. "Not necessarily. Dion Johnson is a year older than Kesha. He's the one who brought her to the mall, and they'd recently fought about her decision to go to school and leave him behind at the local college. He wasn't happy about it."

"What actual evidence did you have against him?" Nikki asked, tired of the detective's blasé attitude.

"Nothing solid, or we would have charged him. Just a feeling more than anything, not to mention it made the most sense."

Nikki doubted that, but she decided not to argue with him until she'd thoroughly looked at the file. "I assume you've kept an eye on him the last month?"

"As best we could, but it's a busy time of year. He said he took leave from work and school, and the local police have kept up with his movements. He hasn't done anything suspicious, but they weren't able to watch twenty-four hours a day. He goes to work, school, home. He does have a sealed juvenile record."

"We're aware," Nikki said.

"Are you also aware that Dion's been participating in a brain study of criminal offenders?" Wiley asked with a smirk.

Nikki looked at Miller, who shook his head. "Would you enlighten us?" she asked.

"Dion's been part of a big neuroscience study since his last juvenile offence. His paternal uncle is a violent offender, and this study is looking for biomarkers in juveniles." Wiley took a drink from a blue coffee mug adorned with snowmen. "His mom wanted to find a way to keep him out of trouble, and the study pays a stipend. We tried to look at the records, but the neuroscientist leading the study fought the warrant, citing HIPAA."

Nikki asked for the neuroscientist's contact information and scribbled down the response.

"Look," Wiley said. "We know, in most cases, the victim turns out to be killed by someone she knows, so we did our due diligence." Wiley rubbed his temples. "I'm part of the old guard. Looking back, I'm sure I did make mistakes and assumptions based on race, and that's my cross to bear. But I promise you that wasn't the case with Kesha's disappearance. Her family and other friends were accounted for, Dion was at the mall with her. And if he didn't do it, then how did someone force Kesha out of the mall without drawing attention? She was a runner and took self-defense classes, but she just vanished, almost like she'd been erased."

"Her killer must have had a weapon, knew how to scare her," Miller mused.

"We'll follow up with you if we have further questions," Nikki told the detective. "By the way, did anything about Washington County come up in your investigation?"

Wiley shook his head. "Like I said, the trail was cold as ice from the beginning."

Nikki winced at the play on words. "Whoever did this definitely planned to take someone from the mall that day, probably capitalizing on the crowds and chaos. And you're right, most of the time murders are committed by someone who knows the victim, but I don't know if that's the case with Kesha."

She and Miller thanked the detective for his time and ended the call. Nikki leaned back in her chair and stared at the ceiling, trying to put her thoughts in some kind of order. In her experience, nineteen-year-old men were impulsive. If Nikki's theory about Kesha's remains being left in the ice was correct, she had a hard time seeing a nineteen-year-old who probably hadn't been on an ice lake in his life embark on something that took planning and experience. She could tell that Wiley's opinion of Kesha's boyfriend had already been tainted by his own bias, so she didn't bring it up. Nikki preferred to make her decisions on her own merit.

"Hey, it's getting close to five p.m.," Miller said. "You go ahead to the Todds' and have Christmas Eve with Lacey. I'll call you tonight and we can plan for tomorrow."

"What about you?" Nikki asked.

"I'm going to finish paperwork and then head home," he said. "Now, go before you wind up being late."

FOUR

Nikki tried not to break too many traffic laws on the way to Rory's parents', but she'd promised Lacey that she would be at the Todds' in time for dinner, and she was cutting it close.

Her ringtone suddenly cut through the music. Nikki glanced at the touch screen. Why were the Forest Lake police calling her? Forest Lake was a small town in Washington County, but unlike Stillwater, they had their own police force, and Nikki had heard Miller complain about jurisdictional issues with them on more than one occasion.

She answered the call. "Agent Nikki Hunt."

"I'm sorry to call on Christmas Eve, but my name is Jill Dover. I'm a detective with the Forest Lake police. We heard about Kesha Williams' remains being found at Big Marine Lake."

Who hasn't heard by now, thanks to Mrs. Stanton? "How can I help you?" Nikki asked.

"My boss told me that calling was a waste of time, and that my case couldn't be connected to the Williams case, but I just can't shake the feeling that it must be. Women's intuition, I guess."

"You have a missing female?"

"A missing young man, twenty-five," Dover said. "He's one of the owners of an artists' co-op here in town, and he vanished a week ago, just like Kesha Williams. His name is Parker Jameson."

"He was taken from a mall?" Nikki slowed her speed as she reached the Todds' neighborhood.

"Well, no," Dover said. "But he disappeared from the co-op while he was closing for the day. His car was still in its usual place, and he'd left his cell and wallet in the back room. Security camera shows him lock the door and start closing duties, but then he hears something and goes to the back. And that's it."

Nikki hesitated. She didn't want to blow any detective off, but at this point she couldn't see a connection. "Did he know Kesha or her boyfriend? Or the Williams family?"

"No," Dover admitted. "But he just vanished, like her. And Big Marine Lake isn't that far from here. Are you going to be searching for other victims?"

Nikki knew nothing about Dover, so she wasn't about to answer that question. "Do you have any suspects?"

"His ex-boyfriend has been a pretty strong person of interest," Dover admitted. "They were only together a few months, but it was volatile, according to Parker's family and friends. The ex didn't take the breakup well, and he's got a prior history of stalking, but his alibi is semi-solid."

"Semi-solid?"

"His mother alibied him," Dover said. "That's always an iffy one in my book."

Nikki understood the detective's trepidation. She'd had more than one parent provide a false alibi for their kid. "Why don't you email me a photo of Parker and a copy of the case file? I'll have my partner take a look at it and see what he thinks." That would give Liam something to do and hopefully kill two birds with one stone. Parker's disappearance did sound odd, but they didn't yet have any evidence to suggest that Kesha had been killed by a serial murderer, and if she had, the vast majority of serial predators stuck to one gender. Richard Ramirez was the only one she could think of who openly enjoyed killing both men and women and didn't appear to have any real pattern other than dissimilarity.

"With all due respect, Agent, I feel like you're blowing me off," Dover said.

"I'm not," Nikki said. "You're asking for our help."

"Parker is a missing person," Dover said irritably. "No offense, but Kesha Williams can't be saved. Parker may still have time."

Nikki gripped the steering wheel, trying to think of a way to be firm and still diplomatic. "I assure you, whether Parker is a victim of the same killer or not, my office is happy to help. But we need the file first. We'll get into our databases—"

"All of that's been done," Dover snapped. "We've combed the entire town and most of the county. He just left everything behind and walked out the back door, which is something his friends and family insist that he would never do. I think there's a good possibility Parker was taken by the same person Kesha was."

"Why?" Nikki asked point blank. "Despite the information you gave me, when it comes down to it, there aren't enough similarities to suggest that. We don't even know if Kesha's killer knew her or not, so if there is no connection between Parker and Kesha, I can't just shift all our resources. Send the information to us, and I will assign an agent to go through it. I assume you've covered the usual bases regarding missing persons: financial records, phone records, text messages, social media, that sort of thing?"

"We have," Dover said. "No red flags at all. APBs out in Minnesota and Wisconsin."

"Good," Nikki said. "I'll make sure an agent follows up with you on the twenty-sixth, Detective Dover."

"Fine," Dover said. "Be prepared to be hounded by me if they don't. Parker Jameson was taken, period."

Nikki wanted to ask her how she could be so sure, but her brain was deluged with information and the memory of Kesha's body. She would make sure the FBI was at Forest Lake's disposal, but right now, she had to focus on her daughter's Christmas.

Rory's parents lived in a gated community in Stillwater, in a modern ranch with a large backyard, a pool and now-dormant flower gardens that Lacey had helped with over the summer. Multi-colored Christmas lights covered the pine trees on either side of the house, and Rory and his brother, Mark, had strung lights along the roof and windows. The solar lights along the brick path in the front yard had been changed to red and green, casting a pretty holiday glow over the white snow.

Nikki parked behind Rory's truck and tried to gather her thoughts. She'd always excelled at compartmentalizing, but putting on a happy face after the last few hours seemed like a herculean task. She found her mascara and powder compact in her bag and freshened up as best she could and then ran a brush through her tangled, dark waves.

She hadn't had a chance to put on anything nicer, but her jeans and long, ivory sweater should be sufficient. Despite the new, fancy house, the Todds were as down to earth as they had been before Mark's multi-million-dollar settlement from the state. He'd bought the house for his parents and was currently living in the guest house to help out with things when he wasn't working with Rory.

This would be the first time Mark had celebrated Christmas outside of prison in twenty years, and Nikki was determined to keep things light, especially around Lacey. Her first Christmas without her father was hard on them both, and Nikki knew that her late ex-husband would be happy that Lacey had a big family to celebrate with instead of just her mother.

Nikki headed up the freshly salted brick path, balancing her bag and the liter of soda she'd just picked up at the gas station. Just as she made it to the first step, the front door opened and Lacey bounded out of the house, dressed in the red and green dress she and Nikki had picked out for dinner. Her dark curls had been brushed into silky waves, and the bells on her elf slippers jingled merrily.

"I'm so glad you're here." Lacey wrapped her arms around Nikki's waist. "I was starting to get really worried."

"Well, Sheriff Miller needed my help, and traffic was terrible," Nikki fibbed, too tired to make up any better excuse. She forced a smile for Lacey. "You look very festive."

"That's what Granny Ruth said." Lacey pulled her toward the house. "Come on, it's cold out here."

Nikki followed her daughter inside, slipping off her boots in the foyer and lining them up next to Rory's and Lacey's. *A Christmas Story* played on the flat screen in the living room, but everyone had gathered in the open kitchen and dining area. Rory slid off his barstool and kissed her cheek. "You made it."

She leaned against him for a few seconds, wishing she could strip off her armor instead of putting on a happy face. "Thanks for picking up the slack."

Rory squeezed her shoulders. "Any time."

"Nikki." His older brother, Mark, waved to her from his perch at the bar. Since his release from prison, Mark had been working for Rory's construction business, slowly putting his life back together. He put his arm around the willowy woman standing next to him. "Come meet Jessie, my girlfriend."

Nikki tried to remember what Mark had told them about Jessie. She was an accountant for some of the larger firms in the

Stillwater/Washington County area, didn't have children, owned her own home. She was tall and slim, with chestnut hair and dark eyes that bored into Nikki.

"Nice to meet you." Nikki smiled. "I've heard so many great things about you."

Jessie's smile didn't quite reach her eyes. "You as well."

Nikki pretended she didn't notice the way Mark's girlfriend had looked her up and down, as if sizing up someone she planned to chew out later. "How did you guys meet again?"

Mark had won a very sizable settlement from the state over his wrongful incarceration, and Nikki's guard had automatically gone up when she first heard Jessie was an accountant, but she'd told herself to remain impartial. Just because Mark had money didn't mean the woman was trying to cash in on the situation.

"A mutual friend," Jessie said. "What about you and Rory?"

"Babe, you know that already," Mark said, his cheeks growing pink. "We talked about this."

"I'm just making conversation," Jessie said with a forced smile. "Why ignore the elephant in the room?"

"What elephant?" Caitlin had appeared seemingly out of nowhere with a glass of red wine, which she silently handed to Nikki. "What did I miss?" She smiled sweetly at Jessie, her tone just perky enough for Nikki to pick up on the sarcasm. Liam lingered behind her and grinned at Nikki.

She forced a return smile, but the guilt inevitably welled up at the sight of him. Liam's concussion had happened because Nikki had sent him alone into a situation, and Liam had been lucky he hadn't been beaten to death. He'd told her a thousand times that she'd made the right decision splitting them up, and that he would have done the same thing at the time. It didn't help alleviate much of Nikki's guilt.

"Tell me, what's the elephant?" Caitlin pressed again, looking straight at Mark's girlfriend.

Jessie shrugged. "Just how Nikki and Rory met."

"We all know the answer to that." Caitlin sipped from her own glass of wine, her arm linked through Nikki's.

"Liam, how are you feeling?" Nikki changed the subject before the tension got any worse.

"Pretty good today," he answered. "I only had a couple of dizzy spells. I had cognitive therapy yesterday, and my memory's improved significantly. The issue is the headaches and falling asleep, but that's gotten better in the last week or so."

"Only because I watched you 24/7 and made sure you didn't exert yourself," Caitlin said. "He's the worst patient. I'm thinking of slipping him an Ambien so he'll stay in one spot for more than thirty minutes at a time."

Nikki laughed. "Good luck. He's so tall it would probably take a massive dose. Then there's the ginger thing. No soul makes it harder to get the dose right."

Liam rolled his eyes. "Like I haven't heard that a hundred times in my life." He glanced at Lacey as she skipped by with napkins and silverware. Ruth had taught her how to set a fancy table, as Lacey called it, and she took the job seriously.

"She doing okay?' Liam asked quietly.

Nikki nodded. "We've tried to encourage her to talk about how she feels without constantly reminding her that Tyler's gone."

Rory's mother announced dinner and shooed them toward the table. "Dinner is a bit unconventional." She laughed. "I cooked a ham, but since it's Mark's first Christmas home, I also made homemade lasagna. It's his favorite. And, of course, Lacey wanted lots of sweets, so we have lots of sugar cookies."

"I'm so glad she has sweets here since we don't have any at home," Nikki said dryly. "But that's only because she and Rory hoover up a batch of a cookies in minutes if I don't keep an eye out."

As the plates were filled and various dishes passed around, Nikki tried to focus on the food and conversation, but her thoughts refused to cooperate. She couldn't stop thinking about Kesha's battered and defiled body or the pain in her parents' faces when she and Miller had spoken to them earlier. Christmas would never be the same for any member of Kesha's family, for Dion and his family, along with Kesha's friends. For the rest of their lives, the holiday would be tainted with the memory of Kesha's life being cut short.

"Nikki, are you crying?" Rory's dad asked. He was the quiet one in the family, but he was also extremely perceptive.

Lacey's fork paused mid-bite. "Mommy?"

"No, no." Nikki dabbed at her eyes. "Just allergies."

"In December?" Jessie asked.

"I guess so," Nikki answered. Jessie gave Mark a knowing look, but he shook his head and pointed to Lacey.

"Ooh, Santa's delivering presents in the UK right now." Rory held up his phone. "Santa tracker."

"How come they get stuff first?" Lacey asked.

"Because over there, it's almost midnight," Rory said.

"Oh yeah, time zones. We learned about those in school." She speared a large piece of ham from the platter. "I'm still starving."

"Me too." Rory helped himself to a large portion of lasagna, earning a dirty look from his brother.

"That's for me, and I want leftovers," Mark said.

"There's half a pan left," Rory retorted.

"Yeah, and if no one pays attention, you'll eat it all."

"Now I might." Rory took a large bite and smirked.

After the apple and chocolate pies had been decimated, Nikki and Caitlin started cleaning up the table. Jessie rose to help, but Caitlin insisted she stay with Mark.

"We can handle it." She smiled sweetly, plates stacked high in her arms.

Nikki grabbed as many dishes as she could carry and followed Caitlin into the kitchen. "Smooth."

"I thought it was," Caitlin whispered, glancing out at the busy dining room. "She just wants to get you alone and discuss the past. It's not happening tonight. You have enough to deal with."

Nikki felt tears building in her eyes again. "Thanks."

"Lacey seems to be doing okay," Caitlin said.

"She's struggled some, but kids are resilient." Nikki told her about Lacey seeing the cardinals earlier. "Part of me felt bad leading her on, but—"

"You weren't," Caitlin cut her off. "Lots of people believe that about cardinals, and since we'll never know the truth, it's not a lie. It's a kindness to her."

Liam appeared with the ham platter and casserole dishes. He set them down next to the sink and leaned against the counter. "Okay, brief me, please. It's killing me not to know everything about the case."

"I can't right now," Nikki said. "We're doing dishes."

"And I'm here, dummy," Caitlin said affectionately. "Don't put her in that position when a member of the media is right here." She shooed him out of the kitchen. "You'll get your chance."

Liam grumbled something under his breath and went back to the dining room.

"I'll wash, you dry," Nikki said. "We'll put the smaller stuff in the dishwasher."

Caitlin grabbed a towel off the counter. "Have you heard of Doctor Alex Roth?"

Nikki scraped chunks of hash brown casserole off the glass baking pan. "The name sounds familiar. Who is he?"

"He's a neuroscience researcher working on mapping the brains of criminals. He worked on the Kasey team at the University of New Mexico, but he returned to Minnesota a few years ago to open a new facility and expand on his research. I caught part of a true crime show yesterday that he'd consulted on. The research is really interesting. He's focused on juveniles."

Nikki stopped scrubbing. The study Caitlin was talking about sounded an awful lot like the one the Bloomington detective had said Dion participated in. "What exactly is his research looking for?"

"It focuses on brain development in minors, looking for patterns of psychopathy and predatorial behaviors. He's trying to identify them in juveniles, compare them to adults, and then develop some sort of biomarkers, with the eventual goal of prevention."

"Prevention of what?" Nikki asked. "Violent crime?"

"That's my understanding."

"Why are you telling me all of this?" Nikki passed her the glass dish. "You never bring something like this up just to make conversation. What are you getting at?"

"Fine." Caitlin paused for dramatic effect. "I found out that Kesha's boyfriend has been in the program."

"We know," Nikki said. "I intend to ask the boyfriend about it, but unless we get real evidence against him, we'll never get his medical records."

"I just think Doctor Roth might be a good resource, since he's interviewed and scanned over a thousand murderers in the last decade," Caitlin said. "With Liam gone and so much on your plate, consulting with Doctor Roth could make sense on this. He's in these guys' heads on a regular basis, you know? The stuff he's sat and listened to would turn your hair white."

Nikki finished cleaning the stockpot and gave it to Caitlin to dry. "And the caveat?"

"What caveat?" Caitlin asked innocently.

Nikki snorted laughter. "I trust you and consider you a friend, but you're also a smart and savvy journalist. You want an interview with Roth. A connection through me would help you get it."

"What makes you think I can't get that on my own?" Caitlin asked. "My documentary on Mark's exoneration earned me a major media award."

Nikki grabbed another heavy dish and started washing. "Translation: you're working on something new, and Doctor Roth would be a great addition to it."

"Only if it's something he's interested in." She smiled sweetly and set the big cooking pot in the rack to dry. "I just thought this might kill two birds with one stone."

"If I decide to reach out to him, I'll give him your name. But you're on your own otherwise."

Caitlin grinned. "Deal."

FIVE

"She's finally asleep." Nikki went to the front closet and found the presents she didn't intend to wrap. "I thought she was never going to give up," she said as she started putting the gifts in front of the big Christmas tree that she and Lacey had helped Rory cut down.

"You aren't wrapping those?" he asked.

Nikki shook her head. "Tyler liked to leave a few unwrapped out for her, from Santa. That's how his parents did it." She looked around at the various sections of the dollhouse he'd bought for Lacey. "What do you need me to do?"

Rory scowled as he studied the directions. "I build million-dollar houses for a living. Why is this freaking dollhouse so hard?"

"Because the people who design them want to make sure parents are a stressed-out mess before Santa finally shows up." Nikki took the directions and tried to read them, but they might as well have been written in Greek.

"I don't need directions, anyway." He searched through his toolbox. "If you want to organize them according to size and shape, that would be great."

After she had all the parts organized for him, Rory got to work. Nikki loved to watch him tinkering, his face pinched in concentration and the tip of his tongue sticking out of the corner of his mouth. Her gaze drifted to the pretty tree, with its multicolored lights and hodgepodge collection of ornaments, including some that Nikki had had since childhood. Her mother had bought an ornament every year for Nikki, and she'd done the same with Lacey. The ornaments from the small tabletop tree that Tyler had last year were at the top, near the angel. Nikki still felt like crying every time she thought about Lacey telling Rory about each ornament and why she wanted her daddy's hung by the angel. Instead of feeling threatened or intimidated, Rory had lifted her up so she could hang them where she wanted.

Nikki wasn't sure the two of them would have made it through this Christmas without Rory.

"What are you thinking about?" he asked, reaching for the flathead screwdriver.

"Fate, I guess," Nikki answered.

"Oh yeah?"

She nodded. "You know, everything that happened this last year would have happened whether you and I got together or not, including Mark's release and Tyler's murder."

"But I convinced you Mark was innocent, and you spoke to the court."

"The DNA exonerated him, not me. The point is, if I hadn't decided to stop at that gas station and fallen on my ass, we might not be here right now." She grinned, trying to lighten the moment. "Lucky you."

Rory shifted to his knees so he could kiss her. "Lucky me indeed."

Nikki squirmed as his lips trailed along her jaw and down her neck. "Behave. We need to finish this so we can sleep too." Not that she expected to be able to rest tonight. Her shoulders already felt the weight of sitting around being happy while Kesha's body was in the morgue and her family's lives shattered. The only way Nikki could deal with the guilt was to keep reminding herself that Christmas was important for Lacey. She needed some normalcy.

"I've been thinking," Rory said, pulling away, his cheeks flushed, "that you should sell your house in St. Paul and officially move in here with me. You guys are always here anyway. You're throwing money away on the mortgage."

Despite the reasonable point he'd made, excuses started to form in her mind. She liked having the house in case she wound up stuck at the office and didn't feel like making the hour drive to Stillwater.

"The market's red-hot right now," Rory said. "You'd probably make some serious money off it."

Tyler had left a sizable inheritance for Lacey, and Nikki had still been the primary on his life insurance policy. She'd put it all into Lacey's college fund.

"Nik?" Worry had crept into Rory's voice. "Was it a bad idea to ask?"

"No, of course not. It makes sense." She bit her lip. "I just wonder if that will negatively affect Lacey, you know?"

"She's never there," Rory said.

"I know, but so much has changed for her in the last few months," Nikki said. "I just don't want to do anything that could harm her recovery, you know?" Did she sound as silly to Rory as she did to herself? Lacey rarely even talked about the St. Paul house, because she had so many memories of Tyler in it. She'd probably be relieved to know they wouldn't live there again.

Her phone rang, startling them both. Miller's number flashed on the caller ID. "Sorry, I have to take this." She slid her thumb across the phone screen. "Hey, Kent. I hope you're bringing better news than you did the last time you called."

"We caught a really lucky break," Miller said. "My friend Reuben can bring his dog out tomorrow."

"On Christmas Day?" Nikki was surprised. "How'd you pull that off?"

"He's divorced, and his kids are with their mom until middle of the week. He'll have them over New Year's. He's meeting me at the lake at eleven a.m."

"What about your family?" Nikki asked.

"They understand," he said. "My girls are past Santa Claus. Presents and food are the mainstay of their Christmas. Plus, they're old enough to understand that what I'm doing is helping another family who's suffering right now."

"Lacey's grandparents are picking her up at one thirty tomorrow afternoon. I can't leave before then, but I'll come out to the lake as soon as she leaves. Did your friend say how long it would take to search the lake?"

"An hour, hour and a half if the dog doesn't hit anything. Then we'll let him start in the parking area and go from there."

Nikki glanced at Rory still working on the dollhouse. "Are you able to help search tomorrow afternoon? Miller has a K9 lined up. We'd probably have to drive separately since I can't leave until Lacey's picked up in the afternoon. But if you can go earlier, Miller needs all the volunteer manpower he can get."

"Is that normal?" Rory asked. "Am I even allowed?"

"I just need the manpower," Nikki said. "Any other time of the year, we'd have deputies and other volunteers to help search, but there's no way we'll be able to put together anything official tomorrow. This will just be as many people as Kent and I can cobble together to walk through the frozen slough around the lake. Fair warning, though, there's a chance you'll see something awful, so I totally understand if you don't feel comfortable."

Rory shook his head. "I'll go with you."

"Would you be able to come earlier than one thirty?" Miller

asked, obviously picking up on Rory's voice. "I understand Nikki has to wait for Lacey to get picked up, but Reuben thinks we'll be done with the lake by noon. We'll hit the ground right after."

"I'll be there," Rory said.

Nikki told Miller she'd update Liam and see if he could come out and help search too. "That makes you, me, Reuben, the dog, Rory and Liam, assuming he's able to come tomorrow. I'd say that's enough. We don't want to attract more media attention. I haven't heard anything on the news about Kesha's hands and feet being cut off, and I'd like to keep it that way."

After she finished talking with Miller, Nikki called Liam. "Kent and I had assumed we wouldn't be able to search until Sunday, but his friend with the dog came through." She explained the plan for tomorrow.

"What time and where?" Liam asked.

"Miller's going to work with the DNR to get the cadaver dog on the lake first, and then the immediate perimeter, working out from there. If he catches any kind of scent, we'll search on the ground. Rory's going to be there by noon, so plan on that. The handler says too many people on the boat distracts the dog. Will Caitlin be all right with you helping out? We can't have her there since she's technically part of the media."

"She'll be fine. She'll have her family here, and she and Zach have a Monopoly tournament planned. I have a feeling it's going to get ugly."

Nikki couldn't help but smile. The relationship between Caitlin and her son, Zach, was complicated, and Zach had been the target of a deranged pedophile earlier in the year. It was good to hear he was doing well enough to act like a normal teenager.

"Like I said, this is off the books," Nikki reminded him. "As long as no one but Miller and I touch any actual evidence, we're fine. I'm hoping it will be nothing more than a wasted Saturday.

Did you get the email I forwarded from the Forest Lake detective?"

"Yeah," he said. "I'm going to read through it in the morning. My head's killing me right now. Was fine until we got home."

"Too much stimulus," Nikki said. "If you can't make it tomorrow, I understand."

"I'll be there, and I'll be up to date on this Forest Lake file too," he said, a razor-sharp edge in his voice. "If someone needs to go out there and meet with them in person, I'll send an agent."

Pushing the issue would only rile him up, so Nikki told him to get some sleep.

"He cut off her hands and feet?" Rory asked when she'd finished the call.

Nikki nodded. "I shouldn't have said that in front of you, so please don't repeat it."

"I won't." He shuddered. "I'm close to finishing this if you want to go through your notes or whatever. I know sitting here not working is killing you."

"Thank you." Nikki leaned over and kissed him hard. "And we can talk about the sale after this case, I promise."

Rory smiled and nodded at her, but Nikki had the distinct feeling he knew she was dodging the answer. What the hell was wrong with her?

Rory managed to finish the dollhouse by midnight, and he fell asleep immediately, but Nikki lay awake, reading over the information Detective Wiley had emailed.

While the public often focused on the gruesome details of a murder, victimology was the key to a profile and, often, to solving the case.

Kesha was a high school senior from a small suburb, but

she'd been taken from a packed mall on the busiest shopping day of the year. The high-risk action showed Nikki the killer was organized and meticulous, managing to avoid not only mall security but he'd kept Kesha in check enough that police hadn't been able to spot her leaving with the killer, despite the amount of CCTV at the Mall of America. Kesha's parents said that she and Dion had planned the Black Friday shopping trip just a couple of days before Thanksgiving. According to the phone records shared by Detective Wiley, Kesha had only told a couple of her close friends about the trip, and they'd already been alibied. What little information they had suggested that the killer had probably chosen Kesha at random that day, possibly after witnessing her discussion with Dion and noting her frustration with her boyfriend. Predators excelled in spotting vulnerability, and many enjoyed the thrill of the hunt. Nikki was certain Kesha's killer had been planning on taking someone that day, but had Kesha been in the wrong place at the wrong time, or did she have a connection to her killer?

SIX

CHRISTMAS MORNING

Freezing water struck like exploding shrapnel, sending her nervous system into overdrive. The heavy weight attached to her ankles dragged her slowly into the depths of the lake, the water filling her lungs. She pawed at the twine around her ankles, somehow breaking free of the gravity pulling her down. She kicked hard, her arms flailing against the water as she struggled to reach the top. Her fingers brushed against something solid and cold. She dragged her fingernails helplessly against the jagged ice, pounded on it with her fists. Couldn't anyone hear her, trapped beneath the wall of ice?

The water was going to win, after all.

Warm hands closed around her arm, a deep voice calling her name.

"Nicole, open your eyes. It's a dream, baby."

Rory's voice shattered the ice, and Nikki sat straight up in bed, gasping for air. Cold sweat had soaked through her T-shirt and shorts. She pulled her knees to her chest and wrapped her arms around them. "I'm so cold."

Rory's strong arms pulled her to his chest, and he jerked the blankets back over her. "Just breathe." His big hands rubbed her back.

Nikki buried her face against his bare skin, inhaling his familiar scent. He kissed her forehead and tucked the blanket around her so that she was cocooned in warmth.

Nikki refused to close her eyes, afraid the imaginary, crushing weight of the water would never go away. She kept her gaze on the bedroom window, watching as daylight began to peek through the blinds.

Rory finally broke the silence. "You okay?"

"I don't feel like I'm in the lake anymore."

He stroked her damp hair. "I can't believe Lacey didn't wake up."

"I screamed?"

"More like gasped and grunted, and you were kicking and throwing your fists. I think you hit the headboard a couple of times."

"No wonder my right hand hurts." Now that her fear was gone, embarrassment crept in. She sat up, her clothes sticky and her hair matted from lying against him. "Sorry if I scared you."

"Don't apologize." Rory shifted and turned on the light next to his side of the bed. "Let me see your hand."

She showed him her right hand. The knuckles were red and sore, but she could move her fingers well enough so Nikki knew she hadn't broken anything.

Rory traced her hand with his index finger. "I know you don't want to hear this, but do you think this case is one you should work? It's already got you way out of sorts."

"I have to work it," Nikki said. "It's not the case, anyway. I think it's more being on the ice yesterday and remembering what happened last winter."

"Just promise me that if it gets to be too much, you'll hand it off to someone else. You've got so much emotional stuff on your plate right now, no one would blame you if you stepped back."

There was no chance in hell she'd step back, and with Liam out of the field, Kesha's murder would be shifted to an agent in major crime who was probably juggling ten plus cases already. Nikki's behavioral violent crime unit had been established to assist in cases involving serial and violent criminals, and they were uniquely qualified to work on cases like Kesha's. After Liam's injury, Nikki had convinced her boss to recruit two new agents into the fold, but working that into the budget had taken weeks, and they wouldn't be interviewing potential candidates until early in the new year. But she knew what Rory needed to hear, so she nodded. "I will. Don't worry about me. What time is it?"

Rory grabbed his phone off the nightstand. "A little after seven. What time does Lacey usually wake up on Christmas morning?"

"Depends," Nikki said. "She'll let us know, I promise."

Less than ten minutes later, Lacey's squeal of delight brought them both out of bed. Rory yanked on athletic shorts and a T-shirt and ran out to join her, while Nikki grabbed her robe and phone, trying not to think about the dream or what they might see this afternoon.

The morning passed in a blur, with Lacey tearing through her gifts. Nikki loved seeing her little girl so happy, but every second was juxtaposed with what she knew Kesha's family was enduring. While Rory and Lacey played with the various new toys, Nikki made chocolate chip pancakes and a pot of coffee. Time ticked away quickly, counting down to Lacey's departure.

Nikki had made sure that Lacey's things were packed and ready last night, but of course she wanted to take her new doll and the tub of Polly Pocket toys from Santa.

Rory and Lacey played a furious game of Go Fish before he headed to the lake. Lacey surprised Rory by wrapping her arms around his neck and telling him how much she'd miss him before he left to help Miller, and Nikki was pretty certain she'd spotted moisture in Rory's eyes.

Now, she checked her phone to see how much time they had. She'd sent Lacey to brush her teeth and make sure she had everything before her grandparents arrived. It was almost one p.m., and she'd given Kesha's boyfriend enough time on Christmas. While Lacey was running around getting last-minute stuff, Nikki fired off a text to Dion.

Hi, Dion, this is Agent Nicole Hunt with the FBI. Kesha's parents asked me to give you time, and I want to honor that since you've been cooperative, but I do need to talk face to face with you as soon as possible so we can make sure our information is accurate.

She started to put her phone back in her pocket when Miller's text came through.

No remains in lake. Found burial ground. Come ASAP.

SEVEN

SUMMER, 1989

Emmanuel peered through the tall weeds, watching his older sister Diana slowly peel off her short shorts and skimpy tank top. He didn't understand why he suddenly felt butterflies in his stomach when he realized she wasn't wearing a bra. She sat down on the towel she'd brought to the secret cove the two of them had found a couple of years ago, before she stopped doing fun things like spending their days trolling the lake for big northerns or searching the woods for old arrowheads. Last summer, Diana had understood his need to run untethered all day, without the watchful and prying eyes of the babysitter.

A tall, older boy suddenly burst through the bushes on the other side of the small beach. Emmanuel had seen the boy around the little town they lived near, working at the gas station —that's how he'd met Diana. His name was David, but everyone called him Davey.

His sister had recently started spending less and less time with Emmanuel and more time with Davey, even though their mother forbade it when she found out.

Diana raced into her boyfriend's arms, wrapping her legs

around his waist. David's hands grabbed at her butt, and his erection was evident through his running shorts.

Emmanuel had only just started dealing with those uncontrollable things. He'd woken up to a mess in his sheets more than once. He'd tried to hide it but sharing a room with a younger sibling made that impossible. Stupid baby brother had told Mom, who'd taken Emmanuel into the bathroom and make him take a shower so hot he looked like a lobster.

While he showered, she sat on the toilet and explained that he had to control his urges, especially around girls. What he'd done was unclean and embarrassing, and God saw everything.

Then she'd made him pray with her, asking for forgiveness for the impure thoughts that had invaded his dreams.

The next time, when he asked why his special part got hard and sometimes hurt before it made a mess, his mother hit him upside the head so hard Emmanuel saw stars. Diana had tried to come to his defense, telling her mother that if Emmanuel understood his body, he might be able to control it.

Their mother had locked his sister in her room for the night. "That girl is trouble," she had told Emmanuel. "She doesn't care that God is always watching."

Now, he watched his sister toss her golden hair over her shoulder as the older boy playfully dropped her onto the big blanket. His sister's face was flushed with excitement, her eyes on the older boy as he quickly undressed and crawled on top of her. Diana gasped and huffed, her fingernails digging into his back. The boy moved back and forth, grunting like Emmanuel heard his father do.

The two teenagers writhed on the towel awkwardly, making gross noises. It was over in minutes, and his sister and the boy ran into the creek, naked and laughing. Emmanuel watched as they splashed each other for a while and then ran back to the towel. They lay naked beneath the shady trees, talking about what was going to happen next. Their plan would work, his sister told the boy.

"Then it will just be the two of us, right?"

"I bet I can get a job in the city," the boy said. "There are places called hostels where we can stay until we make enough money to get a little apartment. We don't need our parents."

"Especially my mother," Diana said, resting her head on the guy's scrawny chest. "She's just mean and miserable. I'm not going to waste my life like she did."

"What about your siblings?" Davey asked.

"Emmanuel can take care of our little brother." Diana started chewing her fingernails like she did when she was nervous. "She's mean to him too, but he'll get bigger. He'll be able to fight back. If I stay, she'll end up beating me to death or murdering me in my sleep, especially if she finds out about you." She sat up abruptly and looked down at Davey. "Let's do it tonight."

"Run away?" Davey looked shocked.

"Why not? I'm sick of putting it off. We can take the late bus to Minneapolis. Your dad and mine will be passed out drunk before nine, and my mother has her precious bingo in Stillwater tonight. She won't be home until after eleven." Diana brushed his hair off his face and then leaned down to kiss him. "Please, baby. I can't spend another night in that house."

Emmanuel's hand drifted to the Bowie knife he carried everywhere, just in case he might need it.

He knew what he had to do.

EIGHT

Nikki parked next to Rory's white pickup and slipped on her winter hiking boots and heavy coat, making sure she had her phone and an extra set of gloves in her canvas bag. She checked her phone, unsurprised that Dion Johnson hadn't returned her call. Waiting to talk to a potential suspect went against everything Nikki had been taught, but given what the K9 had found this morning, she felt justified. It was looking more and more like Kesha had been taken by an experienced serial killer. Her stomach knotted at the thought of these new victims. How long had someone like that been operating in Washington County, right under their noses?

"Fancy meeting you here."

Rory's voice made Nikki jump. "Holy God, you scared me."

"Sorry." He grinned sheepishly. "Miller said he gave you directions to the clearing, but it's kind of a tough slog, so I decided to come back and walk with you."

Nikki locked the jeep and kissed his cheek. "My knight in shining muck boots. How are you doing?" She couldn't discuss case information with Rory, but over the summer he'd been part of the cold case murder of his high school sweetheart, whose remains had been located on a development site Rory had bid for and won. He'd gone to some therapy sessions and seemed to be doing better, but today couldn't have been easy for him.

"Okay." He pointed to the northeast. "When I got here this morning, Miller and his friend with the K9 were just coming off the lake. As soon as the dog got out of the boat, he hit on something and was off. It was sad and awesome to watch."

"Dogs are amazing," Nikki agreed. "They can find decades-old bodies with no organic material left on them."

"The easiest way to get to the site is to walk along the road you just came in on—"

"Is that the route the dog took?" Nikki asked.

Rory shook his head. "No, he beelined through the woods, kind of skirted around the boggy area, and back to the high ground. That's where he lay down and Miller used the ground-penetrating radar."

"Then that's the route I want to take," she said. "It's likely the one the killer took, and I want to have some idea of what it would take to walk through there, carrying Kesha's weight." She said the words matter-of-factly, the same way she would have if she'd been talking to Liam or Miller. Rory's expression made it clear he hadn't thought about that aspect. Nikki felt like a jerk for putting the visual in his head.

She followed Rory off the trail and into the deep thicket of trees, her mind racing with everything that needed to be done. The ground would have to be thawed before the medical examiner and forensic anthropologist could do anything, which meant it could be days before Nikki could officially link Kesha's murder to the bodies in the woods. The large patch of wooded area to the northeast of the lake was easy enough to trudge through, but Nikki's focus was on the boggy area Rory had talked about. She'd studied the satellite images of the reserve, and the wetland was situated right in the middle of it. Getting through wouldn't be so bad in the winter, as long as everything had been frozen. Nikki pointed to the red tape tied around a couple of trees. "Any idea what those are for?"

Rory pointed to the long, curved line of frozen cattails. "That's the edge of the slough. Lacey do okay leaving?"

Nikki nodded. "Better than me. I think if Miller hadn't texted right before Tyler's parents showed up, I would have been a bigger mess."

"Did you put the phone in Lacey's backpack?" When Nikki had gone back to work after Tyler's murder, she'd given Lacey a cell phone so she could text her mom whenever she wanted to make sure she was okay. Lacey believed the phone couldn't connect to the internet, but it was enabled. Nikki just hadn't installed any apps and made sure the phone had parental controls enabled.

"GPS is on, and so is Life360," Nikki said. "She knows to charge it overnight and put it back in her backpack. As long as she does that, we'll be able to know where she's at most of the time."

"Should have just put a regular tracker on her," Rory said. "Like in a watch or something."

Nikki laughed. "She'd definitely forget that. Her backpack has snacks. She never forgets those."

"True." They walked a little way in silence. Nikki watched a hawk circle the trees, eyeing nests to raid. "How far in do we need to go?" she finally asked.

Rory veered to the left. "Not much longer. It's maybe five minutes from the parking lot to the clearing where the dog caught the scent."

A few minutes later, the frozen weeds and trees thinned, and Nikki could see Miller's tall form standing next to Liam on a small, uneven tract of land. Calling it a clearing was definitely a stretch, Nikki thought. It couldn't be any larger than the average bedroom and a couple of dead tree stumps meant a root system to deal with.

"Nikki." Liam skirted around the perimeter tape and headed towards them. "Glad you made it."

Nikki scowled at Liam's pale face. Circles rimmed his eyes, and his breathing appeared labored from the short walk over to them.

"I told you to take it easy," Nikki said.

"I am," Liam retorted. "Before I forget, the background check on Danny Stanton came back. He had a DUI a few years ago, and he's been busted a couple of times for fighting, but he's kept a low profile since. No red flags."

"What about other missing women in the area?" She fell into step next to him.

"Several, but most of them have a history of running away or falling off the grid. I'm going to work on separating those and narrowing down the list."

Stomach turning, Nikki moved closer to the site, stepping over the crime scene tape. What looked like a heavy, black blanket, covered the marked-off site. She'd read about ground-thawing blankets, but this was the first time she'd seen one used. "How long does the Powerblanket take to thaw the ground?"

"Twelve to twenty-four inches in twenty-four hours," Miller said. "I talked to Blanchard. She said there's no point in coming out until they can dig. We need to keep an eye on the soil for the next twenty-four hours."

"Is there a chance the dog hit on something else?" Nikki asked. "What about Kesha's hands and feet?"

"Haven't found them yet," Miller said. "We cleared as much snow as we could before using the ground penetrating radar so the heating blanket could work faster and didn't see any sign of them. But if he came here first, intending to dig, and then had to readjust because the ground was frozen, he might have dumped them somewhere else. The dog didn't hit on anything else in the lake." Miller looked down at the ground, the ear flaps on his winter hat moving in the gusty wind. "I confirmed with the ground penetrating radar. From the looks of it, there are at least six bodies—or things shaped an awful lot like bodies. Maybe more, depending on how deep it goes."

"Six?" Nikki echoed. "Laid side by side?"

Miller nodded and lifted up a corner of the Powerblanket. "After the snow and ice started to melt, we saw these marks. I think he tried to dig recently and gave up pretty quickly. I think that's why he went to the lake this time. I brought part of the bag Kesha's body was in with me this afternoon, and after we came off the lake without finding anything more, let the dog sniff it. He set out like a house on fire and led us here. He either caught her scent and followed the path the killer took to the lake when he couldn't break through the ground here, or he was following the bag's natural scent. I can't tell for certain with the GPR, but it looks like the bodies are contained in something."

"Like a body bag?" Nikki asked, thinking of Kesha.

"Possibly," Miller said. "The frozen ground and snow made getting back here easier than it would be any other time of the year. The water table's high, and it's very much like a slough. That's why it's prime duck hunting area."

"Great," Nikki said. "So water probably compromised the remains."

"Maybe," Miller said. "But this is actually the high point of the entire area."

"Still, why choose this area?" Liam asked. "If it's not easy walking back here, imagine carrying a dead weight. Seems like there are a lot of other areas with easier access."

"I can think of at least ten," Miller said.

"This area means something to him," Nikki said. "Choosing it has to be significant. How soon before you'll be able to start recovery?"

"The ground's frozen three feet deep at least," Liam said.

"GPR showed the bodies around that depth. Depending on how the medical examiner wants to handle it, the ground probably won't be thawed enough until tomorrow night." He shivered.

"We have a bigger problem," Miller said. "Normally, we'd have some kind of structure to put up to protect the site. But the way back here is such a hassle there's no chance of getting any sort of big equipment in to build something that can protect the site and the diggers once things start. With the way the media's been acting on this case, I'd really like to have this blocked off in case someone tries sneaking back here."

"I can help with that," Rory said. "Mark and I can put something together. I've got enough heavy-duty vinyl sheeting to block the area off. I just need to secure it." He circled the crime scene tape, his gaze darting from one side of the small clearing to the other. "We can use the trees as posts."

"Really?" Nikki asked.

"This wouldn't be the first secret hideout I've built in the woods," he said. "Yes, with the right tools, we can get something up in a few hours." Rory checked his watch. "Maybe before dark, if I move quickly enough."

"Do whatever you need to." Miller looked at his watch. "You've got maybe ninety minutes of daylight left."

"Not a problem. But what about Mark?" he asked. "I know there's protocol, but he's trustworthy, and this will go a lot faster if I have him to help me."

Miller thought about it for a moment, and then nodded. "As long as you can vouch he'll keep the information to himself, it's fine. But no one without a badge and field clearance"—Miller glanced at Liam, who rolled his eyes—"can be on the inside of this tape."

"I'm going to the truck to double-check what I've got, and then I'll call Mark and go get the rest of it." Rory disappeared through the trees.

"I'll make sure I've got deputies posted once Rory's finished," Miller said. "One in the lot and one here. It's a tough walk from the road, but it's not impossible, and we need someone to check the soil from time to time."

Liam scanned the area. "It's snowed at least twice since the lake froze, so anything the killer might have dropped or any physical evidence is covered in a foot of snow. Once the ground is thawed, the body recovery process is going to be crucial. Blanchard and the forensic anthropologist will have their protocol to follow, but we need to make sure a member of the evidence response team is here tomorrow night, assuming that's when the digging starts."

"Courtney's back in town tonight," Nikki said. "She'll be here to run point on that."

Miller looked up from his phone. "I've posted a deputy on the road behind the nature reserve, so we should be able to wait in the parking lot for Rory. He and Mark will need help carrying everything back here, anyway."

While they waited for Rory in the warm SUV, Nikki checked her email to see if the medical examiner had responded about the bag containing Kesha's remains.

"Blanchard answered my email. Kesha's remains were in an emergency disaster body bag. The brand is one that is heavily used and available in bulk from Amazon."

"He intended to bury her, then," Miller said. "Why else take the time with the bag when he's going to weigh down the body for the lake?"

Nikki shook her head. "I don't know, but I'm glad we've got an answer before we start recovering the other victims. The body bag may be part of his signature. Liam, widen your net for missing persons. Search statewide, missing women ages sixteen to thirty. Keep an eye out for women from other parts of the state who disappeared from the metro area, like Kesha."

He twisted around in the passenger seat. "You think he's deliberately not taking locals?"

"I don't know," Nikki said. "But this guy is definitely a local. He chose this area to leave his victims because he's familiar with it. He knows how to fit in with the community, how to blend in. That's how he managed to bury multiple people in this relatively small and well-trafficked reserve. What do we know about the houses that border the area?"

"A retired surgeon owns the property northwest of the site," Miller said, his eyes on his computer. "Looking at property records, it's probably less than three hundred yards from the burial. But that area is even harder to get through than coming from the lake. He leases it to duck hunters during the season."

"Is he home?" Nikki asked. "I could go talk to him while we wait."

"I spoke with him this morning," Miller said. "He and his wife winter in Florida, and they pay their neighbor on the other side of the road to keep an eye on things. She's a realtor, no kids. I left a message for her, but the owner said he'd never had any issues with people trespassing, though he always accepted it might happen, given the reserve. As long as he didn't hear gunshots out of season, he honestly didn't pay much attention. After all, Washington County is a safe area." Miller's sarcasm didn't do much to lift Nikki's mood.

Hollywood had given many people the idea that serial killers operated over wide geographical areas like Bundy in the western United States or Hansen up in Alaska, but in reality, the majority chose to operate close to an anchor point like a job or home and family that helped keep up their facade of a normal life. Like Nikki's mentor had once said, *strangers stick out, locals are invisible.* "We need to re-interview everyone in Kesha's life."

Miller glanced at her in the rearview mirror. "As much as I disliked the Bloomington detective's attitude, I read the reports. Their questions were pretty thorough. Of course, if you read the newspaper this morning, it's a racial issue."

"You don't agree?" Liam asked.

"After reading the detective's notes on the case and the report, no. They didn't have anything to go on, and the boyfriend was the only person of interest." Miller shrugged. "I just don't want to say a case was mishandled because of race when I don't agree. It's like crying wolf, and it takes away from the cases that are affected by race."

"I read his notes, and I agree with you," Nikki said. "The bottom line is that a serial killer is using this area for his personal cemetery, which means he's likely from here. The Bloomington detective wouldn't have had any reason to ask about Washington County or Stillwater, but we do. That's why we need to re-interview everyone in Kesha's case."

"How many is that?" Liam asked.

"Ten, maybe twelve," Miller said. "Including parents, family, boyfriend, friends, co-workers. All of them had been ruled out as suspects except for the boyfriend. I think they're reaching, but he's someone I'd like to interview in person if possible."

"We already asked Kesha's parents about connections to this area yesterday," Nikki said. "Let's divide and conquer the rest first thing tomorrow."

"I'll do it." Liam spoke up. "If they've been cleared as suspects, calling them and asking them about ties to Washington County isn't a big deal."

"Just make clear you're asking if Kesha or anyone in her life spent time here, has property here, did she come here for summer camp, stuff like that. Think local."

"If he's local, then why didn't he come back and bury Kesha

before the ground froze?" Liam asked. "He had time the first week of December at least."

"Maybe he couldn't get out here," Nikki said. "He might live in the metro area now, but I think he chose this area for a reason. There are dozens of areas he could have found that were easier to reach and probably less chance of being discovered, not to mention the St. Croix River is just a few miles east of us. It's something about this place specifically, I think. Either way, we've got to make sure we cover all our bases."

"So, what about Dion then?" Miller asked.

"I sent him a text earlier today, asking him to get in touch," Nikki said. "If he doesn't reply by tonight, I'll try again." Nikki massaged the knot that had formed in her left shoulder. "Just so we're all on the same page, Liam's going to search for missing persons in the state and he's going to contact everyone police interviewed about Kesha to see if he can find any connection to Washington County. I'm going to the mall in the morning, and we're working on the burial site. Courtney will be able to test the blood from Stanton's truck tomorrow, so we can hopefully rule him out."

"Hang on." Liam went back to his laptop and searched through his open tabs. "I did a property search this morning and had started working up a lead before Caitlin's family arrived. There was something about Stanton's wife... it was important. I can't believe I forgot to come back to it."

"Isn't that part of your post-concussive issue?" Miller asked.

"I guess," Liam said. "Most of the time it's headaches and random blurred vision. Okay, here it is. The wife's maiden name is Blaine. Her cousin owns the goat farm just down the road. It's a five-minute drive, and an hour's walk. Big coincidence, especially given how fast she asked for the reward."

"Maybe," Miller said. "But these little towns in the northern part of the county are pretty insular. A person could probably throw a rock and hit someone they're related to."

Liam looked back at Nikki. "Still worth checking out the goat farm, right?"

"It's worth me checking out," she corrected him.

"Right now?" Miller asked.

"Might as well," Nikki said. "Rory won't be back with the equipment for at least another half an hour. Hope they don't mind me knocking on their door on Christmas."

NINE

Nikki turned off Mayberry Trail Road and onto the dead-end gravel road that led to Blaine's dairy goat farm, which was surrounded by open land and public trail. It would be tough going, but an experienced hiker or hunter could make the trek through the reserve to the burial ground. Blaine's farm looked like any other Nikki had been on, with three metal barns, a couple of grain silos, and a fair amount of equipment scattered around. It probably looked quaint in the summer, but dismal in the winter, like everything else. A small line of fir trees separated the house from the barns, and the cottage-style home appeared to be well maintained.

Nikki spotted a familiar minivan in front of a locked greenhouse. "Fantastic," she muttered. "The Stantons must be here celebrating Christmas."

As soon as she stepped out of the jeep, Nikki heard the shouts of kids playing in the yard, followed by several loud barks. A big, furry, black dog raced around the house, barking. Nikki moved to hop back in the jeep, but a man slammed the front door open and came out onto the porch.

"Sandy, come."

The dog slowed down and veered right. She raced up the porch steps and lay down next to the man's feet. "Good girl. Stay."

Nikki slowly approached. "That's a well-trained dog."

"She's a good watchdog," he said. "If she thought you were a threat, she would have ignored me. So, what can I do for you, Agent Hunt?"

"I guess the Stantons know I'm here. Are you Mr. Blaine?"

"Call me Tanner," he said.

Nikki stopped at the porch, her eyes on the dog. "Would she mind if I came in?"

"Probably not, but my cousin would. Danny had to stop her from coming out."

A gust of wind sent the snow flying off tree branches and the roof. Nikki pulled her hood up and zipped her coat to her chin. "Can we talk on the porch?"

"Sure, but what's this about? Danny said you guys wouldn't be able to do anything until tomorrow. He wouldn't hurt a fly, by the way. How'd you know he was here?"

"I didn't." Nikki walked slowly up the steps, making sure to stay clear of the dog. "You're the closest neighbor who isn't in Florida. I wanted to ask if you or anyone in your family ever noticed people in the woods at night, in the reserve or on the lake?"

"Like sneaking around?" Tanner asked, stroking his scruff. "We can't see the lake from here, obviously. I haven't seen anyone out in the reserve, but I go to bed fairly early. Let me ask everyone else real quick." He turned to go back inside.

"It would be great if I could talk to them," she said.

Tanner shook his head. "No offense, but I don't want to deal with my cousin's temper any more than I have to. I'll be right back." He slipped inside, opening the door just wide enough to squeeze between it and the frame.

Nikki's eyes watered as the scent of marijuana rolled out of the house. Guess she didn't need to ask where Stanton got his pot or why the greenhouse was locked.

Tanner came back outside, followed by a teenaged girl wearing sweats and a fleece hoodie. She was the spitting image of Tanner, sans the beard. "Your daughter?" The girl might be old enough to drive, but she definitely wasn't old enough to smoke, despite her red eyes. Tanner and his wife were either the kind of parents who'd rather their kids did illegal stuff at home, or just didn't care.

He nodded. "Chelsea, this is Agent Hunt. Tell her what you saw."

Chelsea stuck her hands in her pockets. "A couple of weeks ago, my boyfriend and I were driving around, just hanging out, and I saw light in the trees. Not like a flashlight, but a lantern. So, my boyfriend stopped and we went to check it out."

"Hang on," Nikki said. She unlocked her phone and found the screenshot she'd taken from Google Earth. She moved so that Chelsea could see the screen. "This is your house, and this is the lake. Where were you guys?"

"Around there." Chelsea pointed to the area of Mayberry Road that bordered the reserve. The burial site was located due south, less than three hundred yards from the road. "We had just gone into the woods when all of sudden a guy comes out of the trees, holding a big camping lantern. He said he'd been out walking his dog and something scared the dog and it took off. He was looking for him, so we offered to help."

"What did the man look like?" Nikki asked.

"He had on work coveralls, the heavy kind, and a black coat with a high collar. It went up to his nose, and he had a hat on. All I can say is that he was white and tall."

"How did he react when you offered to help?" Nikki asked.

"He seemed surprised, but he accepted the help. We split up, my boyfriend and me walking the road while the guy looked for his dog in the woods."

"Did he say why he wanted to walk in the reserve?" Nikki asked.

"He said he grew up around here and that he could walk through blindfolded and still find his way back to his truck."

"Did you see the vehicle?"

"No, and we weren't sure how we were supposed to tell the guy if we saw his dog, because he didn't have his cell phone with him. Maybe a half hour later, he comes out of the woods and said his dog went back to his pickup at the north entrance. He thanked us for our help and told us to get home before we got lost or hurt." Chelsea shivered. "It was weird, because we'd driven by the north entrance to the lake right before we first saw the light in the woods, and we didn't see a vehicle. I just figured we didn't notice it. Either way, it was cold and I had homework to get to, so we came back here."

Nikki wanted to tell her they'd probably escaped a serial killer that night, but she didn't want Mrs. Stanton going right to the news. "Thank you for the information," she told Chelsea. "Did you notice any other details? Like his eye color, or his eyebrows? Were they weird shaped? Fuzzy? Or even the brand of his hat or coat."

Chelsea shrugged. "It was dark. He had on darker Carhartts, like overalls. I remember thinking he looked close to my dad's age. Which is forty-two." She grinned at her father, who rolled his eyes. "He also got pissy when we shined the flashlight at him so we could see his face. He said the light hurt his eyes or something."

"Did you two even think that guy might be up to no good and might have a gun or something?" Tanner demanded of his daughter.

"He looked like half the people I know when they go hunting," she said. "He was friendly and thankful for our help." Chelsea looked up at her dad. "Didn't you say we should always help neighbors?"

"Yeah, but this guy didn't say he was a neighbor, did he?" Tanner asked.

"He said he grew up here. Since he was out there at nine o'clock at night, I figured he must live nearby." She rolled her eyes.

"You can drop that tone and go back inside unless there's anything else you need to tell Agent Hunt."

Another shrug from Chelsea. Is that what Lacey was going to be like when she was a teenager? Aloof, reckless, sassy... Nikki's heart sank. Of course she would be, because Nikki had been the same way. And Lacey was definitely a mini version of her. "Take my card." Nikki fished a business card out of her pocket and handed it to Chelsea. "If you or your boyfriend think of anything else, call me."

Chelsea nodded and went back inside.

"Sorry about her attitude," Tanner said.

"Don't worry about it. I was a teenage girl once. Please let Danny know we hope to have the testing done Monday. Thanks for letting me bother you on Christmas."

"Hey, no problem." Tanner glanced behind him. "My cousin is betting you found more bodies. That's why you're out here today." He flushed. "She watches a lot of true crime shows."

"Have a good night, Mr. Blaine."

Nikki turned and hurried down the steps before he could remind her that she hadn't answered his question.

By the time she returned to the burial site, Mark and Rory were back and the makeshift shelter, which consisted of fastening strong vinyl sheeting between the trees, forming an oblong border a few feet outside of the crime scene tape, was mostly done. Nikki argued with Miller that she could take the first shift, but he insisted on staying.

"My county, and my responsibility," he'd said. "I've got it worked out."

Nikki could tell Liam was exhausted, but she knew he'd never leave the scene unless she did, even though he wasn't supposed to be in the field. "All right, we'll head back. Everyone has their assignments, right? Liam, contact everyone the BPD interviewed after Kesha disappeared and ask about connections to this area, and keep searching for possible additional victims. I'm going to keep trying to reach Dion, and I'll let Courtney know what she's in for once the ground is ready to dig."

She and Liam walked back to the parking lot together, his steps slow and methodical.

"I don't want to leave Detective Dover hanging after she asked for my help with Parker Jameson's disappearance, so I'll also follow up on Forest Lake—"

Liam rubbed his temples. "I went through the details while you were gone. Parker disappeared on December seventeenth from his small shop and no witnesses spotted him leaving. He's responsible and has no known enemies. He co-owns the Artists' Co-op with two other artists, both female and alibied. Business is in its first couple of years and doing all right, their operating costs are low so no major financial issues for the business or Parker. Like Detective Dover said, they've exhausted their resources and done everything right."

"None of that really jives with what happened to Kesha," Nikki said, nearly slipping on a dirty chunk of ice in the gravel lot.

"Except the vanishing without a trace," Liam said.

"Right," Nikki agreed. "But how many disappearances start out the exact same way until more evidence is uncovered? We just don't have enough to suggest these are tied together. I want you to focus on Kesha and the things we talked about for now, as long as you feel all right."

He glared at her. Nikki stopped walking and craned her

neck to give him a dirty look right back, her hands on her hips. "It's not an insult. You aren't a hundred percent, and that is okay. I just don't want you to do too much and set your recovery back."

Liam's expression softened. "I know." He pressed his lips together, and Nikki could see tears forming in his eyes. "I just want to get back to normal, and I'm stuck."

She tried to think of something to say that would make him feel better, but what could she say other than to hang in there? Head injuries, despite ridiculous amounts of research, were still hard to predict. The doctor said Liam would get back to full functioning, but he'd cautioned there would likely be setbacks.

"It's going to get better," Nikki finally said. "But not if you push too hard. You have to balance on a very fine line right now."

Liam found his keys and remote started his Prius, and Nikki did the same with her jeep. "Call me if anything comes up," she told him. "I'll be at home going through everything for the hundredth time."

"By home, do you mean your house or Rory's?" Liam's eyes shined, a smile playing at the corner of his mouth. "I heard you were thinking about selling your house in St. Paul."

Nikki gritted her teeth, trying not to get frustrated with Rory's blabbing after he'd helped out so much today. "Go home and rest, Liam."

TEN

Rory had left the area before her, so the house was blazing with light and hopefully hot food when Nikki turned into the driveway. Lacey's phone number popped up on her caller ID. "Hi, baby," Nikki said. "Are you all settled?"

"Mommy, Florida is so pretty. I can hear the ocean waves from my room."

"That's great, Bug." Nikki grabbed her bag and headed into the house. "How was the flight?"

Lacey had only flown once before, when she was three, and barely remembered it. "Awesome," she said. "The flight lady asked if I wanted my wings since it was my first real flight. I said yes, and she came back with plastic wings like the ones on her vest. It's cool, but I was kind of disappointed because I thought she meant chicken wings, and I was hungry."

Nikki laughed, feeling some of the stress ease off her shoulders. She found Rory in the kitchen, plowing into a plate of leftovers. "Made up a plate for you. It's in the microwave."

"Tell Rory about my wings," Lacey shrilled.

"Why don't you tell him? You're so much more entertaining

than I am." She put her phone on speaker and set it on the table in front of Rory. "She wants to tell you about her wings."

"You got wings, Lace?" he asked.

Lacey launched into her story again, earning a loud laugh from Rory. They chattered with her while they ate the leftovers, her sweet voice making Nikki miss her.

"I'm glad you're having fun," Nikki said. "How are Grandma and Grandpa?"

"Fine," Lacey said. "They didn't say anything mean about you, and Grandma asked me if I wanted to talk about Daddy instead of just blabbering on."

"That's good," Nikki said. "If you feel like it, you should ask her about taking Daddy down to Florida when he was a kid. I know there are lots of good stories she'd love to share, but only if you're ready."

"I'll think about it," Lacey said. "Grandma is telling me to clean up because we're going to get something to eat. I'll talk to you later."

Nikki and Rory barely had time to say goodbye before Lacey ended the call, chattering excitedly to her grandmother. "Kids are so resilient, it's amazing."

"I'm glad she's doing so well." Rory eyed her. "What a freaking day."

"Thanks for your help," Nikki said.

He shrugged. "I wish we'd had time to build a proper shelter, but at least the area's blocked off now. Hopefully Miller and his deputies will get a break from the wind too."

"I wish Liam had been cleared for the field," she said. "Having him work from the office is better than nothing, but it's different."

"I can see that," Rory said. "You guys read each other well, and you trust one another. But he was tired today, Nik."

"I know," she said. "He swears the headaches are coming

less and are less intense, and he stopped getting blurred vision a few weeks ago so he can drive. He's just impatient."

"I would be too." Rory spoke between mouthfuls of leftover cheesy hash brown casserole. "I have to tell you, today was really sobering. Even though I didn't see anything graphic, just knowing what's in the ground and what you guys have to do, it's amazing and sad at the same time. How do you not get emotionally involved? As soon as Miller said the GPR showed multiple human remains, I teared up. I kept hoping someone would say they're old or maybe historic Native American, even though I know that's unlikely."

"Very much so," she said. "Buried together the way they are, at the depth... this is likely an active grave. Thankfully, Miller has the Powerblanket. There's no other way to get to these victims without thawing the ground out."

"I kept thinking, why would this guy wait until the middle of December when there's snow on the ground, but then I remembered that we didn't have all that much until last week. Seems like it's been months of snow already."

"Because winter's miserable," Nikki said. "And who knows why he waited? Maybe he travels for his job, that sort of thing."

Rory nodded. "I should probably stop talking about it. I know you can't share much information and you want to relax."

Nikki snorted. "Relaxing never happens on a case, but you're right, I can't share much."

"I probably don't want to know any more anyway," he said. "Today was enough."

A video call prompt flashed on her phone. "I have to take this." She headed into the living room. "Dion, thanks for calling back. I didn't expect a FaceTime, but that's okay."

"You said that you wanted to talk face to face," he answered. "I work tomorrow and don't know when I'll be available." Dion spoke softly, emotion in his voice.

Nikki remembered that Dion worked part-time at a local

gym. "Your employer won't give you the day off considering everything that's happened?"

Dion shook his head. "I need the money, and he's already short on staff. Besides, if I don't work or go to school, I'm thinking about Kesha." His voice caught. "I loved her. I don't know why the Bloomington police wouldn't look at anyone else but me, but I would never hurt her."

Nikki grabbed her notebook and a pencil and then propped her phone up with the napkin holder. "Tell me what happened that day, Dion."

He nodded and took a deep breath. "We got to the mall around two, and it was still crazy crowded. I tapped out pretty quickly, so we grabbed something to eat. She wanted me to walk with her to the other stores, but I hate shopping." Dion wiped the tears brimming in his eyes. "So, I told her to go without me. She wasn't happy when she walked off. That's the last conversation we had."

"How long before you realized something wasn't right?" Nikki asked.

"Probably after around forty-five minutes. I figured that she was just mad and taking more time, so I decided to wait a bit, but then I texted. She always texts back, even when we're arguing, but every text I sent stayed on 'delivered.' That's when I found a security guard. Me and him walked the route Kesha would have taken, checking with the stores she told me she'd stop in."

"Did you check in with her parents or friends to see if she'd contacted them?"

"Her best friend, Noni. She hadn't talked to Kesha since before we left for the Mall of America, and Kesha wasn't responding to her texts or calls. I didn't want to check with her parents at first because I kept thinking Kesha was going to show up, and they didn't need to get upset over nothing. But Noni called them, and they hadn't heard from her, either. She was just gone."

"Kesha's parents think a lot of you," Nikki said.

"They're good people," he choked. "She was the best. I still can't believe someone did this to her."

According to the report, Bloomington police had taken Dion to the precinct for further questions. Kesha's parents arrived sometime during that time and had been livid the police were wasting their time on Dion instead of looking at the mall and surrounding areas. "The police report says that you admitted the two of you had argued more lately."

He rolled his eyes. "I told that to the mall security guard when we first searched, because I still hoped she was just not answering. He must have told the police."

"What did you tell the police when they asked you?"

"The truth," Dion said. "We'd gone through a bit of a rough patch because she decided to go to Mankato State instead of staying close like we'd talked." He dragged his hand over his short hair. "I acted like an ass when she first told me about Mankato State, that's true. I panicked and felt dumb for being in community college, so I took it out on her. But that was a month before Thanksgiving. We'd worked through it, mostly because I had no reason to be mad."

"Don't feel dumb about community college," Nikki said. "It's still higher education, and it's smart financially. You will have a lot less debt doing only two years at a community college. Kesha got along with people at school and work? Did she ever talk about someone bothering her or being afraid of anyone?"

"No," Dion said. "Everyone liked her."

"What about Stillwater or Washington County? Can you remember her ever talking about coming here?"

Dion thought about it for a few seconds. "No."

"The BPD said you changed your version of events that day," Nikki asked.

Dion rolled his eyes. "I was freaked out and forgot about going to the bathroom and looking for a damned Pepsi. But the cop only cared that I forgot to tell him that. I guess stress can't apply to black people."

Nikki tried to word her next question carefully. "This next question is kind of difficult, and I may have to ask it again after the medical examiner is finished, but do you know what you were doing the first two weekends this month?"

"I think the first weekend, I was still taking off work and classes because of everything going on. I went back on December eighth, and I worked five days straight trying to make up for lost time and keep my mind off things."

"Ever been ice fishing?" Nikki watched his expression carefully, searching for any involuntary sign of deceit.

"Hell, no," he said. "I don't like to fish period, but ice fishing is like Russian roulette. I don't care how thick it is, shit happens."

"That it does," she agreed. "Did Kesha ever mention Danny Stanton?"

Dion briefly closed his eyes. "I know that's the guy who found her, and ever since I heard his name, I've been racking my brain, but I don't remember her saying anything about him."

"We'll double-check with her friends tomorrow," Nikki said. She wasn't going to give up her poker face just yet, but unless the GPR had made a mistake, they were looking for a serial killer, likely homegrown in Washington County. And Dion didn't match the description of the man that Chelsea had told them about earlier today. "The BPD mentioned a violent crime study you were participating in?"

"Not because I committed one," Dion said quickly. "I did some dumb crap a few years ago, and my mom was freaked out I'd end up like my cousin."

"Your cousin served time?"

"He's still in prison," Dion said. "Three counts of rape and one of murder two."

"Whose study is this?" Nikki asked him.

"Doctor Roth," Dion said. "He's an expert on violent offenders, plus a neuroscientist. He's studying people between twelve and twenty, so I only have one year left."

"How does the study work?"

"I don't know how it works for everyone, but I had a lot of interviews with Doctor Roth the first couple of years, but now I just do a monthly check-in."

"Meaning you're supposed to report committing a crime?" Nikki asked dryly. "Criminals don't exactly do well with the honor system. How'd you end up in the study again?"

He smacked his forehead. "My mom would kill me if she knew I was talking to you without a lawyer."

"She wouldn't be wrong," Nikki said.

Dion looked frustrated. "So I'm still considered a suspect?"

Nikki hedged. "Because I can't definitively rule you out without more information from the medical examiner, technically, yes, you are."

"You mean from the autopsy?" Dion asked softly.

"Yes."

"Did she die quick, or did she suffer?"

"I don't know," Nikki said. "Since her body was left in water, the medical examiner may not be able to answer that question. What I can tell you is that Sheriff Miller and my team will do everything possible to locate the person who did this, no matter how long it takes."

"I guess that's all I can really hope for," he said. "I mean, you're supposed to be innocent until proven guilty but... you know how that goes for some of us."

"Not when my office is involved," Nikki said firmly. "I solve crimes based on real evidence, not opinions or bias."

"Thank you," he said. "That's all I ask. Kesha deserves justice."

ELEVEN

SUNDAY, DECEMBER 26

Nikki trudged into the lobby of the FBI's massive building in Brooklyn Center, a picturesque suburb of Minneapolis. The rectangular building's uniformly shaped windows reminded Nikki of the Bureau office in D.C., but the campus was more like a mini Quantico, adjacent to well-maintained walking trails and a beautiful lake. She waved at the security guards and signed in at the front desk. The receptionist was on the phone complaining about how unfair it was that the day after Christmas wasn't considered a federal holiday.

Nikki held back her laugh and headed up to the top floor to major crimes. She headed straight for her boss's office.

Hernandez looked up at the sound of Nikki's knock. "How was your holiday, sir?"

He motioned for her to come in and sit down. "Better than yours, I'm guessing. How are you doing?"

"I'm okay," Nikki answered. "Lacey had a good holiday, and she's on vacation with Tyler's parents right now. As much as I miss her, the timing couldn't be better. This case is going to take every second of my time, especially with Liam working in a limited capacity."

"That's actually what I wanted to speak with you about," Hernandez said, his eyes on his monitor. "After our conversation on Christmas Eve and the speculation I've seen in the media in the last day, I think we need to bring in an outside consultant."

Nikki hedged. Major crimes agents were all capable, but she and Liam were trained profilers. His background in behavior science was almost as strong as Nikki's, and he'd started as a junior agent on her team when she'd returned to Minnesota several years ago. The idea of working with another agent sounded more stressful than Nikki taking on an extra workload, but she knew Hernandez wouldn't see it that way. She mentally ran through the list of agents working in major crimes; they were all solid, but none stood out to Nikki as good or bad options. "Who are you considering?"

"I assume you're aware that Kesha's boyfriend is a part of Doctor Alex Roth's study?" Hernandez asked. "He's a neuroscience researcher who worked on the criminal mind mapping program in New Mexico until a few years ago, when he returned to the area to open up a facility of his own."

"Yes," Nikki said. "It's my understanding that he's looking to establish biomarkers for juveniles."

"Yes, but that's just one part of the study," Hernandez said. "And he's a strong advocate for racial equality and change in all of our institutions. That's what gave me the idea. I checked with some colleagues before I spoke to D.C. Doctor Roth has assisted the St. Paul police with some pretty big cases over the past few years. Roth has probably spoken with more convicted, violent criminals than all of us combined, including you. In the past year alone, he's been going to Midwest prisons and jails, focusing on child killers and pedophiles. He's trying to find biomarkers to predict future behavior, which is all well and good. He's already been vetted. I ran it by the brass in D.C., and they loved the idea."

"I'm sure they did," Nikki said. "I understand your point, but I don't feel comfortable bringing someone into the field when I haven't worked with them."

"You don't need to," Hernandez said. "He can do his thing without being in the field, he's not an investigator. He's a behavioral psychologist and neuroscientist."

And it really didn't matter if Roth could be helpful or not, Nikki thought. It made the Bureau look good, so the consult was going to happen. "What about a conflict of interest regarding Dion?"

"He's not a patient of Roth's," Hernandez reminded her. "This is voluntary reporting, and I've already confirmed with Roth's office that Dion hasn't spoken with Roth in over a year. At this point in the study, it is Dion just self-reporting. Roth's office said that they run the names of all their participants every month to make sure they aren't lying and jeopardizing the study."

"Dion told me the same thing last night." She briefed her boss on the surprise video call from Dion. "We're talking with friends and associates to see if we can shake something loose, but despite the minor inconsistencies in Dion's story, I don't think he's good for this, especially now that we know there are more victims."

Hernandez nodded. "Just meet with Roth, Nikki. We need all the help we can get on this, especially considering the likelihood more victims will be unearthed."

Nikki wasn't going to waste any more energy on a losing battle. "Would you mind if I waited to speak with him until after we've learned more about the victims buried in the area around Big Marine Lake? Since the dog tracked Kesha's scent to the site, we're pretty confident her killer intended to bury her in that same area but miscalculated how hard it would be to dig, so he improvised with the lake. I'm almost certain these victims have been killed by the same person, but I'd like to have that confirmed by the medical examiner and forensic anthropologist before I speak with Doctor Roth."

Hernandez thought about it for a few seconds. "According to your email, the plan is to start the recovery process tonight, when the ground should be thawed enough?"

Nikki nodded. "This is the first time I've used a Powerblanket to thaw ground, but Miller's confident it will work. We've already created a makeshift windbreak that blocks the site from prying eyes, and Miller is keeping deputies posted."

"I'll set the meeting up with Roth for tomorrow morning, at the Washington County Sheriff's Office so Sheriff Miller will hopefully be able to attend. With the media breathing down our necks, I don't want to wait any longer than that. We're drafting a press release right now letting people know we're bringing in another expert."

"Assuming we're dealing with a serial killer, Kesha is still the most recent victim," Nikki reminded him. "Our current investigation revolves around her, so the press needs to know she is the priority."

Hernandez leaned back in his chair. "Any word on the autopsy results?"

"Doctor Blanchard is doing it today," Nikki said. "She's coming in on her holiday and she's going to be at the dig site tonight, so I'm hoping to get a full report then."

"What about the guy who found Kesha?"

"Danny Stanton," Nikki said. "After we're finished, I'm meeting Courtney in the lab. Hopefully she's got enough information that we can clear Stanton."

"You believe him then, even though it looks like his wife is the one who called the family before they could be informed by police?"

"I think so," Nikki said. "The dynamic between him and his wife is strained, and she seems to bulldoze her way over Danny.

That said, if Courtney has found anything significant, I'll have Stanton brought in for questioning today."

"Sounds like a plan," Hernandez said. "Keep me in the loop."

Nikki bypassed Courtney's office and went straight to the lab. The wall of bullet-proof glass that protected the lab also made it visible to passersby, and Nikki could see Courtney peering into the microscope, bouncing along to the music that always played on low in the lab. Nikki waved her badge in front of the security door. Courtney buzzed her in without looking up from her microscope.

"I brought Christmas cookies." Nikki held up the tin. "Where can I put them?"

"Right next to me," Courtney said. "I'm starving. What kind are they?"

"Sugar, rum balls, gingerbread. Save the rum balls for home."

Courtney popped a gingerbread cookie into her mouth. "Yum."

"Thanks for cutting your trip short."

"Thanks for asking me to," Courtney quipped. "I couldn't leave fast enough. And I can tell you that the blood in Stanton's truck was animal blood. Same with the knife, but I did find trace amounts of human blood at the hilt. I can compare them to Kesha's once Blanchard is done."

"It's a fillet knife," Nikki said. "It's not hard to cut yourself on those, especially if you're not sober. What about the hair and fibers from the truck?"

"The fibers are pretty innocuous," Courtney said. "The hair found doesn't look African American to me, but we'll test against Kesha's to make sure. Without her hands and feet, I can't compare fingerprints." She shuddered. "Why mutilate her if he was just going to dump her in the lake?"

"We're pretty sure the lake was plan B after the ground froze," Nikki answered. "And he might have also been afraid of DNA under her fingernails."

"Why her feet, though?" Courtney asked. "I guess we'll have to wait and see if he did the same thing to the other victims. How's the burial area coming?"

"I checked in with Miller this morning and things were progressing as he'd hoped. He's expecting we'll be able to start recovery by this evening. We'll need you there, and Blanchard is coming, along with the forensic anthropologist." Nikki leaned against the long counter next to Courtney. "Hernandez is bringing in a neuroscientist who's also a psychologist to consult since Liam is still stuck behind a desk."

"He's also covering the Bureau's ass," Courtney said bluntly. "Thanks to the MNPD, we're all under a fresh microscope. Who's the consultant?"

"Doctor Alexander Roth."

Courtney looked up from the microscope. "I saw him on the news a few months ago, talking about his study. He reminded me of the new digital image of Alexander the Great. You know the one where he's ridiculously attractive? If I was interested in men, he'd be on the top of the list."

"I thought you were bisexual," Nikki said.

"Yeah, and right now, men piss me off."

"And women don't?" Nikki asked.

"They don't mansplain or struggle with toxic masculinity." Courtney grinned. "And women are better at sex."

"That I believe," Nikki said. "I'm going to brief Liam and his rookies. Call me with any results."

.   .   .

While major crimes occupied the top floor of the building, Nikki's small team was situated in the eastern corner, with a beautiful view of the campus thanks to the impressive wall of windows. The bullpen outside Nikki's office was small; she and Liam were the two primary profilers, along with two junior agents normally tasked with a lot of research and grunt work. Their dedication and efficiency had impressed Nikki, but she hadn't had enough time with either one of them to know if they were ready to start working with a profiler in the field.

Of the two, Kendra Gray had seniority by a few weeks. She'd assisted Liam on a couple of cases when Nikki had been on leave several months ago, and he'd been impressed with her organization and her ability to make a suspect feel comfortable. The thirty-year-old was single, no kids, her sole focus on her career, which concerned Nikki. As much as it might make the job easier given the uneven hours, it was important for an agent to have a support system. According to Liam, Kendra had a couple of close friends who worked in social services, so she did have someone to lean on when a case got bad.

Jim Barker had joined the team this fall, and while he was efficient and almost as good with computers as Liam, his field experience was limited.

He and Kendra barely looked up from their work when Nikki passed, both muttering distracted greetings.

Liam's large cubicle was right outside Nikki's office, and she could see his red head sticking up over the gray wall. She motioned for him to follow her into her office.

"Close the door, please."

"Am I in trouble?" He sank into the chair in front of Nikki's desk, rubbing his temples. "I probably gave Kendra and Jim too many things to chase down, but there are a lot to go through."

"Of course not," Nikki said. "I put you in charge of them because I trusted you. I'd actually debated bringing Kendra in the field on this one, since your being stuck here means I'm solo, but Hernandez is one step ahead of me." She told him about Roth's impending visit. "Hernandez wanted to bring him in today, but I convinced him that it made more sense to meet with Doctor Roth tomorrow, when we have a better idea of how many people are buried in the reserve."

"I'm familiar with him," Liam said.

"Hernandez insists that even though his current study is mostly focusing on juveniles, Roth has still spoken with more serial violent offenders than any of us, so I'm interested in what he has to say, but I'm not sure it will ultimately help us," Nikki said. "Hernandez is giving him limited clearance, so he won't be in the field, but he'll be able to look at reports and photos. At any rate, I managed to put off dealing with him until tomorrow. Hopefully we'll know a lot more about the remains in the woods by then."

Liam nodded. "I've got Kendra and Jimmy helping me comb through blogs and message boards for Minnesota fishing, looking for anyone who mentioned going to Big Marine in the last month. They're also working on a list of sporting goods stores in Washington County, starting with the one closest to the lake. You want me to have them look in the metro area too?"

"It's probably too big of a net, even if that's where he went to buy stuff," Nikki said. "What about fishing licenses?"

"You think the killer took the time to get one?" Liam asked.

"If he's smart—and it appears that he is," Nikki said. "He doesn't want to draw attention to himself, so the last thing he wants is the DNR creeping up on him. That said, I don't even want to guess at the number of fishing licenses the state issues every year. I'm not sure going through them is worth our time."

"Minnesota issued almost two million fishing licenses this year," Liam said. "Breaking down by the county is still thousands of names."

"Waste of time then, unless we have an actual name to search for. Where are you with missing persons?"

"In the last year, one hundred and sixty-five people have gone missing in the state. More than a hundred were women between the ages of fifteen and thirty. I'm working on weeding that down into known runaways, people who've been located, and women whose disappearance has any sort of similarity with Kesha's." Liam stretched out his long legs. "And don't forget the current missing person, Parker Jameson, from Forest Lake. I know we're focusing on Kesha right now, but given the timing, I wanted to look more into that case."

"Skin and hair color are one thing, but different sexes?" Nikki asked. "I don't know."

"Neither do I," Liam confessed. "But since we know there are more victims in the woods, I thought it was worth noting. I did find out that Parker's ex-boyfriend's mother owns the restaurant next door to the Artists' Co-op, and the breakup was contentious. He's the main suspect, because his mother is the one who alibied him. Said he was home with her, watching a Hallmark Christmas movie."

"Thin alibi," Nikki said. "You and I both know how far mothers have gone to protect their children."

"I thought the same thing." Liam sucked on a piece of candy. "According to friends and family, Parker's relationship with"—Liam paused to check his notes—"Colton Troyer was rocky from the start. Colton wanted commitment, Parker wanted to see other people. They only dated three months, but Colton didn't take the breakup well."

"More reason not to lump him in with these victims. Assuming the bodies in the woods are actually related to Kesha's murder," Nikki said. "Logic and circumstantial evidence say they are, and the dog tracking Kesha's scent from the lake makes me pretty confident the same person's responsible for those bodies, but I want to make sure we have solid forensic evidence before that news gets out."

"Caitlin's freelancing now, but she still keeps up with her

news contacts," Liam reminded her. "She got a call this morning asking if she knew what was going on in the reserve, because the area was closed off and law enforcement spotted, blah, blah, blah. Caitlin said she didn't know anything, but I don't think Miller will be able to keep a lid on it much longer."

Nikki barely heard the timid knock on her office door. "Come in."

"Agents." Kendra practically danced with excitement. "I just found a poster on one of the local fishing message boards that talked about fishing Big Marine since the ice came in. I cross-referenced our sex offender list, and he's a Tier 2, soliciting minors under the age of eighteen. He lives in the southern part of Washington County."

"Great work," Nikki said. "How old is he?"

"Twenty-two," Kendra said. "Should I contact him for an interview?"

"No," Nikki and Liam answered in unison. "A registered sex offender isn't going to be very eager to come down to the FBI office. Email me the information, and I'll see if Miller can check it out," Nikki said.

Kendra looked disappointed. Nikki smiled at her. "Seriously, this is a good catch. And if this case wasn't such high profile I'd probably send you to talk to him, but not without Liam or myself. I'm headed to interview people at the mall, and then I've got to speak with Danny Stanton. All of the blood turned out to be deer blood, save for the human blood on the hilt," Nikki said, looking at Liam. "Courtney said it's older but not significantly. I'm waiting on the warrant for his DNA."

"He's going to love that," Liam said.

"It's for his benefit," Nikki said. "At least, that's the angle I'm going with. Kendra, keep up the good work. Once things settle down a bit, you can come into the field with me and hopefully Agent Wilson."

"Thank you, Agent Hunt. Do you want the door open or closed?"

"Open's fine."

"I can't take much more of just sitting in the office," Liam said after Kendra left the room. "My next evaluation is in two weeks. If I have to fake feeling good, then I will."

Nikki rolled her eyes. "Like you can hide that from me or Caitlin. You know we aren't going to let you get away with that."

"I'm doing all of the eye therapy and other exercises, and I don't have any vision issues. Every once in a while I get dizzy, but the headaches are getting better and I'm having less. They've got to let me work."

"In the meantime, you're stuck here," Nikki said. "I want you talking to any potential witnesses from the fishing boards, preferably over Zoom. I'd have you contact the sex offender too, but I don't want to spook him. And check in with Forest Lake police, let them know where we are. Don't mention the mass grave—Parker's only been missing for a week, so even if he turns out to be a victim of the same guy, he's not going to be buried in the woods." Personally, Nikki was hedging her bets on something domestic with Parker, especially after Liam's update.

"Fine," Liam said. "I'm not sure the sex offender's a good suspect given his age. Chelsea said the guy looked like he was in his early forties. He told them not to shine the flashlight directly at him because he had sensitive eyes, right?"

"We don't know for sure that was the killer," Nikki reminded him. "But, yeah, I have my doubts on someone so young being this organized, but I want someone with experience sitting down with him. With you sidelined, Miller's the only one I trust to do it. He's got enough experience to play it cool, and it's not unusual for the county sheriff to check in on sex offenders. The FBI, not so much."

TWELVE

Nikki hadn't been to the Mall of America since last spring, when Frost had targeted Lacey. She'd never been a fan of the place, and now it represented more than crowds and commerce to Nikki. Her life had changed forever in this mall, just like Kesha Williams'. She chugged down the last of her coffee and forced herself not to think about what Frost could have done that day. Since the Mall of America would be insanely busy today, she'd arranged to meet security before the mall opened. Still, shoppers were already waiting in their cars when Nikki drove past them down to the separate entrance for security.

Unlike most shopping centers, the Mall of America's security team was a nationally recognized department, patrolling both the interior of the mall and the maze of parking garages. They also employed a K9 unit and had a state-of-the-art dispatch center located in the basement.

"Agent Hunt, it's good to see you again. How's your daughter?" Head of Security Ashley Stack greeted her at the security office entrance. Stack had been part of the team that helped Nikki search the mall in the spring when the serial killer Frost had spoken to Lacey when she'd become separated from Rory and Nikki.

"She's good," Nikki answered, hoping Stack didn't bring up her ex-husband's murder. "Thanks for meeting with me on such short notice."

Stack ushered Nikki into her office. "Of course. I'm still sick we weren't able to keep Kesha Williams and her kidnapper from leaving the mall that day."

"Try not to be too hard on yourself," Nikki said, double-checking the notes app on her phone. "Can you walk me through that day?"

"Of course." Stack opened the file on her desk. "At 2:32 p.m. on November twenty-seventh, Dion Thompson flagged down a security guard and asked for help finding his girlfriend. She wanted to shop a couple of stores not far from the area, and he didn't feel like going, so he decided to wait. He played a game on his phone, not paying any attention to the time. When he realized Kesha had been gone for around forty-five minutes, he texted her."

Nikki had already looked at the phone records from the Bloomington police's file on Kesha. "He texted her seven times in the next twenty minutes, with no response."

Stack nodded. "During that time, he left the food court and went in the same direction she did, checking stores." She grabbed a map of the mall and turned it around so that it faced Nikki. "They had eaten here, at the pizza joint on the first floor, before he found a place to sit and wait for her nearby." Stack traced a route on the map with a pencil. "It's not far to Victoria's Secret, maybe five minutes. She also mentioned that she wanted to stop at Bath and Body Works and Barnes and Noble, which are here, near the east parking ramp. While my officers helped search for Kesha, I pulled up CCTV footage. The mall was busy, so we never found her in any corridor videos, but she went into Bath and Body Works and purchased lotion. Then she went to Victoria's Secret and picked up a bra and some perfume. We never saw her enter Barnes and Noble, and I'm confident that we would have seen her on the CCTV if she'd made it to the bookstore. There's only one entrance."

Nikki studied the map. "Kesha could have taken a few different routes towards the bookstore—"

"We checked and confirmed with the store that she never came in," Stack said.

"What about Dion?"

"We confirmed he was sitting near the pizza place during the time, but he did get up and walk away for about fifteen minutes. He said he went to the restroom, but we didn't pick him up on security cameras. That said, the mall was busy, and the men's room was heavily trafficked during the lunch hour, so it's possible we could have missed him or he went to a different bathroom."

"But he came back to the same spot?"

"Near it," Stack said. "The seat was taken, so he found another place to sit, and we were able to confirm that."

"What about all of the exits?"

"We didn't pick her up on any of those cameras, but it would have been easy to miss her given the foot traffic."

Which was likely the reason Kesha's kidnapper had chosen that day to act, whether he'd been following Kesha, or she'd been a victim of opportunity.

Nikki knew Stack had worked for the Bloomington police before joining the Mall of America's security team. "Do you still know anyone over at Bloomington P.D.?"

Stack snickered. "I left because of racial tension and harassment. They don't like it when a black woman stands up for herself. Or they didn't back then, but that was probably fifteen years ago. I'd like to think they've changed, though I will tell you that the main culprit is now heading the investigations division."

"Fantastic," Nikki said, handing Stack one of Liam's cards. "Would you mind emailing all the footage of both Kesha and her boyfriend to my colleague? He'll want to get fresh eyes on it."

On the way to her jeep, Nikki checked her email. The warrant had come through, so it was time to pay Stanton a visit.

Danny Stanton lived outside of Marine on St. Croix, a tiny village in northeast Washington County and only a short drive from the lake. The craftsman-style house had seen better days, its wooden siding badly in need of a fresh paint job. The property was at least two acres, with the house, a detached garage, and a big yard with a rusting swing set. A tire swing hung forlornly from the oak tree in the front yard.

A red Honda Civic was parked in the driveway, but Nikki didn't see the minivan Mrs. Stanton had been driving. She took a photograph of the Honda's plate with her phone just in case they needed to run it later. Walking to the front door, the quiet struck Nikki as odd. The Stantons had three kids under ten on holiday break, so she would expect to see some sign of them.

She knocked, trying not to wrinkle her nose at the heady scent of weed seeping from underneath the door. The door swung open, and Danny Stanton stared at her with bleary eyes. He hadn't bothered to put a shirt on before he answered, and his thin sweats didn't leave much to the imagination.

"Uh, hi, Agent Hunt. I thought the sheriff was going to call me when I could have my truck back." He wedged himself between the door and its frame, blocking Nikki's view inside.

"We're still working on processing the evidence," she said. "I have some follow-up questions."

He glanced over his shoulder, his teeth digging into his lower lip. "This isn't really a good time."

"It never is," Nikki said, keeping her voice pleasant. "It will just take a few minutes."

He sighed. "Let me put a coat on and I'll come outside."

"Actually, can we talk inside?" Nikki asked. "It's just so cold and windy."

Stanton hedged, reminding Nikki of Lacey when she'd been caught in a lie.

"I assume your wife and kids aren't here?"

"They're at her mom's for the next few days. My wife hasn't seen her mom in months, so I told her to take advantage of a few extra days off."

Nikki gestured to the red car she'd parked behind. "At least you have a third vehicle so you aren't stranded while we process your truck."

Stanton nodded. "You sure we can't do this outside?"

"Look, Danny." Nikki had grown tired of dancing around the obvious. "If you've got another woman in there, I don't care. It's none of my business."

His face turned red, his eyes looking furtively between her and the car. "I don't know what you're talking about, Agent."

"Danny?" A younger-sounding female voice drifted from inside the house. "I have to get back to work."

He flinched.

"Who is that?" Nikki asked.

"You just said it wasn't any of your business."

"I changed my mind once I heard her voice."

A pair of dark brown eyes peered over his shoulder. "I'm eighteen. He's not my authority figure, so we aren't doing anything wrong."

"I'm going to run your license plate, so the two of you might as well let me inside."

Defeated, Danny opened the door and walked down the hall, his head hanging and the girl staring at Nikki. She looked younger than she claimed to be, but so did most high schoolers in Nikki's opinion. But she was more concerned about the girl's physical appearance. Her skin tone and wavy, dark hair were reminiscent of Kesha's.

"What's your name?" she asked as she entered the hallway.

"Maria." The girl thrust out her license. "I turned eighteen in October."

Nikki studied the license. "I see that. How did you meet Danny?"

"I don't have to tell you that," Maria said stubbornly. "He's a good man, and I'm not going to get him in trouble with his wife."

"I'm not sure if you're aware of this, but I can do enough digging and find out if you were having sex with Danny before you turned eighteen. So, I suggest you cooperate."

"You mean when I was seventeen, which is the legal age of consent in Minnesota?" Maria smirked.

Nikki tried another tactic. "You really want me poking around in your life?"

Maria glared at her. "I met him at work, and all we did was flirt. I never even let him know I was interested until I was legal. I'm going to be a lawyer, by the way."

"That's great," Nikki said. "But you're still a high school student. That said, I'm not here to bust you or Danny for that, but I will if I find out you're lying." She wanted to tell Maria that she was just setting herself up for a big fall, but Nikki knew that once she started in on the girl, she wouldn't be able to stop, and she didn't have the time to be distracted. "Where do you work?"

"West End Diner."

"Is that in Marine on St. Croix?"

Maria shook her head. "You can Google it."

"I want to show you a photo." Nikki opened her phone and showed the girl Kesha's photo. Maria's facial features were nothing like Kesha's, but she had a similar build, hair and skin tone. All three often played a large role in victimology. "Do you recognize her?"

"From the TV, and I know Danny found her." Maria shuddered. "He's a wreck about it."

"How long have you known him?"

Maria shrugged.

"Are you the only girl he's seeing?"

"I better be."

Nikki didn't bother to point out her hypocrisy. "You've never felt unsafe around him or noticed anything that set off alarms?"

Maria shook her head. "I really need to get to work."

Nikki gave her back the license along with a business card. "If you think of anything else, call me."

"Sure. But you need to promise you won't say anything to my parents."

"I don't have to promise anything of the sort," Nikki said evenly. "But your cooperation goes a long way."

Maria flipped her shining hair over her shoulder. "I know he's a good guy that's treated like crap by his wife. She's the one selling—"

"Maria, you're going to be late for work." Stanton reappeared wearing a black sweatshirt.

Maria smiled smugly at Nikki. "See you around. Danny, call me later, okay?"

He grunted a response. Nikki didn't try to hide her disgust as Maria sauntered to her car.

"Agent, I know what it looks like—"

"I don't want to hear it," Nikki said flatly. "She might be legal, but it's disgusting. And if you had sex with her when she was still a minor—"

"I didn't, I swear."

"Is she the only one?"

"Why does that matter?"

"Because I asked."

"Yeah, fine. It's obviously just a physical thing—"

"Again, gross," Nikki said. "I'm here to get a DNA sample to test against the blood found."

He stared at her. "It's deer blood, Agent."

Nikki nodded. "Our lab confirmed deer blood in the bed of the truck and on the knife's blade. But there's human blood on the hilt."

"It's a fillet knife," he said. "I've nicked myself hundreds of times."

"Which is why I'm hoping you will give us your DNA. If you're innocent, then this will only help to get us off your back."

"I don't want to give my DNA."

"Why not?"

"Because I don't have to," he snapped back. "I'm not going to let you get my DNA and then pin something on me."

Nikki unlocked her phone and showed him the cued-up warrant. "All I'm trying to do is clear you, Danny."

"You won't run it through all your databases?" he asked. "You people keep track of everything."

"Legally, I can't do that," she said. "This warrant is very clear that it only covers DNA taken to compare on the fillet knife." That didn't mean that she couldn't act if a hit came back, but Danny didn't need to hear that right now.

"Fine," he relented. "But no needles."

"No need." Nikki put on latex gloves and then opened the package containing the swab. "Open your mouth, please." She swirled the Q-tip twice and then put it back in the secure container.

Danny wiped his mouth. "Gross."

Nikki ignored his complaint. "Your wife sells the pot, then? Does her cousin grow it?"

"I don't know what you're talking about." He stuck out his jaw, arms across his soft chest. "You got your DNA, Agent. I'd like you to leave now."

"See you soon, Danny."

THIRTEEN

1992

Emmanuel sat on one of the hard, plastic chairs in the school's main office, waiting for his turn with the principal. Stupid Mrs. Martin. Emmanuel's notebook was his property, and he could draw what he wanted in it. Why was he in trouble for some dumb girl looking over his shoulder? Stupid bitch should have minded her own business.

But no, she had to get all prissy and pissy and tell the homeroom teacher. Now he was sitting here instead of in math, where he was already struggling.

The principal's door opened, and Emmanuel tried not to stare at the pretty freshman walking out. Her hair was so dark and wavy, like his grandma's had been. She flicked her hair over her shoulder and plopped down next to him with a dramatic sigh.

His entire body tensed when she sat down. He waited for her to give him the same look as most other kids and move down a chair. If they weren't making fun of his clothes, they pointed and laughed at his pimple-ridden face.

"What are you in for?" she asked.

Emmanuel stared at her. Was she just making conversation, or setting him up only to make fun of him later?

"What?" she demanded. "Do I have a booger or something?"

He tried to laugh, but it sounded more like a dying gasp. "Uh, no."

"Then answer my question."

"I drew things in my notebook the teacher didn't like."

She twisted to face him, her striking blue eyes laser-focused on him. "Oooh, a naked lady?"

Emmanuel nodded.

The girl laughed gleefully. "Which teacher?"

"Mrs. Martin."

"Ugh, that old bat needs to retire."

Emmanuel nodded. "Why are you here?"

"I skipped the first two periods." She shrugged. "Freaking gym and English. Big deal. But I'm sure Valerie will ground my ass again."

"Valerie?"

"My mom."

Emmanuel found that interesting. As much as his mother drove him crazy, he'd never think of calling her by her first name. His father or Grandpa Nelson would slap him across the face if he did. "Why did you skip?"

The girl shrugged again. "Gym sucks, for one. And my ex-boyfriend makes English class miserable."

"You just stayed at home?"

"Of course not," she said. "I got on the bus, and then I snuck off campus before the last bell rang. It's not hard."

Until they called around looking for her, Emmanuel thought. "Where'd you go?"

"I walked a couple of miles down the road to a coffee shop." She twisted a lock of hair around her finger. "I wrote a note from my mom, too, but the principal didn't buy it. Oh God, speaking of Valerie..."

A woman in beige slacks and a purple shirt stormed into the main office. Her hair wasn't as long as her daughter's, but they looked almost exactly alike.

Valerie glared down at her daughter. "Car. Now."

The girl rolled her eyes and slowly stood, stretching her arms over her head. Emmanuel stared at the sliver of soft, creamy skin on her belly.

"Nicole."

"I'm coming, Valerie," she mocked, grinning down at Emmanuel. "Good luck in there."

She sauntered past her mother, who launched into a rant about disrespect. The girl—Nicole—seemed totally unbothered by her mother's anger. She probably didn't have to worry about getting her ass beat at home.

"Manny." The principal stood in his open doorway. "Let's go."

He scowled at the childish name. The nickname had died along with his sister three years ago. Emmanuel walked slowly, dragging his feet. He sat down in the chair that was still warm from Nicole sitting in it.

Principal Gustafson studied him, the dislike scrawled across his face. "You want to tell me why you're drawing these revolting images of nude people?"

"Nude drawings are a kind of art," Emmanuel said.

"Not when they depict grotesque and violating acts," Gustafson snapped. "You need to see a psychologist, Emmanuel —a real one, not a school counselor."

"What if I don't want to?" Emmanuel demanded, knowing full well his family didn't have the money and wouldn't spend it on him if they did.

"Then I won't be surprised if you're in prison by the time

you're an adult." He held Emmanuel's red notebook up. "These drawings are not normal. You need to get help before it's too late and you do something you can't take back, boy."

Emmanuel smiled. Principal Gustafson was so stupid.

FOURTEEN

Miller had convinced the DNR to close the entire reserve for the next couple of days so the victims buried in the clearing could be recovered without the prying eyes of nosy onlookers and media. The sheriff had placed deputies on the road and trail bordering the reserve in case someone tried to get a better look while the DNR manned the entrances to the lake.

Nikki put a couple of bottles of water and granola bars into her backpack, along with extra gloves and a flashlight. The wool winter hat made her scalp itch, but it was the warmest one Nikki had. She started down the path into the trees, her flashlight on the highest setting.

With the moon hidden behind a heavy cloud layer, the woods looked much darker and dense, but once Nikki got past the thatch of full pines that bordered the woods, the yellow light from the clearing glowed in the naked trees like a campfire.

The light did nothing to ease her sense of dread. How many victims would they find? Would Blanchard be able to establish any timeframe for their deaths or burial? Would the remains tell them anything other than confirming that a serial killer was operating in close-knit Washington County?

The privacy shelter Rory had put up was still in place, and she could see Courtney setting up to collect evidence.

"That coat looks like it weighs more than you." Nikki shrugged out of her backpack and placed it against a tree, out of the way.

"I don't care," Courtney said. "It's damn cold out here. I can't believe that thing thawed the ground."

"Technology is a wonderful thing sometimes." Nikki pointed to the vinyl barricade. "Miller and Blanchard in there?"

"And the forensic anthropologist," Courtney said. "Blanchard had the body bag Kesha was in sent to the lab. I found particles all over the inside of the bag, like something had been put in with her, possibly to help neutralize odor. I should have test results back in the morning."

"Miller said it looked like the bodies could be in bags on the ground-penetrating radar," Nikki said. "Which would be consistent with our theory that the killer originally intended to bury Kesha here but couldn't get through the ground." Another reason to believe that he was local and had some outdoors experience. Walking out on the ice and drilling a hole took care and guts, and Nikki was betting the killer had ice fished before. She wished they could figure out if he'd gone out on the lake the same night he'd come to bury her or if he'd come back the next night. Chelsea and her boyfriend might have spooked him enough to wait a couple of nights, but Nikki was more interested in whether he had the ice equipment on hand or had to purchase it.

The two of them went into the makeshift enclosure Rory had constructed. According to the ground-penetrating radar, the victims appeared to be lying side by side in roughly an eight by eight foot grave. Rory had blocked off double that amount of space, so they all had plenty of room to move around inside.

"How close are we?" Nikki asked.

Miller wiped sweat off his forehead. "Doctor Willard didn't

want us using large shovels, since the bodies don't appear to be much deeper than three or four feet. We're down to the last few inches of earth, so Doctor Willard and her assistant took over the digging."

Nikki had worked with the forensic anthropologist a few times since she'd returned to Minnesota six years ago, and she'd been fascinated with the woman's knowledge about skeletal remains. As the only certified forensic anthropologist in the state, she'd worked on several high-profile cases. She'd also done her graduate work at the University of Tennessee with Dr. Bass, the creator of the Anthropological Research Facility, better known as the Body Farm. Dr. Willard's experience with remains in all states of decay made her invaluable to the investigation.

"Doctor Willard, good to see you again. Can you bring me up to speed?"

Dr. Willard sat back on her heels. Her auburn waves peeked out from her wool hat. "We're removing shallow amounts of dirt with buckets. My graduate student, Omari, is pouring the dirt into a sieve, looking for anything we can test, like buttons, bits of fabric or jewelry. We've got a receptacle for inanimate objects and one for flora, fauna and any sort of seeds. At this point, everything we can take out of the ground, including the dirt itself, is evidence."

Courtney snapped on a pair of gloves and examined the bits and pieces Omari had taken from the dirt. "Are these parts of shotgun shells?" she asked eagerly.

"This is all popular duck-hunting ground," Miller said. "I'm surprised there aren't more. So don't get too excited just yet."

"Did you have a chance to talk to the sex offender who posted on the fishing forum?" Nikki asked him. Miller's unassuming manner and his ability to connect with just about anyone had made him a better candidate to talk to the sex offender than Nikki's trainees.

"He was out of town for Thanksgiving and had credit card receipts to prove it," Miller said. "He was on the lake the weekend of the fourteenth and fifteenth, but he worked both evenings until midnight. His boss confirmed."

"Nikki, I'm glad you're here," Blanchard said. "I finished Kesha's autopsy. Her stomach and her bowels indicated she'd last eaten pizza. Sheriff Miller said she ate at the mall shortly before she disappeared, but she didn't die that day and probably not the next. Digestion takes about thirty-six hours. Her bowels hadn't been emptied since she ate the pizza at the mall, so she likely died within the first twelve to twenty-four hours after the kidnapping. Cause of death appears to be asphyxiation. I didn't find any fibers or residue around her mouth and nose. Between that and the bruising on her neck, I'm pretty confident he strangled her. We're still waiting on toxicology."

"Any idea how long she might have been in the water?" Kesha had disappeared on Black Friday, but her body didn't look like it had been in the water that long.

"There were signs of very early decomposition, suggesting she'd been stored somewhere cold, and she may have been frozen at one point. If he put her in the water shortly after her death, given the water temp, I'd expect to see adipocere because cold speeds it up. But there isn't any, which again makes me think she might have been kept frozen. Given the condition of her body, I doubt she's been in the water more than a week, two tops."

"What about sexual assault?" Nikki asked.

Blanchard nodded. "Tears on the inner walls of her vagina and rectum suggest that she was, and I found spermicide still inside of both."

"So we need to look for all of that on these victims," Nikki said. "If they're skeletonized, how much will you be able to tell about the bodies, Doctor Willard?"

"Knives often nick bone, as do bullets. If there is any soft tissue remaining, we can test it and the bones for signs of poisoning. If the method of killing is strangulation, that often results in the hyoid getting broken," Willard said. "It looks as though the grave has been extended as each victim was buried, sort of like a trench."

Dr. Willard gently probed the remaining soil. "I can feel something solid right here, so we're close. Omari, make sure we're keeping an eye for any sort of tool marks along the edges of the grave."

Within minutes, dirty material started to become visible beneath the loose dirt.

Nikki crouched next to Willard. "That doesn't look like a body bag."

"It's not," Willard answered. "It looks like a big towel, and it's pretty degraded. But the one next to it is an emergency disaster body bag."

"Same on this end," Dr. Blanchard said. "Emergency disaster body bags."

"Like Kesha's," Courtney said. "I'll compare the two and confirm the match. You should be able to track who purchased them, right?"

Blanchard snorted. "You can buy body bags on Amazon, especially this kind. Good luck getting a subpoena through their legal department."

"How is the death industry not more regulated?" Courtney asked in surprise. "I mean, very few people are going to buy a body bag for non-nefarious reasons, it just seems bizarre."

"Sadly, Blanchard's right," Willard said. "You'd be looking for the proverbial needle in a haystack. These bags are water-proof, though."

"Kesha's would have been too," Nikki said. "But something ripped the bag, which caused the weight to slip out." She hated to think how long her body would have been in the lake if that hadn't happened. It was likely none of them would be out here in the freezing dark right now.

Nikki took photos of everything while the others worked.

"This is a skeleton, and the towel is falling apart, so we can't just pick it up and put it on the tarp." Willard worked to extricate the rotting material until the full skeleton was visible. "These bones have probably been here a decade or longer. I'll know more after we've thoroughly examined them."

"Can you tell anything about the material they were wrapped in?" Nikki asked. "The part you peeled away is pretty degraded but maybe if there's print left we might be able to date it."

Willard shined her LED flashlight on the bones inside the towel, gently shifting them around. "There is some kind of print left on the fabric. It's too hard for me to make out to even hazard a guess at the pattern, though."

"Once you've taken all the bones, I'll collect the towel," Courtney said. "Hopefully I'll be able to see something under the microscope."

"We'll obviously need to sift the dirt beneath this victim carefully, but I don't think we've got half a skeleton here. Likely animals carried off the rest of the remains."

Thanks to the ten inches of ice and snow on the unthawed ground, searching for scattered bones wasn't an option. They were stuck with what they found, at least until spring. And even then, Nikki doubted the search would yield many results. Small bones ended up in various critter nests, and an animal could have carried the larger bones miles away.

After Willard made sure the remaining bags weren't compromised, Miller and Omari carefully removed the second body and placed it on the tarp.

Nikki held her breath as Dr. Willard opened the bag. "Skeletonized, head to toe, but see the difference in the bones? They look more recent," Willard said. "These were in body bags, however, so that could make a difference. The less water and heat, the slower the decomp."

"Any idea how much of a difference?" Miller asked.

Dr. Willard shrugged. "Depends on how long they've been here, how many different seasons they've gone through. Given Minnesota's average seasonal weather and the depth this person is buried at, my best educated guess—and that's all this is right now—is that this victim's been here through a few seasons. There's no organic material or insect activity, but the bones themselves look fresher, for lack of a better word. But I can't tell you anything with any certainty until I've thoroughly examined the bones in the lab. And wrapped in any sort of plastic, which is essentially what body bags are, will slow decomp, especially if the victim is buried in the fall or early winter."

Miller put a red tag on the bag. "Red goes to your lab, Doctor Willard. If there's enough organic material left, blue tags mean Blanchard's lab."

Willard studied the third victim, who also appeared mostly skeletonized. When she got to the fourth victim, she said, "I don't think this one has been here more than a year or so. There are intact dead beetles, which suggests some organic material was left on the bones fairly recently." She touched the long, glossy black hair. "He stripped her like the others, but she's wearing a silver bracelet with some beautiful inlaid design. I've seen similar ones at the Shakopee Sioux events."

Like all tribal reservations, the Shakopee Sioux, located south of Washington County, fell under the jurisdiction of the FBI. They didn't have their own police force like some reservations, but they did have an officer liaison from the local police. "If she's missing from the reservation, why haven't we heard about her?" Nikki asked.

"Maybe they don't trust the government," Miller said wryly.

"I don't blame them, but this is different. She's a missing person, and we're here to help." She texted Liam and asked if any of the missing women he'd found in the database were Native American. He must have been waiting to hear from her, because the reply came back right away.

"Liam says a twenty-six-year-old female disappeared from Mystic Lake Casino about thirteen months ago. She worked there and clocked out. Security footage showed her heading toward her car, but she walked out of the frame. Her car was found in the lot the next morning."

"The last bag is a lot larger than the others," Courtney said. "I hope there isn't a mom and a kid inside."

It took Miller, Willard and Omari to remove the wide third bag. "No way this one is skeletonized," Willard said. "It wouldn't be this heavy." She carefully unzipped the bag, the faint scent of decomposition hanging in the air.

"Holy God," Blanchard said.

The five of them stood in silence, trying to comprehend what they were seeing. Like Kesha, the victims were nude. Instead of a heavy person, two people occupied the bag. They lay facing each other, their bodies covered with a waxy substance and in advanced decay, but the genitals of both were still visible. The man's dark hair was flecked with gray, the female's long hair in a braid.

"They might be siblings." Courtney finally broke the silence. "Or friends. It doesn't mean they're a couple, does it?"

"No, but that doesn't matter in terms of a profile." Nikki barely managed the words, still trying to comprehend what she was seeing. "It's a biological male and a biological female. That is... rare for this sort of serial killer, to say the least."

"Will you be able to tell if they were assaulted?" Courtney asked.

"Possibly," Blanchard said. "But I'd think the removal of clothes suggests they were."

"Or he wanted to humiliate them before he killed them," Nikki said.

The medical examiner pointed to the male's belly, where lividity marks could still be seen. "He either died face down or was turned that way shortly after death, because the lividity on his stomach is fixed, and you can also see some on his upper thigh." Blanchard motioned for Dr. Willard to help move the male onto his side. The fatty tissue on his rear end had marbled, and what looked like a mix of dried blood and body waste were visible on his upper thighs. Nikki looked away as Blanchard worked to get a better look at the man's injuries. She hated the undignified way victims often had to be examined.

"He was probably assaulted." Blanchard sat back on her knees. "There appears to be external injuries around the rectum, but I'll have to confirm at autopsy."

"Is there any obvious sign of death on any of them? If these are execution-style murders, then different sexes aren't as much of an issue." Nikki heard the worry in her own voice. Nothing about the bodies suggested something as merciful as execution. They appeared to have been beaten and tortured, most likely raped.

"These two have marks suggesting asphyxiation," Blanchard said, gesturing to the couple in the body bag. "But I need to confirm that on autopsy."

"I can't tell you anything definite about the skeletal remains right now, either," Willard said. "Finding cause of death is going to be difficult at best."

Both doctors shook their heads. "Hopefully we will find it once they're X-rayed."

"Look at the body bag," Blanchard said. "That's either blood or fecal matter. The latter happens with decomposition, but bleeding out of this area doesn't unless there's trauma."

"If he was sexually assaulted, the bleeding would stop after he was killed," Nikki said.

"Yes, but the body's still going to expel any fluid. He could have had an ulcer or something, but his wrists and hands are still bound with some kind of wire. I'll see if I can find any trace of semen or spermicide from a condom. Hopefully I'll be able to tell more on autopsy."

Courtney peered over Blanchard's shoulder. "What are all of those granules? It looks like there are some in all of the bags. I found something similar with Kesha, although the water had liquidized most of it."

Blanchard picked up a handful of the granules and sniffed. "My bet is Neutrolene. The smell's just barely noticeable, but we use it so much it's ingrained in my memory."

"Now that's a smart criminal." Willard shook her head.

"What's Neutrolene?" Nikki asked.

"A godsend," Blanchard said. "It's an organic odor neutralizer used in funeral homes, hospitals, refrigerated morgues—any place that deals with death. It's the only thing I know of that doesn't mask the odor—it actually neutralizes it, and it works."

"Please tell me you can't buy that on Amazon too," Miller said.

"No, but anyone can purchase it off Neutrolene's site. Gas stations are starting to use it in restrooms. I've suggested it to a couple of friends with pet odor issues, and that's what they did."

"It works on pet odors?" Courtney asked. "Surely not cat urine? That's its own molecular beast."

"My friend claims it does, and so do a lot of reviews," Blanchard said. "It's a powerful product. And it wasn't introduced until 2012. I was doing my fellowship as a pathologist, and the difference it made was incredible."

"It looks like there are granules with every victim except the one wrapped in the towel," Nikki said.

"I'll test the towel for it," Courtney said. "Can you tell the sex of the partial skeleton?"

Willard looked up from examining the remains. "No, not without testing. Given the number of bones missing, don't count on dental records, either. I'm only seeing a partial jaw."

"The dog scented this site, even though five out of the six are in body bags with the odor neutralizer," Miller said. "Can a dog sniff out old skeletal remains after more than a decade?"

"They're training cadaver dogs to work on archeological sites," Willard said. "A few years ago in Croatia, a trained cadaver dog led researchers to a site dating back to about seven hundred B.C. Even if the dog did follow the scent Sheriff Miller gave him, it's fully capable of sniffing out all six of these—even with the Neutrolene. It's made for our noses, not animals'."

"We need to prioritize dental records," Nikki said. "The sooner we identify them, the better. Victims' remains always tell a story about their killer."

The story these victims told scared the hell out of Nikki. Assuming Willard was correct about the age of the remains in the towel, they were dealing with someone who came back years later to bury more victims. That told Nikki that he was not only a local, comfortable enough to move around without drawing attention, but the older remains could very well hold the key to the killer's identity. This wasn't the only place to dispose of his victims, which meant he'd come back to Washington County and this location because this first victim meant enough to their killer that he'd remembered where he'd buried her, something many serial murderers forget over time, because the disposal wasn't important to them. It was the control and power over the victim that mattered. Disposal was about not getting caught.

They were dealing with the rarest kind of monster, and Nikki needed all the help she could get.

FIFTEEN

Nikki stepped out of the tent to get some air and try to clear her mind. She'd worked several serial cases and countless other homicides. She'd seen men and women killed together and whole families wiped out. She racked her brain trying to think of sexually motivated serials who had sought out both men and women to rape and murder. None came to mind, but maybe the cold and shock were just numbing her memory.

Ramirez killed men and women, but he'd only raped women and young girls. Dahmer, Gacy, Nilsen, and Bonin, better known as the Freeway Killer, had raped and killed men and boys, but not women. Spree and mass murderers were different beasts entirely. Rader—known as BTK—had raped and killed women, as had Bundy, the Hillside Stranglers, and so many more serial killers.

The longer she tried to think of names, the more confused she felt. There had to be precedence for a killer like this. She took her phone out and called Liam.

"This is bad," she burst out before he finished saying "hello." "There's at least one man in the pit, buried with a woman. We don't know about sexual assault yet, but it's likely. None of the victims appear to have been shot. I sent photos over the secure server." Her chest felt tight with anxiety.

"I'm looking at them now," he said. "Christ Almighty, this is even worse than I thought. Maybe the guy was killed out of necessity when he tried to protect the woman he's buried with." His tone sounded about as hopeful as she felt. The idea that serial killers were only motivated by sex was a myth. Some serials killed for revenge, financial gain, or attention, and some killed solely for the thrill. The D.C. Sniper case and the Son of Sam were the first two that popped into her mind. Both had killed indiscriminately, by gun. Only the worst of the worst were sexually motivated, and of those, the vast majority chose victims based on sexual preference, regardless of what their public lifestyle might have been. Nikki knew she should wait for the forensic reports, but in her experience the absence of gunshot wounds suggested some sort of poisoning, which may or may not be personal and sexual. Stabbing and strangulation almost always meant the killing had been intimate, even if done by a stranger. Nikki's usual confidence in her investigative abilities had started to shrink with each victim that had been uncovered. She kept trying to tell herself she was jumping ahead, but every instinct in her body told her they were dealing with a predator unlike any other, including the Frost Killer.

"What about the hands and feet of these victims?" Liam asked.

"They all seem to be intact," Nikki said.

"So why cut off Kesha's?"

Nikki had been asking herself the same thing since they'd gotten their first look at the bodies. "Assuming he intended to bury her, whatever he used to bring her out on the lake may have been too small. I'm not sure we'll know that answer until we catch the guy. And sex is the key."

"I'm sorry?" Liam asked.

"Sexual motivation, I mean. If that's all there is, and we're dealing with someone who doesn't care—male, female, white, Hispanic, how old the victim is—we're in over our heads."

"No, we aren't," Liam said firmly. "I can do plenty from the office. We can and will figure this out. We always do. What else did you guys find?"

His calm voice and confidence helped Nikki get back on track. She told him about the victim in the towel and the lack of granules around the bones. "We'll have to wait for official results from Willard and Courtney, but Blanchard is positive about the Neutrolene. It came on the market in 2012."

"Meaning the first victim is likely older and someone close to him," Liam said. "Unless Willard's estimate is wrong and the remains aren't as old as she thinks, but looking at the photos you sent, the towel is decaying, and the bones don't look like the second skeleton."

"And they've been disturbed," Nikki said. "The others had a body bag and an odor neutralizer, but it seems impossible that at least some animals wouldn't catch the scent and start digging."

"Hey, Nik." Courtney's voice behind her made Nikki jump. "Sorry to sneak up on you, but after Blanchard said animals could probably catch the scent even with the Neutrolene, I started examining the fauna and flora they've taken out of the dirt. I'm going to test it and see if something toxic was deliberately planted. Wild animals are usually smart enough to avoid plants that will kill them. None of the body bags look like anything has tried to get into them, which tells me that nothing's messing around back here. I'd like to know why."

"Good idea," Nikki said. "Liam, did you find out anything new?"

"I spent the day combing through fishing forums, along with Kendra and Jim," he answered. "We contacted a dozen people who've posted about fishing Big Marine since Thanksgiving. Most of them didn't see anything suspicious, but I did talk to a guy who said he was out on Big Marine last weekend, and he remembered a guy putting up a new ice shack. After he brought the plywood out, it didn't take him long to put it together. He definitely knew what he was doing, but the witness said the guy carried his equipment in one of those huge, heavy-duty rolling totes. It struck him as odd because he never opened the tote while he was building the shack, but he never thought any more of it."

"Did the ice fisher talk to the man?"

"Unfortunately, no," Liam said. "A lot of the guys know each other and chat, but this guy was standoffish, didn't come over and introduce himself. He did say the guy wore a neck gaiter up to the bridge of his nose, so he didn't get a good look at his face. He wore worn Carhartt coveralls and all-weather boots. I had him look at a photo of the lake, and he put the guy around the area where Kesha's body was found."

"That sounds like the man Chelsea Blaine and her boyfriend encountered less than a week before. Your witness have any idea of his age?"

"He didn't see him well enough, but he said he was tall, probably around six feet. Definitely white."

"What about a vehicle?" Nikki asked.

"Old, dirty white pickup," Liam said. "The ice fisher thought it was probably a mid-eighties Chevy, but he didn't get that good a look."

"Danny Stanton's is a white 1976 Chevy Scottsdale," Nikki said.

"I already sent him a photo of it," Liam said. "He said it could be the same truck, but he thought this guy's looked like it was in better shape than Stanton's."

"Still, that's a big coincidence, and he said he didn't get a good look." Nikki told him about her visit with Stanton earlier. "The girl showed me her ID, and it looks legit, but run her name and the plate number."

"Gross," Liam said. "You don't think he's our suspect, though?"

"At this point," Nikki said, "I'm not sure." She hugged her chest as the wind screamed through the bare trees. "Plan on being at the Washington County sheriff's in the morning and be ready to try to work up a profile. Doctor Roth is going to meet us there."

"You think he'll be able to offer something we can't?" Liam asked.

"He's the serial killer whisperer," Nikki said. "And right now, we need all of the help we can get."

She ended the call and went back into the shelter. Their small group spent the next two hours photographing each victim along with the entire burial area, examining soil and taking as many evidence samples as possible. Once Willard and Blanchard were confident everything had been collected, the bodies were secured on stretchers and taken out of the area one by one. The DNR had managed to keep the media out of the parking lot, but two news vehicles were parked across the entrance, cameras rolling.

A stocky reporter from Channel 9 called her name, but Nikki pulled her hood up and continued helping secure the bodies for transport. Willard and Blanchard left first, but the media remained, shouting questions at them from their perch across the road.

"Are Parker Jameson's remains in the reserve?" the Channel 9 guy called out. Nikki thought about ignoring him, but she could put that rumor to rest. She walked across the lot but remained on her side of the road. If she crossed the line the DNR had set up, Nikki would be swarmed with questions she couldn't answer.

"We didn't find his remains today, no. That's all I can tell you."

"Agent Hunt, the Forest Lake police claim they asked for your help, but you refused on the basis the person responsible for Parker's disappearance couldn't be the same one who killed Kesha Williams."

Nikki felt like she'd eaten a mouthful of sand. She had to keep her composure, but she couldn't let this rumor gain any traction, and if she had to guess, the Forest Lake police had involved the media as a means of forcing her to get involved. "That is false," Nikki said. "A member of my team has been talking with the Forest Lake police since they first contacted us, which was Christmas Eve. At the time, we believed Kesha Williams likely knew her killer."

"Is that no longer the case?" the Channel 9 guy asked.

"It's much less of a possibility," Nikki said.

"But the remains in the woods are connected to Kesha's murder?"

"No comment."

"Is it true your team is consulting with Doctor Alex Roth to help crack this case?" The woman from the CBS affiliate finally squeezed in a question. "The press release issued this afternoon insinuated as much."

"No comment." Nikki headed back to Miller, more irritated than she should be with her boss. Hernandez's attempt to make the FBI look good had wound up making her team look incompetent.

Miller jerked his chin toward the reporters. "Did they say something about a consultant?"

"I didn't get a chance to tell you earlier, but Hernandez is bringing in a neuroscientist who has worked with the St. Paul police and others. He's talked to more murderers in the last decade than just about anyone else, which is part of the reason

Hernandez thinks it's good for our image, given all the media attention."

"I hope he's got some kind of magic formula," Miller said dryly. "We also need to get on this Parker Jameson thing. I'd like to know why the Forest Lake police called the FBI first instead of getting my help since the county is my damn jurisdiction."

"Until we found the male's remains tonight, there was very little information to make me think Parker could be another victim. Liam followed up with the detective, and he agreed, especially since Parker's ex is still considered a suspect," Nikki told him.

"And now?" Miller asked as she climbed into the jeep and turned on the engine.

"I'm not convinced yet, but we need to follow up with Parker's case. If his ex isn't involved, Parker's been missing for about a week, so there's a chance he could still be alive."

Nikki prayed she hadn't made a decision that wound up costing Parker Jameson his life. "I'll see you bright and early tomorrow morning, Kent."

Nikki drove home on autopilot, her mind consumed with the bodies in the woods until everything tangled together in a messy heap, just like this case. Rory would still be up, and she had no idea what to tell him about today. She couldn't share details, but Rory had helped yesterday and would want to know what they'd found. Until her ex-husband's murder, she always talked through heavy cases with him. His job in white-collar crimes gave him a different perspective, and Nikki could share the gruesome parts of her job without worrying about Tyler's reaction. He knew what questions Nikki could answer and which ones she couldn't, and he'd helped her through more than one heinous case. Rory insisted he wanted to do the same, but Nikki always refused to burden him with the horrors running around her head.

Light glowed in the kitchen window, and despite the turmoil in her head, the sight of Rory's house gave her a sense of calm. He'd texted about keeping a plate of leftovers warm for her, so Nikki went straight from the garage to the kitchen. The downstairs television blared one of the zillion bowl games played after Christmas, so Nikki grabbed the plate of food and a beer and started for the stairs.

"Hey." Rory was already halfway down the steps. "Is the food hot enough? Mom swears by those warmer thingies, but I've never tried one."

Nikki nodded, her mouth too full to speak. Rory kissed her temple, grabbed a beer, and they sat down at the kitchen table. They sat in companionable silence as she scarfed down the food. Nikki topped things off with a long chug from her beer bottle.

"I take it tonight wasn't good," Rory said.

"Six victims," Nikki said. "GPR was right on that." She drank the rest of her beer to keep from spilling painful details to Rory.

"I saw something about a missing guy from Forest Lake too," Rory said.

Nikki nodded.

"Sorry," Rory said. "I know you can't tell me anything. I just can't help but feel personally invested."

"Why wouldn't you?" Nikki asked. "You guys were a huge help. I have no doubt the media would have been breathing down our necks if you hadn't put up the shelter."

"I talked to Lacey a little while ago." Rory grinned. "She had an encounter with a manatee. I only understood about half what she said, she talked so fast."

"I spoke to her for a few minutes, and we've texted a few times." Being able to text her mom had helped alleviate some of

Lacey's fears about Nikki's safety. "I'm so relieved she's having fun." She started peeling the label off the brown bottle. "And a little jealous, I think. Maybe that's not the right word."

"She's in paradise and you're in the frozen north working a nasty murder case. Why wouldn't you be jealous?" Rory got up and tossed his empty bottle in the recycling bin.

"Right." Nikki shook her head, handing him her own empty bottle. "Does it make me a bad person if a tiny part of me is sad she's not pining for her mom?"

Rory massaged her shoulders, his warm fingers igniting an electric current inside her. "Nope. It makes you human." He leaned down until his lips grazed her ear. "Why don't we go to the bedroom, so I can give you a massage?"

Nikki rolled her eyes at his obvious innuendo. Doing normal things like sex and sleeping during a big case always made her feel like a lazy cop, but a little self-care could also do wonders for a tired brain. She stood and took his hand. "All right, but only if it's a full-service massage."

SIXTEEN

MONDAY, DECEMBER 27

After her "massage," Nikki had spent at least two hours going over her notes, searching for anything they'd missed, including the information Forest Lake had originally sent about Parker's disappearance. That jettisoned her into worrying that she hadn't taken that information seriously enough, which led to going back and forth about giving her boss a heads-up on the police's claim she'd ignored them. He'd know it wasn't true, but a big part of his job was about making the Bureau office look good. She eventually sent him a short text and forced herself to at least try to sleep a couple of hours, but she tossed and turned, falling asleep an hour or so before her alarm.

Hernandez's early morning call also came before her alarm sounded. "What the hell is happening with the Forest Lake police? Is there a missing person we need to be concerned about?" He sounded like he'd been running, but Hernandez always sounded like that when he was upset. From the clinks and clangs on his end, Nikki assumed Hernandez was still at home and getting breakfast.

"Honestly, sir, I don't know." She grabbed her notebook off the nightstand and went through everything they knew so far. "When you look at the big picture, including Parker's trouble with his ex, there's still a strong chance his disappearance isn't related. But Liam is working with Forest Lake from the office, and I will be going to Parker's work and the diner later today."

"This is a PR nightmare," Hernandez said. "Without evidence he's been taken by the same person, it doesn't look great that we're stretching resources between him and a black woman's murder."

"I know," Nikki said. "But that's our best shot right now. And I didn't ignore the Forest Lake police, by the way."

"I believe you, and I believe in you and your team. Stick with the plan right now, but I want you to run it all by Roth this morning. How soon will Blanchard be able to tell us if the male victim you found last night was sexually assaulted? That's the key to what kind of person we're dealing with."

"She's rushing it," Nikki said. "But that's all I can tell you right now."

"Stay on her," Hernandez instructed before ending the call. *Right*, Nikki thought. Because Dr. Blanchard responded so well to being pushed. Still, she left the doctor a message, making clear the male victim needed to be priority, all the while envisioning the medical examiner rolling her eyes.

Numb with exhaustion, Nikki loaded up on coffee, showered and dressed and then headed towards the sheriff's station. They were meeting with Roth at nine a.m., and she wanted to have plenty of time to go over the case with Liam and Miller before the doctor arrived.

Nikki followed the smell of donuts to the conference room, her stomach grumbling. "Food?"

"They're incredible." Liam spoke around a mouthful of pastry. "Miller's wife got up and made them this morning. He also brought in fresh coffee." He took another bite and moaned. Liam's relationship with food was always a sight to behold. He could put away more than anyone she'd ever met, including Lacey, who seemed to be constantly ravenous.

"What an angel." Nikki poured a fresh cup of coffee and dumped sugar and powdered creamer into it. "I don't think I slept more than a couple of hours." She sat down across from him.

"You sounded kind of spooked last night," Liam said.

"Aren't you?" She told him about her conversation with Hernandez. "Until we know if the male vic was sexually assaulted, we're spinning, but it sure looks like that's going to be the case. And if Parker Jameson turns out to be another victim..."

"Boss," Liam said. "I went over that file, and so did Kendra and Jim. Sheriff Miller, too, since I emailed it to him last night. Parker did 'vanish,' but that doesn't mean his ex—whose jacket is more extensive than I thought—isn't responsible. Statistically, that's the most likely scenario."

"Stats aren't looking that helpful right now, are they?" Nikki grabbed a glazed donut and ate half in two bites. "That's going to sit in my stomach, but damn, it is good. Where's Miller?"

"He went to call Reynolds to tell him to check on the site and make sure no one's been snooping. He should be back in a minute."

Nikki opened her notebook and tried to decipher the notes she'd taken at three a.m. "We need to get everything we know on the board. My mind is so jumbled and tired, I'm having trouble keeping everything straight."

While they waited for Miller, Nikki went to the whiteboard and wrote down what they knew so far.

- *Black Friday, Kesha disappears*
- *Big Marine at least four inches of ice by mid-December*

- *December 12, Chelsea and boyfriend meet suspect in woods looking for dog*
- *December 14, ice fisher observed building shack and hauling tote. Witness said driving old white truck*
- *December 17, Parker Jameson goes missing, possible victim, age 25. Disappeared leaving Artists' Co-op in downtown Forest Lake*
- *Christmas Eve, Kesha's body found*
- *Christmas Day, burials found. 6 victims total. At least one male, possible sex assault. One victim may be Native American. Kesha is black, couple found in decomp white, suggesting no preference regarding ethnicity and appearance*

Possible suspects

- *Danny Stanton—human blood on knife, found body, pickup similar to the one observed on Dec 14. 5'7", 150lbs*
- *Man building shack on lake—closer to six feet per witness*
- *Chelsea described the man she saw in similar way*
- *Parker Jameson's boyfriend Colton Troyer*

"That's it?" Liam asked when she stopped. "What about Dion Johnson?"

"No one in Kesha's life raises red flags, and her boyfriend is frankly too young and the wrong race to have killed all of these people. Unless her murder is separate from the others—and I don't think it is—Dion's in the clear." Still, Nikki added Dion's name to the suspect list, along with an asterisk. "Not to mention he doesn't fish and is adamant he wouldn't go on the ice for anything."

"Fair point," Miller said as he joined them and helped

himself to a donut. "Everyone would remember a young black man on the lake, and the man described by the ice fisher and Chelsea is white and larger than either Dion or Danny Stanton."

"Danny Stanton also has an eighteen-year-old girlfriend." Nikki told Miller about her encounter with Stanton. She hadn't had a chance last night, and after the bodies had been unearthed, she'd been so rattled she'd forgotten. "Liam, did you run that plate?"

"The Honda Civic is registered to Javier Lopez, forty-eight, of Forest Lake. His daughter Maria turned eighteen in October. She works part-time at West End Diner in Forest Lake, which is right next to the Artists' Co-op. And Parker's ex is the diner owner's son."

"The Artists' Co-op?" Miller asked. "My wife always has to check out the inventory every time we're in Forest Lake."

"Parker Jameson, part owner." Liam flipped through his notes. "He and two female artists opened the business a couple of years ago. Parker disappeared on December seventeenth, and while the Forest Lake police have no leads, they also had no interest in the FBI's help until the detective called Nikki on Christmas Eve after she heard about Kesha's remains being found in the lake."

"I spoke to the Forest Lake Chief of Police that same night after I called about getting the K9," Miller assured them. "He said the detective didn't know what she was talking about, and they were confident it was his ex-boyfriend. They've been tailing him for the last week."

"With no results." While Nikki hadn't appreciated the insinuation she'd ignored the situation, she also didn't like the police chief's word choices about a female detective, but since her nerves felt like they'd been flayed, she was probably overreacting about that. "I plan to go to Forest Lake today. Now that I know Maria works at West End Diner and is sleeping with

Danny Stanton, that's a loose connection between Kesha and Parker I want to check on," Nikki told them. "She said she met Danny at work," Nikki said. "My gut feelings about Danny aside, if the first body is pre-2012, like we think given the absence of the odor neutralizer, that means he would have been twenty-one at the oldest at the time of that murder."

Liam grunted and started leafing through his mess of notes. Before the attack, his organization had been impeccable. Now, he needed to have visual reminders in front of him. "Remember I did the background check on Stanton? He was born in Wisconsin and moved to Stillwater with his wife and kids in 2014. Not exactly the local type we've been talking about."

"He could be the scout of sorts," Miller said. "He helps find the victims and tees them up for his partner to take care of." He looked at his phone. "Doctor Roth is here. I told the desk sergeant to send him straight back."

The man who appeared in the doorway possessed the confidence of an experienced academic and leader in his field, but without the stuffiness Nikki always associated with researchers. He'd dressed in dark jeans, a white Oxford shirt, and fading leather loafers. "I'm looking for Sheriff Miller?" His sunburned fair skin complemented his sandy blond hair. Courtney had been right—he did remind Nikki of the Alexander the Great digitized photo.

"That'd be me." Miller shook the doctor's extended hand and introduced everyone. "Looks like you have been somewhere other than here."

"Treated myself to a vacation in Puerto Rico. Unfortunately, I'm not very good at reapplying sunscreen." Roth's gray eyes landed on Nikki. "Agent Nicole Hunt, I have to admit I was surprised when I heard you needed me to consult on a case."

"Why is that?" Nikki asked, motioning for him to take a seat across from her. "I'm certain we haven't met before."

Roth smiled. "You and your team's reputation precede you, especially after the last year you've had."

"It has been challenging," Nikki admitted. "I'm not usually anxious for the new year, but I'll be happy to turn the calendar on this one." She pointed to Liam. "Agent Wilson's still on restricted duty, and, frankly, after last night, we need help. You've consulted with the St. Paul police before, correct?"

"I have," he said. "Along with Milwaukee and Madison, over in Wisconsin. At any rate, I'm well-versed in the rules of working with law enforcement." He smiled, his gaze on the whiteboard. Then Roth's thick eyebrows furrowed together. "Am I reading this board correctly? You have male and female victims?"

Nikki and Miller walked him through what they'd found last night. Miller had drawn a map of the burial scene on the board rather than show actual photos. Nikki slid the photos she'd printed off this morning across the table to Roth. "As you can tell, we're still in the early stages of identifying these victims. We're waiting on confirmation from the forensic anthropologist, but the remains in the towel are older, and possibly a key to the killer's identity."

"You believe he knew them?" Roth thumbed through the pictures of the mass burial. He stopped at the photo of the male victim. "He's much more recent than some of the others. Do you know if the woman he was buried with was related to him?"

"Not yet," Nikki answered. "To answer your first question, as I'm sure you know, it's not uncommon for a serial murderer to start displaying worrying behavior during adolescence. That's usually where we see the cruelty to animals come in, and there's often predatory behavior in their background that was swept under the rug or explained away as a one-time mistake. People don't like to believe evil walks right under their noses."

"That's very true," Roth said. "Especially if the perpetrator's young. That's one of the core parts of my research—preventative actions that can be taken so that issues are spotted earlier and, hopefully, parents have some resources on how to deal with whatever's happening."

"That all sounds great," Liam said. "But what about people who live on the fringe of society or don't have access to insurance? If they can't afford to go to the doctor for strep throat, how are they supposed to afford a special psychologist for their kid?"

"They can't," Roth said. "We're working on an outreach program that would offer a lot of resources to the community, pro bono. Mental health is important to everyone, not just those who are better off than others." He flushed. "Sorry, my soapbox is sidetracking us. Assuming you're correct and your killer knew his first victim, that victim's identity is crucial. I assume you believe the killer's a man?"

"Eyewitness reports suggest so, as do statistics." Nikki looked ruefully at Liam. "At this point, we know Kesha was strangled. Doctor Blanchard found some evidence of asphyxiation in the male and female victims who were in the same bag, but we don't know how the others died. No sign of an execution-style killing. We don't know if the victims in the woods were sexually assaulted, but the medical examiner is making the male victim priority. We need to know if he was killed protecting someone, or because he was in the wrong place at the wrong time, or if he was targeted."

Roth leaned forward in the chair, fascination in his eyes. "Just to clarify, this killer is sexually assaulting and killing both men and women?"

"We're waiting on the autopsy report," Nikki clarified, "but there is evidence to suggest there's a strong sexual component to all of his attacks, yes. It also appears that he's not picky about ethnicity, physical attributes or age."

Roth was silent, digesting the information. Nikki debated

giving him more details, but they still had parameters to stick to. "All right, then," Roth said. "Assuming your hypotheses hold, the question is, does he take both sexes because he doesn't care who he kills, or because he's bisexual and probably sexually repressed in his real life?"

"We're hoping the medical examiner will have an answer for us soon," Nikki said. "As I'm sure you know, very few serial killers have taken victims from both genders, and the few that have weren't up close and personal kills."

Roth nodded. "Son of Sam, D.C. Snipers, those types of killers may be labeled as serial murderers, but they are categorically different than sexual sadists like Gacy or Dahmer. They're driven to commit sexual acts that cause the psychological and physical suffering of their victims. That power and control gets these guys off."

Dr. Roth stood and walked to the whiteboard. He crossed his arms over his chest and tapped his finger against his lips. He bounced on the balls of his feet. "Traditionally, those types stuck to whichever gender they were attracted to. Gay men, almost always closeted and full of self-loathing, chose males they wanted to have sex with but knew the person would never consent. For that sort of killer, control is the key."

Roth spoke with confidence, but he didn't come across as an academic who thought he knew more than the cops on the ground. He'd also probably dealt with more killers than the vast majority of law enforcement officers saw in their entire careers. During her time at Quantico, Nikki had gone to interview a few violent offenders with her mentor. She'd quickly learned that connecting with an inmate sentenced for murder, when there were few, if any, benefits to the inmate, required an entirely new skillset. Nikki had watched her mentor pretend to empathize with more than one violent criminal in order to gain their trust. Roth impressed her.

"How many violent offenders have you interviewed?" she asked him when he returned to the table.

"I think all of them at this point," Roth said with a small grin. "Beginning with my time in New Mexico in 2011, upwards of two thousand, including some of the ones well known to the public. If they were still living when I started, then I probably talked to them." Roth shifted in his chair. "But the less well-known ones are just as scary."

"What about single-victim killers, like domestic cases?" Miller asked. "Are those included in your study?"

Roth nodded. "Since I started with the New Mexico team over a decade ago, my goal has been to talk to every convicted murderer and rapist, no matter the victim count, as these are vastly different personality types, even after spending years in prison. Those who've killed multiple people are just a different breed."

"Exactly," Nikki said. "And the worst part is, we believe this killer is from Washington County."

Roth looked at her, surprised. "Really? You've come to that conclusion with so many unknowns?"

"It's the location of the burial pit." Nikki explained the difficulty of navigating the area because of the water table. "He knows the area. He may not be a born local, but I believe he lives in the area and understands how to blend in."

"Have you managed to put together a full profile?" Roth asked.

"Limited," Nikki said. "White male, thirties or forties. Organized, financially stable, possibly drives a white 1980s Chevy pickup but likely has a nicer vehicle as well."

"Why the second vehicle?"

"Given his likely age and the planning he's exhibited, chances are he's not driving that Chevy to work." The body bags and odor neutralizer weren't cheap, and a killer's financial situation almost always made a difference in the choices they made. Serials always lived two different lives, and the successful ones appeared so benign they flew right under the radar.

"You mentioned the first set of remains are much older, so I assume that's part of your age estimate?" Roth steepled his fingers together, resting his chin on top.

Nikki nodded. "If they started in their mid-late teens, our killer has to be at least mid-thirties, even if he was a young teenager when that victim was killed." Nikki glanced at Miller and Liam, silently reminding them of the decision to keep the odor neutralizer between them. Roth was a respected doctor and an asset, but Nikki knew nothing about his inner circle. She couldn't risk that leak and the Neutrolene could end up being the smoking gun.

"A teenager?" Roth echoed. "They're impulsive and disorganized."

"They are, and if they do kill at that age it's almost always someone they know, someone accessible, which is why the oldest set of remains are so important. We do believe a significant amount of time passed between the first murder and the second, but that could be a year or fifteen at this point. The forensic anthropologist hopes to figure that out in the next day or two."

"Good," Roth said. "I take it from your bullet list that you believe Kesha could have been put in the lake after the lake iced over?"

"We're almost certain of it," Miller said. "The autopsy supports it, and we've got a witness who saw a man building an ice shack and hauling a tote shortly after full ice-in."

Roth stared at him. "You're saying that you believe this man got rid of her body while others were around?"

"It's a strong possibility," Miller said. "The DNR would have noticed a light on the lake at night, just like Chelsea and her boyfriend noticed the one in the woods. But you build an ice shack during the day, and no one thinks anything of it."

For the first time, Roth seemed unnerved. He worried his lower lip, locking eyes with Nikki. "That's a level of confidence you don't see very often. Have you established any sort of time frame in terms of how often he takes victims? There's no chance he's got someone now, is there?"

"We're not certain." Liam explained Parker Jameson's disappearance and the early theories the Forest Lake police had.

"I'm heading up there right after we finish here," Nikki said, feeling defensive. She'd been obsessing about it all night. What if she'd blown off the Forest Lake detective when she called on Christmas Eve and Parker was out there right now, being tortured by the man they were hunting—or worse? "Finding the male in the grave yesterday has obviously changed a lot about the investigation."

Roth's sympathetic glance only made Nikki feel worse. "Hindsight's always twenty-twenty, Agent."

Nikki forced a smile, but she hated being so easily read by a stranger. Roth struck her as the kind of person who might not say a lot in a social setting but saw everything. He'd probably recognized the reek of shame around her as soon as he'd come in. Maybe that was a bit dramatic, but they'd been far behind the killer from the beginning, and she was starting to think her decisions had only made things worse.

"It's such a shame to see beautiful natural resources used for acts of evil," Roth said. "I believe it's significant that he remembered where the first body was buried after an extended period of time and chose to continue using that spot."

"Exactly," Nikki said, glad to hear they were on the same page. "As soon as we get a better time frame, we'll start pulling up cold cases and see if we can identify them. We're still waiting on identification and estimated time of death and burial for the others, but the body bags are important too."

"He can afford to buy them," Liam said. "And he's likely got a place in a rural area where he keeps the victims."

"Do you believe the bags have other significance, Agent Hunt?" Roth asked. "Perhaps you're dealing with someone in the death industry? Or he's got a contact within that community. You can't just buy those off Amazon." Roth chuckled, glancing at Nikki. When she didn't smile, his eyes widened. "Surely you aren't saying that body bags are available online, for any consumer?"

"Yep," she said. "I think he used body bags because he's smart and wanted to do everything he could to keep the bodies undisturbed. That's one of the main reasons he's never gotten caught."

"Well, tell me what I can do to help," Roth said. "I'm not sure I can provide anything you don't already know, but I'll do my best."

"Dion Johnson, Kesha's boyfriend, is part of your study, correct?" Nikki asked.

"He is," Roth answered. "The juvenile program I've created in Minnesota is aimed at identifying predictive behaviors and looking for biomarkers that suggest a propensity for violence has a genetic component. In Dion's case, his mother was concerned with his family history, but I can't tell you more than that, I'm afraid. Privacy reasons, I'm sure you understand."

Nikki nodded. "But you do confirm he still participates?"

"Since he's past eighteen, he's in our self-reporting group, but, yes, he does."

"Do you provide behavioral therapy as well?" Miller asked.

"Our institute does," Roth said. "I'm very much research based, but I've got three outstanding psychologists and a psychiatrist on staff. Dion's been working with one of our more experienced therapists, and the police did interview her, I believe."

"Yes, we've read those notes. She didn't believe he was capable of harming Kesha, but she also admitted that as his ther-

apist, it was impossible for her not to be biased." Nikki appreciated the therapist's candor, but it had also given the BPD reason
to write off her opinion on Dion. She opened the article on
Roth's brain institute she'd found last night. "Correct me if I'm
wrong, but it seems like your research is sort of like what Ressler
and Douglas originally did when they created profiling, but
with much more recent killers."

"That would be partially accurate, yes," he said. "When the
research first started in New Mexico, my mentor did study
criminals from Ressler and Douglas's research, but his approach
was to test a much broader sample. My research is similar, but I
approach it from a neurological standpoint. There are definitely
neurological similarities among murderers, with even more
defined similarities between psychopaths. I won't bore you with
the science since we can't solve this case by looking at your
suspect's brain." Roth grinned. "But wouldn't it be nice if we
could? Anyway, my focus is now on inmates who've been incarcerated in the last twenty years, because like the rest of the
world, the serial killer is evolving."

"How so?" Miller asked.

Roth drummed his fingers on the table. "Many of the serial
predators who've been incarcerated in the last two decades are a
different breed than those the Behavioral Analysis Unit originally studied. Of course, most of the things people like Douglas
and Ressler wrote about are still very much true and in play.
But the new ones, they have so many options at their fingertips.
Many of them are Gen-Xers or Millennials, meaning they've
come of age at the same time as new technology like smart-
phones and the internet took over the world. They know how to
use those tools, and this often changes their approach." Roth
waved off the donut Nikki offered.

"No thank you," he said. "If I eat that I'll be in a sugar coma
in thirty minutes." He laughed for a few seconds before his
handsome face became deadly serious. "Now, you can find just

about anything online—including body bags, apparently. I'm not talking about what goes on the dark web. There's a wealth of published research right at these guys' fingertips, ways to study how not to get caught, ways to study themselves, really. Because of the BAU's early efforts, we knew enough about serial predators by the late nineties that the playing field seemed to even out just a bit. Then came the internet, and a new breed of criminal was born."

"That's true," Nikki said. "Gen-X and Millennials definitely see the world differently. And it's impossible to stay ahead of the technology and dark web. So much information is passed over foreign servers we have no access to."

"Exactly." Roth nodded. "That said, many of the standards established by Ressler and Douglas still stand true: most of the time, serials are men killing women, sometimes gay men, most still stick to their own race. And if they veered from those things, it was out of necessity to survive, not for personal stimulus. To see someone so driven to kill that literally any person could become his victim is—and forgive me for this—fascinating from a neuroscience point of view. It's interesting given our societal issues too. Gender is recognized as something fluid for many people, along with sexual orientation. I would think, however, that these murders are likely to be at least partially sexually motivated."

"As violent as this guy has shown to be, he's got to have some serious trauma in his past," Miller said. "Isn't that usually the case with serial killers?"

"Nature versus nurture is a bit of a battleground subject in my profession," Roth said. "Statistically, regardless of what generational bracket they're in, most people who commit these kinds of crimes do have childhood trauma, and often it's severe. But on the other side of the coin are all those individuals who experienced terrible abuse as kids and didn't grow up to be murderers. Nature does play a role, and that's part of what I hope to show with my research," Roth told them. "But I've encountered more and more murderers who came from a relatively normal upbringing. They're still in the minority, but there are a few I've studied in the last couple of years who came from as good a home as I did, which is why I believe in the next few years we are going to have to seriously rethink nature versus nurture, because we're seeing more and more criminals who never should have turned to crime, but did anyway."

Miller had been furiously taking notes. "And the choice to kill males and females? Is that something that could happen because of generational differences too?"

Roth considered the question. "To be honest, I don't believe so. Unless the motive had nothing to do with sexual impulse, the criminals I've spoken to—mostly men—would get little gratification from sexually assaulting another man because men in general are stronger and able to fight back. And as we know, sexually motivated crimes are always about control. Out of the hundreds of male violent offenders I've studied, the commonalities are significant. The handful of openly gay men—meaning men who were attracted to other men prior to incarceration, not just because they had no other option—had similar scans as the heterosexual killers. That leads me to believe a person who would assault and kill both is quite possibly struggling with his sexuality and likely always has."

Nikki jotted that down in her notes, hoping she would be able to read her shorthand later. "Self-loathing, possibly the product of a strict upbringing that made him feel compelled to stay in the closet." She tossed her pencil on the table and rubbed her temples. "We're just circling right now."

"I'm sorry I'm not more helpful," Roth said.

Nikki sat up straight. "No, you have been helpful, truly. We just don't know what we don't know, and it may be days before we have forensic details about the other victims, and even longer before they are identified."

Roth nodded, his gaze back on the whiteboard. "Kesha is the only one in the lake, you're certain?"

Miller nodded. "I'm confident the dog would have found any other remains in the lake."

Roth leaned forward, resting his elbows on the table, his lips pursed in thought. "I just keep coming back to Isaac Monday, from Alaska."

"The name sounds familiar," Liam said.

"He's one of the few I can think of who's anything like your offender, and that in itself is disturbing. Richard Ramirez is the only other one I can think of who did just about everything and went after all types, including raping kids. But he never sexually assaulted men. He killed them because they stood between him and whoever he wanted to rape and kill that night." Roth shivered. "I'll never forget sitting across from him with my mentor. He was one of the first murderers I met."

Liam's head shot up from his notes. Liam's fascination with Ramirez stemmed from a friend in college, who claimed to have been among the crowd that chased Ramirez down in 1985, leading to his arrest. Liam would grill Roth for hours on the guy if he had the chance, so Nikki beat him to the punch. "Tell us about Isaac Monday."

"Well, Monday was nothing short of a genius, choosing his victims in one state and burying them in another, often thousands of miles apart. He killed a couple and admitted to raping both the male and female. He also claimed to have raped and killed more men, but he never gave names. Do you have any idea why only the last victim was put into the lake?"

"The ground froze before he got her buried," Nikki said. "But the fact that he improvised a solution speaks to experience and financial stability."

"It does, but I asked because Monday also buried all of his victims, except for his final victim, whom he put into a lake." Roth's eyes clouded with worry. "He admitted that he'd dug the hole on the ice in broad daylight, while other people fished. Of course, this was Alaska, so the ice was much deeper, but the similarity is frighteningly interesting."

"You seem very familiar with the case," Liam said.

"That's because an investigative journalist wrote a book about him about a year ago," Roth said. "It's superb, and the author insinuated Monday isn't as well-known as some other serial murderers because there were major bungles by pretty much every law enforcement office involved, including the Anchorage FBI, and they worked hard to keep that out of the media. Monday didn't want the attention, either, because he had a young child to protect. Given the relative newness of the book and the similarities between Monday and your killer, my curiosity is more than piqued."

"How many people did Monday kill?" Nikki asked.

"They don't know all of them," Roth said. "I believe at least double digits. But he started when he was young—early teens. He raped and killed a neighbor girl. They never found her remains, but he admitted to it after they caught him decades later."

Liam had been concentrating on his phone. "Monday grew up in a rural area, had survival skills. His family was religious, and his childhood definitely wasn't normal."

"No, it wasn't," Roth said. "His parents lived off the grid and homeschooled their children. Religious beliefs caused much of his self-hatred. Unfortunately, he killed himself while awaiting trial. We'll never know what truly went on in his head, and it's a shame. We could have learned a lot, not to mention the victims he didn't admit to killing."

"Antisocial behavior, shooting the neighbor's house and pets with BB guns, torturing a feral cat." Liam looked disgusted. "All of that by the time he was fourteen."

"Antisocial behavior is one that we continue to see, even in criminals from decent homes with no record of abuse or trauma.

It often starts at a young age, and I can think of at least three inmates whose parents intervened multiple times, got them help, the whole nine yards. None of it mattered." Roth shuddered. "Those are the scary ones."

"Well, our killer either cooled off or moved," Nikki said. "Regardless of who the first victim turns out to be, the rest were buried much later, and possibly with months in between. So, he's patient. He knows the kind of victim he's looking for, and he can control the urge until he sees that right person."

Roth nodded. "Think of this person as an alligator, hanging out in the depths of the pond, sunbathing on a log, whatever they do when they aren't hungry. When they get hungry, they strike. But the rest of the time, they're more docile. Doesn't mean they aren't capable of striking at that moment, but they aren't driven by the primordial need of hunger. That's how they hang out in plain sight without being noticed so often."

"Or Nile crocs," Nikki said.

"I'm sorry?" Roth asked.

"*Fishing For Giants*. It's a show on the Smithsonian Channel," she answered. "My boyfriend and my daughter love it. One of the first episodes is about trying to catch Nile perch, which can grow to be more than four hundred pounds."

Roth looked more confused, and Nikki felt like she was back at the academy, taking the long way to answer an instructor's question. "Anyway, he's got to contend with Nile crocodiles, which are more aggressive than American alligators or crocs. There's a scene where he's thinking about getting off the boat and fishing from this shore area where the weeds are tall and brown, but then he sees these crocs watching him. Instead of being intimidated or cautious, they raced past him and the boat, and a couple of them looked like they might attack. They fear nothing and no one."

"Just like the guy we're looking for," Liam said.

The four of them looked at each other in silence for a

moment before the desk sergeant poked her head into the room. "Sheriff Miller, a Forest Lake detective is on line three about Parker Jameson. You want to take the call in your office?"

"No, patch them through."

The phone rang moments later, and Miller put the call on speaker. "Sheriff Miller, here with the FBI and Doctor Alex Roth. You're calling about Parker Jameson?"

"Detective Dover from Forest Lake," the voice on the other end said. "We just got a photo of Parker Jameson. He looks like he's alive, but there's a body bag next to him. He also left a message with the photo," Dover said. "Can your team get to the police station this morning?"

"We're on our way." Nikki was already on her feet. "Doctor Roth, your information has been helpful."

He was already shrugging into his coat. "Of course. Please call if you have additional questions." He worried his bottom lip, glancing around the room. "I don't want to alarm you, but I believe Isaac Monday also sent a photo of his last victim, asking for ransom. She turned out to be dead in the photograph."

"Forest Lake didn't mention a ransom letter," Liam said. "With all the media attention since Kesha's body was found, he's trying to show that he's not afraid of us, that he's still in control. That means he's close to making a mistake, or that he has already. We just have to find out what it is."

Roth nodded. "I'm sure you're right."

Nikki glanced at Liam, who looked more pale and tired than he had a couple of days ago. She knew he was going to be pissed off at her decision, but she wasn't going to stand in the way of his recovery.

His eyes locked with hers. "Don't say it."

"I'm sorry, but I need you to stay here," Nikki said. "You aren't cleared for the field, so we're pushing it with you working here at the sheriff's station."

Liam opened his mouth to argue, but Nikki held up her

hand to stop him. "I need you sharp, not exhausted. Start going through the Violent Crime Apprehension Program and cross-reference as much information as you can with what we know so far."

Liam's jaw set hard, and Nikki braced for the argument, but he knew she was right. Liam grunted something unintelligible and glared out of the window. Nikki figured that was the best she'd get out of him. She didn't like not having him at full capacity any more than he did. Miller was an excellent cop, but Liam had great instincts, especially when it came to serial murders. He'd been in the trenches with her, understanding that profiling was nothing more than another investigative tool. Nikki glanced at Roth, thinking about everything he'd just told them. His wealth of experience and training meant he probably read people better than most cops, including her.

"Doctor Roth, would you mind coming with us to talk to the Forest Lake police?"

Roth looked surprised. "I wasn't under the impression I'd be participating hands-on. I'm not sure what I can bring to your team."

"Another perspective." Nikki explained Liam's medical situation. "Sheriff Miller and I are up to our necks with questions about this case. I'd love to get your impressions about Parker Jameson's disappearance firsthand. Kent, you okay with that?"

Miller nodded. "I'll see you guys over there, then." He left, leaving Nikki standing between Liam and Roth, tension coating the room like body odor after a basketball game. She broke the stalemate. "Liam, I'll touch base as soon as we're done at the police station."

He forced a tight smile, but she could see the frustration in his eyes. "Guess I'll be here, won't I, boss?"

SEVENTEEN

Forest Lake's small police department buzzed with activity. Nikki, Miller and Dr. Roth found themselves crammed into the police chief's small office along with Detective Dover, who'd been working Parker's case. He'd balked when Nikki explained Roth's credentials, but Miller stepped in before things went too far.

"As your sheriff, this is my call," Miller said. "Especially since you requested help from Agent Hunt."

Chief Peek seemed satisfied, but Dover still had a sour expression as Peek ran down the case details. "We received the encrypted photo electronically, sent from a dummy account off a foreign server, so there's no way to trace the sender," Peek said.

Nikki studied the copy of the color photo the chief had printed off. Parker appeared to be hung by his hands, his head resting on his right bicep, staring at the camera. Hanging next to him was a body bag. "He took the picture with a Polaroid, is that what we're looking at?"

Detective Dover nodded. "Why would he do that?"

"Taking a photo with a cell phone makes it possible to study the metadata, possibly tracking down the IP it was sent from. It shouldn't matter since he used a foreign server, but I'd guess he was covering all of his bases," Miller said.

"He's also letting us know that he knows we found his burial pit and that he's not afraid," Nikki said. "Parker co-owned the Artists' Co-op located next to West End Diner, correct?"

Detective Dover nodded. "He was scheduled to work until close at seven, but weather had come in and they weren't getting customers. He texted his partners shortly after five saying business was slow and he needed to run some errands, so he was closing early, which both partners were fine with." She handed Nikki a couple of photographs.

"As you can see, the shop is right next to the diner, and Parker and his partners lease the land from the diner owner. Because the shop was built shotgun style, one security camera catches everything." Detective Dover set up her tablet on the chief's desk and played the security footage.

"Parker locked up and then started his closing duties," Dover said. "In a couple of minutes, he looks toward the back of the building, which is where the office is, along with the back door. The camera doesn't pick it up, but we assume he heard something and went to check it out, because he walked out of frame, to the office, and that's it."

"They don't have a camera in the office?" Nikki asked.

"The shop is small, maybe twenty by ten," Dover said. "The office doesn't even have a desk. It's more like a coat room and extra storage. And the door locks from the inside, so anyone entering through that door needs a key."

"This was a week before Christmas?" Nikki asked.

"Yes," Dover answered. "The time-stamp when he goes to the back room is 5:47 p.m. The restaurant owner called one of the partners around eight that night because she'd noticed the back door to the shop was open. The other two owners came right away and confirmed nothing was missing. Parker's car was still parked on the street, and his phone and wallet were still in his coat, which was still in the shop."

"What about security footage from the building next door?" Miller asked.

"The lighting between the buildings is poor, and it was dark and snowing lightly. It doesn't catch anything useful," Chief Peek said.

"Parker's ex-boyfriend was the initial suspect," Nikki said for Roth's benefit. "Detective Dover, tell us about Parker's ex-boyfriend. How old is he?"

Dover rolled her eyes. "Colton Troyer, just turned twenty-one, thinks the world owes him something. He's been accused of stalking prior partners, and at least one filed a restraining order against him. We spoke to her, and she said that the TRO seemed to shock him into leaving her alone. A few months later, he meets Parker."

"So, Colton's bisexual?" Roth spoke for the first time.

"I would assume so given he's dated both men and women," Dover said. "Why?"

Nikki jumped in before Roth had to answer. She hadn't worked with the Forest Lake police before and knew nothing about Dover or Peek. Given the media leaks in the case, she wanted as much pertinent information kept back as possible. "Colton's mother owns the diner, correct?"

"Yes, and he started working as a cook after he was fired from his previous job," Chief Peek said. "He and Parker got together soon after. Parker broke it off because Colton was obsessive and controlling, they fought. Colton didn't take it well. He showed up at the Artists' Co-op a few days before Parker disappeared, and they got into a big argument in the back room. Parker's co-owners said they tried to ignore it, but they did hear Parker tell Colton to stop following him and showing up at his place."

"Makes sense he's your main suspect," Nikki said.

"He *was*," Dover corrected, her eyes on Nikki. "When I called you and asked for help after Kesha's remains were found, you said the cases couldn't be linked—"

"I said it was unlikely." Nikki tried to keep her tone respectful, but Dover's snide look made it difficult. "And I forwarded your information to Agent Wilson, and we both agreed they probably weren't linked. At that time, we had no idea there were other victims."

"You should have informed me about the new victims as soon as you discovered them in the woods," Dover said.

Miller's head shot up from his notes. "Detective Dover, I don't think you understand chain of command. If anything, as the county sheriff, I should have been contacted first instead of the FBI. And until we were able to uncover the remains, we knew nothing about the victims."

"So?" Dover demanded. "This isn't LA or New York or some other dangerous city. The idea that these weren't related is preposterous—"

Chief Peek's mouth tightened. "Detective, let's remain civil."

"Are you not from this area, originally, Detective Dover?" Nikki asked.

"I'm from Chicago, but that's irrelevant."

"No, it isn't. Coming from a big city with so many police jurisdictions and different types of crime makes Washington County seem idyllic. Bad things don't happen around here and if they do, they must be related because this isn't the big city you used to be in, and there just aren't that many bad guys here."

"That's not what I'm saying," Dover said, her cheeks red. "The circumstances of Parker's disappearance—"

"Enough." Miller's sharp tone silenced everyone. "We're wasting time pointing fingers. The bottom line is that we have new information, and frankly, the photo you received today is the reason we're here. We need the file sent to the FBI's tech experts immediately. We may not be able to trace the IP, but we might get some idea of where the photo was taken from the stuff in the background. Was the back door of the co-op forced open?"

Chief Peek shook his head. "Parker must have opened the door. We initially thought someone he knew might have knocked on the door and needed help or something, but that theory didn't pan out. We canvassed the area, but it's a commercial street in a small town. That time of night, very few businesses were still open. A couple of days after Parker disappeared, a witness claimed she'd seen him in the passenger seat of an old, white Chevy pickup at a stoplight about three blocks from the co-op. It struck her as odd because Parker looked straight ahead, sitting stock-still. The witness couldn't see what the driver was wearing, but she did notice that he had a neck gaiter pulled up to his nose."

"This would have been useful to know Christmas Eve when we were putting together a list of suspects," Nikki said.

"We receive tips like this all the time on cases." Dover's irritated tone matched Nikki's. "Including this particular witness."

More like Dover had screwed up and was trying to pass the buck off to the FBI. "What time did this witness see Parker?"

"Around six p.m.," Dover answered. "The woman was on her way home from work. When we spoke to her, we still weren't sure if Parker had left on his own or if he'd been taken by his ex—"

"You're kidding," Roth interrupted. "Credit cards and his phone could be used to track him, but he's in a short-sleeved shirt in that security video. Why on earth would he leave on his own without taking his coat?"

Dover bristled. "Doctor, I'd like for the law enforcement officials to do the talking."

"Doctor Roth has been brought in by my boss to help with

this case," Nikki said. "If I didn't think he could help us catch our killer, I wouldn't have brought him here."

Chief Peek spoke before Dover. "Parker's had some issues with depression. He and his co-owners have known each other since college, and they said Parker had talked about 'dropping everything and running off,' when he had bad moments."

"Recently?" Nikki asked.

"No," Peek admitted. "But given that he was known to carry cash and the lack of any real evidence, we had to consider the option. With the holiday coming up, we were short-staffed, but we still searched open fields, parks, any place a body might have been dumped, and found nothing."

"You should have asked for my help," Miller said. "The county sheriff has more resources."

"And yet you need the FBI's help," Chief Peek countered.

Nikki bit the inside of her lip to keep from losing her temper. It seemed like the FLPD was as naïve as many locals, who often described Washington County as some kind of impenetrable place where only outsiders did bad things, despite evidence to the contrary. And when bad things did happen, people often looked to outsiders to blame instead of a home-grown citizen of Washington County. "What did the woman notice about the white truck?" Nikki asked, thinking of Danny Stanton's. "I assume she didn't get a license plate."

"No," Dover said. "She said there was a big dent on the passenger side door, but the truck was dirty."

"What about the bed?" Miller asked. "Maybe a toolbox or something else?"

"She said it was empty, as far as she remembers."

"Did the name Danny Stanton come up in any of your investigations?" Nikki asked.

"He's the one who found Kesha's body in the lake, right?" Dover asked.

Nikki nodded.

"He also drives a white pickup similar to the one your witness described, but with a toolbox in the back. It's held together by rust, but there's no dent in the side. Of course, the toolbox is removable and Stanton's a mechanic, so he might have fixed it," Miller said. "A witness from the lake observed a possible suspect a couple of weeks ago driving a junky white pickup, but he was fairly certain it was an eighties model."

"If you've got a photo of Stanton's truck, I can contact the witness and have her take a look," Dover said. "I have her cell number, so I can text it."

Nikki airdropped the photo, and Dover forwarded it to the witness. "I'll let you know what she says."

Miller had pulled up Google Earth on his tablet. The town was named after Forest Lake, one of many smaller lakes that made up the area. The lake and town were at the northern tip of Washington County, about fifteen minutes from Big Marine Lake and the burial site.

"We've searched every open field and wooded area within our city limits," Peek said. "That includes the docks around Forest Lake, boat storage places and part of the public grounds. But as we've already talked about, the holiday has thrown a wrench into everything in terms of manpower. I'm confident we would have seen him if he'd been left in the area. Forest Lake itself is highly trafficked, but the week leading up to Christmas, it wasn't busy, even with ice fishing. We can't get a dive team until January and it's going to be a dogfight to convince anyone Parker's in the lake without more evidence."

Nikki could tell that Miller wanted to remind the police chief that the Washington County sheriff would have assisted in the search had they been informed, but he also knew that he had to keep the peace. The tone in Chief Peek's voice told Nikki that he knew they'd made a mistake in not contacting the sheriff. But dwelling on it wasn't going to help Parker.

"Chief Peek, when you called the sheriff's office this morning, you mentioned a message that came with the photo?" Nikki asked.

"That's right," the chief said. "Once we got through the encryption, we found two files. One was the photograph of Parker, and the other consisted of a single line in a document: 'Guess I will have to find a new place for him. Shame on the FBI for disturbing my dead.'"

"'*My dead*'?" Nikki echoed. "Either the killer wants us to connect Parker's disappearance to the other victims or this is someone trying to manipulate us so that we're looking at the wrong person. You've been keeping track of Colton, the ex-boyfriend?"

Dover nodded. "He lives with his mother above the diner, but he hasn't left the apartment since Parker disappeared. I don't understand contacting the police. This increases the kidnapper's chances of getting caught," Dover said.

"Either he's willing to take the risk, or he doesn't think there is one," Nikki answered. "He wants us to know how good he is, how much he's gotten away with."

"Let's hope his ego helps us catch him," Miller said. "We need contact information for everyone who's been interviewed. Agent Hunt's headed to the co-op and the diner after this, so myself and Agent Wilson, who's back at the task force command center, will split interviewing everyone else. Detective Dover, please let me or Agent Hunt know as soon as you've heard from the witness claiming to have seen Parker that night."

Nikki could tell Detective Dover wanted to stay involved in the investigation, but she had no interest in the detective accompanying her to the co-op. They'd gotten off on the wrong foot, and Nikki wasn't sure she had the energy to focus on both the case and finding some kind of common ground with Dover. She struck Nikki as the type who'd involved other investigative units just to have a scapegoat to blame if Parker wasn't found alive. But her unit had to maintain a decent relationship with the police departments in the state. "Detective Dover, since this is your case, we'll need you to focus on Parker's family and friends since you've already established a relationship with them. I want them to know we are working the case, of course, but dealing with half a dozen different people instead of one just causes more stress. Can we count on you to take care of them?"

Dover's eyes narrowed, her gaze flickering between Nikki and her boss. "What about Colton? I'm the only one he's talked to."

"Which is why someone else needs to sit down with him," Nikki told her. "We all have different strengths. I just think with this case having so much media attention, the family needs to deal with a familiar face." She mustered a semi-sincere smile.

"Dover will handle the family," Peek said. "Colton should be working at the restaurant. His mother seems to be keeping him close by since Parker disappeared." He picked up the photo of Parker. "What do you think the chances are that he's still alive?"

Nikki shot Roth what she hoped was a warning look. She didn't trust Dover not to talk to the press, so the less they discussed theories in front of her, the better. "I'd say fifty-fifty. It's hard to tell in the photo, even though his eyes are open. I'm sure the lousy quality of the photo is intentional." She caught Roth's gaze again, and the worry in his eyes sent a wave of fear through her.

Nikki prayed they weren't too late to help Parker Jameson.

"Well, that was certainty interesting," Roth said as the three of them headed to their vehicles. "I'm shocked this little police department didn't ask the sheriff for help."

Miller shrugged. "It's political. Peek's the old guard and buddies with our former sheriff, who retired in disgrace. He resents having to deal with me."

"Too bad," Roth said. "I wish the photo of that poor kid was better quality."

So did Nikki. "Our computer guys will do everything they can to enhance it. We don't believe there are more remains in Big Marine Lake, and we know Parker isn't buried with the others. It sounds like Forest Lake proper and some of the surrounding areas have been well searched too. So, either Parker's still alive and with our killer, or he's in Forest Lake itself, which is hopefully unlikely."

"Are those the only options?" Roth asked.

"No, but the third's the worst of all," she answered. "If our killer's found a new location to dispose of his victims, it's going to be damn hard to find. Unless he was able to thaw the ground, he couldn't have dug a grave. So he's disposed of Parker's body another way, or Parker's still alive somewhere." She hoped that sounded more confident than she felt.

"Doctor Roth, police decisions aside, what are your impressions?" Miller asked.

Roth's hair stood up at odd angles from the gusting wind. He retrieved a knit cap from his coat pocket and put it on, yanking it down below his ears. "This is why I never go to warm places in the winter. It makes coming back here all the more miserable. To answer your question, the similarities to Isaac Monday's murders in Alaska are disturbing. But as I said during our initial meeting, the murderers I'm interviewing have had access to eons of research on the subject, and a killer who hasn't been caught has access to even more. What's most disturbing is that the author of the book about Isaac Monday, psychologists and law enforcement officers who worked the case, claimed he's in the one percent of serial killers. The author used the word *unicorn*, actually, which I believe to be totally misleading. There have been other known killers who were indiscriminate with their victim choices, and simple logic suggests there are probably more that we don't know about.

The author's word choice lures the public and the entire criminal justice system into a false sense of safety. It's much easier to believe that someone so sadistically cruel is a special case, but like unicorns, such a person doesn't exist, at least in my opinion."

"Serial killers adapt and evolve, just like every other living thing on the planet." Nikki looked up at Roth. "If you have the time to come with me to the co-op and the diner, I'd love a second set of eyes."

He looked surprised. "As honored as I'd be, I have another commitment scheduled at Oak Park Heights Correctional Facility."

A chill went down Nikki's spine. There were plenty of violent felons to interview at Oak Park Heights, including the man who'd killed her parents and the man who'd murdered her ex-husband. If Roth was scheduled to speak with either one of them, Nikki didn't want to know.

"Thank you for your time this morning, then," she said. "I'll touch base tonight or tomorrow, if you don't mind."

"Of course." Roth shook her hand and then Miller's. "Good luck to both of you and stay safe." He jogged over to his black Audi, his head down against the wind.

"I'll head back to the station and get Liam up to speed," Miller said. "I think he and I should be able to split up the interviews of Parker's family and friends. I'll drive out to Parker's parents, but Liam can do some of the follow-ups on the phone. I'm also going to contact the DNR in charge of the lake here. Forest Lake is a popular spot, even with the bass virus spotted in the fish this fall. Fortunately, it's smaller than Big Marine and its location in the middle of town makes it a lot less likely our guy would risk leaving Parker here."

"Agreed, but see what DNR records show, if they keep any. Liam's familiar with the angler and fishing forums, so he can go through them and see if he can locate anyone who's been out on this lake since Parker disappeared." Nikki hit the remote start on the jeep. "I almost feel worse after meeting Roth."

Miller looked at her in confusion.

Nikki shrugged. "He confirmed my worst fears and then some. And he's right. Unicorns are a myth. We're dealing with a sneaky rat who can hide in plain sight."

EIGHTEEN

Maria Lopez's father worked at an auto body shop not far from the Forest Lake police station, so after Miller headed back, Nikki drove to the shop and asked to speak with him. He'd been employed by Danny Stanton, before his shop had gone under, and Nikki hoped he could provide her with unbiased information.

Javier Lopez came into the lobby wearing greasy work overalls, an equally greasy shop cloth in his hand. "Someone asked to talk to me?"

Nikki stood and introduced herself, keeping her voice low. Lopez wasn't a suspect, and she didn't want his employer to get the impression Lopez might be in trouble. Lopez motioned for her to follow him into the hallway where the vending machines were located.

"You said this is about Danny Stanton? He ran himself out of business," Lopez said.

"I know," Nikki said. "This is difficult, and I've gone back and forth about it since yesterday. Legally, there's nothing I can do, but as a parent, I want you to know that your daughter was leaving Stanton's house yesterday when I stopped to question him."

Lopez's eyes glittered with anger. "My Maria? I told her to stay away from him."

"She said they met at work." Nikki had assumed that Maria had meant the diner where she worked part-time, but now she realized that the girl had been referring to Danny's old shop.

"Yeah, I used to work for Danny. She used to come by after school and say hi," Lopez said. "I could tell she had a crush, and I know how Danny is, so I told her to stay away from him."

"And how exactly is Danny?" Nikki asked. "Has he ever been violent with anyone?"

Lopez snickered. "He's too lazy for that. He said the economy ruined the shop, but he didn't take care of the books. He was too busy getting high. Even if he wasn't almost my age, I don't want my daughter with someone like that. She's going to college, wants to be a lawyer. I'm not letting some deadbeat ruin that."

"I don't blame you," Nikki said. "Do you remember if Danny used a lot of chemicals to clean the shop, maybe something to make things smell clean?"

Lopez shook his head. "Only thing I can think of is the bathroom toilet. It plugged a lot."

"Maria works at West End Diner part-time, right?"

Lopez nodded. "She's on winter break now, so she picked up more hours. She's working right now."

"Would she get in trouble if I stopped in to ask her some questions?" Nikki said. "Not about Danny, but about the place next door."

"Yeah, that young man's missing." Lopez shook his head sadly. "When I moved my family here from Minneapolis a few years ago, I thought we were coming to a safe area. Washington County's so beautiful in the summer, the people are friendly. Now we're turning into a murder mecca."

"You're not wrong," Nikki said. "I'd make sure she stays away from him out of an abundance of caution."

"Oh, believe me, she's going to stay away from him," Lopez said grimly. "Do me a favor if you see her and don't tell her that I know. I want to handle it myself."

Like most of the area, Forest Lake embraced their Scandinavian heritage. Nikki's paternal great-great grandparents had settled in Scandia, the heart of Scandinavian Washington County, just a few miles east of Forest Lake, and had been buried in the historical Scandinavian Cemetery. When she was a little kid, Nikki loved listening to her father talk about the stories handed down through his family. Her ancestors had helped build the railroad switch lines. Chicago gangsters had used the area during the 1930s and 40s, and her great-grandmother had allegedly cleaned one of the cottages occupied by Ma Barker during her stay.

West Side Diner was oddly located on the eastern end of Forest Lake, but within walking distance to the marinas on the western side of the lake itself. Nikki could see the ice shanties dotted along the shallow lakeshore, but the wind that whipped across the lake had likely prevented anyone going out today. Nikki drove down North Shore Drive into the heart of downtown Forest Lake. Located in a two-story Victorian with a sign boasting its status as a national historic landmark, the diner appeared to be a favorite of locals. Seating inside was limited, and the outdoor seating reserved for the summer. Nikki bypassed the line of gray-haired ladies waiting for a table and went to the counter, where she asked if Colton was available.

"Who's asking?" A woman wearing a hairnet stuck her head out of the window that connected the kitchen and cashier's counter.

Nikki flashed her ID. The woman immediately scowled. "The police are done trying to railroad my son."

"Ma'am, with all due respect, this is a federal investigation now. I need to speak with your son and get his side of the story. We can talk now, or I can have him brought into the Washington County sheriff's station."

"I'm right here." A twenty-something man with a blue mohawk and neck tattoos appeared next to the woman. "If this helps find Parker, I want to help."

His mother glared at him. "They want to pin this on you. You shouldn't talk to them without a lawyer."

Colton ignored her, his eyes on Nikki. "I'm innocent. We can talk at the break table if you want."

"The break table?"

He pointed down the narrow hall to Nikki's right. "Go through that door, it's the little two-seater table off of the kitchen."

Colton disappeared, and Nikki did as he'd directed. The compact dining made private conversation difficult, even if the table was near the kitchen.

"You sure you want to speak out here?" Nikki scanned the customers. None seemed to be paying any special attention to her. "I have to ask some tough questions."

"It's basically our only choice unless we go out back to the smoking area. It's cold so I wasn't sure if you'd want to do that."

Nikki patted her warm coat. "I think that would be better."

Colton shrugged and motioned for her to follow him down the hall. He grabbed a coat off the hooks mounted near the back door and they went outside. He lit his cigarette before Nikki could shut the door.

"I know who you are," he said.

She smiled. "Well, I did show my ID."

"Yeah, but my mom only saw 'FBI.' She doesn't know who *you* are." He took a long drag and blew out thick, white smoke. "Thank God you're here. Forest Lake police are asshats."

Nikki managed not to laugh. "They still consider you a suspect." She made sure to emphasize "they," instead of saying "we." Colton needed to trust her.

"I might be a stalker, but I'm not a kidnapper." He puffed some more. "I don't think I'm a stalker. I just love hard."

Nikki leaned against the building and waited for him to continue. He wanted to talk, and she was happy to let him.

"Parker told all of his friends that I wouldn't let go, but it's a two-way street. He texted me to come over less than a week before he disappeared."

Nikki tried to remember everything she'd read about the case. "You refused to show the police your phone, so they got a warrant for the records. He asked you to bring him something he'd left at your house, and he would get it when he came to work."

Colton flushed. "That was code. My mom didn't want me to see him because of the TRO."

"Well, that is the point of a restraining order," Nikki said.

"I know, but Parker and I had talked a couple of days before he sent that text and decided to try again. I came up with the code."

"I don't remember seeing that in the detective's notes."

"Because I didn't tell them," Colton said. "Mom told me to keep my mouth shut, that they'd pin it on me if I didn't. Because of my history."

"Right," Nikki said. "Did you see Parker the day he texted about the personal items?"

"I went to his apartment that night and we did our thing," he said. "Then Parker starts in about how it's just sex, and I'm a stalker, yada yada. I'm seriously standing there with my mouth hanging open like an idiot and feeling like I got whiplash. He's the one who wanted to hook up and 'try again.' His words, not mine. Then he changed his mind. And that wasn't the first time, but I told him it was damn sure going to be the last." Colton's eyes filled with tears. "That's the last time I spoke to him."

"Did he ever mention anyone following him or snooping around?"

Colton shook his head. "And like I told the police, as far as I know, he wasn't seeing anyone else. But what do I know?" He lit another cigarette.

Nikki cupped her hands in front of her face, trying to warm her freezing nose. "What about the co-op? You ever see or hear anything?"

"I wasn't working that day," Colton said.

Nikki noticed the back deck had a perfect view of the Artists' Co-op. She'd also noticed curtains and empty planter boxes on the second floor of the Victorian. "This diner's pretty cool. Does anyone live upstairs?"

"Mom and me," Colton said. "Why?"

"So you were home the day Parker disappeared?"

Colton scowled like his mother had. "Yep. Watching a movie with my mom."

Nikki's bones were starting to feel the cold. "Look, Colton. I can't give you details, but I can tell you that I'm on your side. I'm not here to judge your relationship with Parker or whatever mistakes you might have made. I'm here to find out what happened. You work and live right next to the co-op. You've admitted to stalker tendencies. Are you going to tell me that you didn't keep an eye on Parker's work?"

Colton hugged himself, the cigarette balanced between his lips. "Maybe I did."

"Good," Nikki said. "Did you ever see anyone walking around the place when it wasn't open?"

"Like casing it?" Colton shook his head. "It's cold as shit here even during mild nights because the wind comes off the lake. No one's out doing anything if they can help it."

"Parker never seemed worried about his safety?" Nikki asked. "You're certain? Think back farther, before winter. Someone might have been planning this for a while."

Colton worried his bottom lip. He took a final puff and dropped the smoke onto the concrete. He ground the cherry out with his boot. "Maybe."

"Maybe what?"

"Thanksgiving week," he said. "It was the Tuesday or Wednesday before. Me and Parker got into a fight because I thought he'd tried to sneak someone into the building after hours."

Nikki pushed off the wall, her pulse accelerating. "Before Thanksgiving? You saw someone sneaking around?"

"I thought I had," he admitted. "But I'd also been drinking, and Parker insisted he wasn't going behind my back. He's a lot of things, but he's not a cheater."

"Do you remember what the person you saw looked like?"

Colton snorted. "A tall dude in a dark coat with a dark hat. Could have been a shadow, but..."

"What?" Nikki prodded.

"I just remember thinking it was either a creep or a phantom. We didn't have snow then, and it was a really cloudy night, and I thought someone was standing under that big willow tree for the longest time." He pointed to the massive willow about fifty yards from the diner. Its branches were weighed down with ice and snow, and some were so long they reached the ground. A month ago, without the starkness of snow and the benefit of night, someone could conceivably hide around the tree.

"You saw them from here?" Nikki asked.

Colton shook his head. "I was on the second floor, in the living area. So, looking at an angle, if that makes sense. I saw him and called Parker and went off, and I'm looking out the window the whole time, right? Parker's going on about me being drunk and hallucinating, so I come downstairs and turned on the back floodlights. No one was there."

"You didn't mention this to Detective Dover?" Nikki asked.

"I forgot," Colton said. "Nothing came out of it, and I'd convinced myself the booze and scary movie I'd been watching just played tricks with my mind." His voice cracked on the last word. "Do you think Parker's alive?"

Nikki hated giving anyone false hope, and she couldn't tell Colton about the photo. "I hope so. We're going to do everything we can to find him alive."

"Oh my God." Colton's voice dropped to a whisper. "Your team's working that case that's on the news, with all those bodies. You think the same person took Parker, don't you? That's why you're here?"

"I think it's a possibility that has to be investigated," she said. "We haven't found anything that indicates he's buried in the reserve at Big Marine."

That seemed to pacify Colton enough. Nikki gave him her card. "The bottom number's my cell. If you think of anything else, call me, not Dover. Let's go back inside before our faces freeze in this position."

The little hallway was warm and smelled like apple pie. Nikki's stomach growled. The lunch smelled so good that Nikki debated placing an order, when she recognized the dark-haired girl sitting at the break table next to the kitchen. "That's Maria Lopez, right?" she asked Colton. "Can I talk to her at work?"

"If she's sitting there, she's on break, so sure. But she didn't know Parker very well."

"It's actually about another issue." Nikki kept her answer vague. "Thanks for your time." She waited until Colton had gone into the kitchen before approaching the break table at the other end of the hallway.

Maria sat alone, her head buried in her phone.

"Making plans with Danny?"

Maria looked up in shock. "What the hell?"

"I know, you care about him," Nikki said, barely managing not to roll her eyes. "I came here to talk to Colton, but I've got some questions for you too. I'm investigating Parker's disappearance."

The teenager's expression softened. "Yeah, that sucks. But why are you asking about it? Aren't you busy enough down in Stillwater?" She sipped her soda. "I saw on the news that more victims were brought out from the woods during the night. The reporters were talking about thawing the ground." Maria stilled. "Oh my God, that Parker guy wasn't one of them, was he?"

"He's still missing," Nikki said. "Forest Lake police asked for my help. I stopped by to talk with the staff, and I figured I'd start with you since we've met before."

"What am I supposed to tell you?" Maria asked. "I only talked to the guy a few times. He seemed nice."

"Were you here the night he disappeared?" Nikki asked.

"I was with Danny," Maria said proudly. "We met at a bowling alley one county over and then bowled for a couple of hours before we went for a drive." She smiled slyly, obviously trying to get under Nikki's skin. Had Maria deliberately alibied Danny, or was she just talking?

"Which bowling alley?" Nikki asked.

"Why?" Maria asked indignantly.

"Because I need to confirm Danny's whereabouts that night," Nikki answered.

"He didn't do anything," Maria insisted.

"This is how the job is done." Nikki was tired of the girl's emotional back and forth. "Now, I can have my staff call every damn bowling alley in the tri-county area, or you could just answer my question."

"Patty's. It's about ten minutes north of here."

"Thank you," Nikki said. "Now, back to Parker. Did you

ever see him with a white guy, fairly tall, maybe wearing Carhartts or other outdoor workwear?"

Maria shook her head. "I never paid much attention, to be honest. He's not really my type."

Apparently, handsome and clean was the type she didn't like. "What about someone lurking around, either on foot or in a parked vehicle?"

"Well, I worked the night before, after school until my shift ended at seven," Maria said. "When I got here, I freaked out for a minute because I thought Danny had come to see me at work. There was a junky white Chevy pickup parked across the street, which is where Danny usually parks if he comes to eat."

"But it wasn't Danny's?"

"No," she said. "But every time I walked by the big bay window in the dining room, I'd see it out of the corner of my eye and think it was him all over again."

"Did you ever see anyone get into the truck?"

"No, but it was gone when I left," she said.

Nikki spoke to the dishwasher and cashier before she left West End Diner. They'd both been working the night Parker disappeared, but neither one had seen anything. Nikki left a couple of cards with Colton's mother and headed outside.

"Jesus." She hid her face in the high collar of her coat. The wind had picked up since she'd been outside with Colton. She jogged to the jeep, the wind nearly yanking the door out of her hand when she opened it. Nikki slammed it shut and turned the vehicle on. Her cheeks burned from the wind.

While she waited for the heat to kick in, Nikki checked her messages. Rory and Lacey had both texted to check in, with Lacey's text full of her morning exploits at the beach. Knowing that she was having so much fun made Nikki miss her a little less, but she still hated being so far away from her little girl. She texted her and Rory back and then checked her voicemail.

Roth's gentle voice came through the Bluetooth. "Um, hi,

Agent Hunt. I'm just getting ready for my interviews at Oak Park Heights, but that photo of Parker kept bugging me. I knew I'd seen it before. Monday posed his last victim the same way, hung by her wrists, head on her shoulders, the quality of the photo just bad enough it was impossible to tell she was already dead when he'd taken it." He sighed. "I think this is why I went into science instead of criminal justice. Every little thing seems like a sign to me when I'm sure it isn't. But I do think the similarity is more than coincidence. Don't hesitate to call if you need my assistance. I'm tied up the rest of the day, but I will return your call."

Nikki opened the browser on her phone and googled Monday's last victim, but the ransom picture he'd sent of the dead girl posed to look alive hadn't been made public. She texted Liam to call the Anchorage Bureau office and get a copy of the photo emailed ASAP. Roth's message had left her rattled. Their killer had used Monday's tricks to dispose of Kesha and communicate with the police. If the pattern continued, Parker Jameson was probably already dead.

NINETEEN

BLACK FRIDAY, FOUR WEEKS EARLIER

Kesha

Kesha glared down at her boyfriend, tapping her foot. Shoppers trudged along like zombies mindlessly looking for the next deal. "Dion."

He huffed and looked up at her with a dramatic sigh. "What?"

"You really going to sit here while I shop, with all these people around?"

"Babe, the reason I'm not shopping with you is because of all these people." He grinned up at her, but she refused to smile back. Dion had promised to spend the afternoon shopping with her, but he'd only gone into the candy shop and the pizza joint where they'd had lunch. He probably thought she'd rather shop without him since all he did was complain about the people and the prices, but they'd come to the mall together, and she hated dodging the crowds by herself.

"'Sides, I thought you were going to Victoria's Secret to get something for me." Dion wiggled his eyebrows suggestively.

"I'm going because I need new bras." Dion had been sulky

ever since Kesha told him that she planned on going to Mankato
State next year instead of the community college he currently
attended, even though he insisted that he understood her decision. "I thought you wanted to spend time with me today."

"I do," Dion said. "You wanted to come to the mall, not me."

"Because today is the only time I can afford anything here."
She flipped her braids over her shoulder and glared down at her
boyfriend, who'd already started a new round of Diablo on his
phone. "Whatever, D. I'll be back in a little bit."

"Just text me when you're done shopping and I'll meet you,"
Dion said.

Kesha grumbled her agreement and left him sitting with his
stupid phone, playing his dumb game. She dodged a mother and
daughter carrying at least ten bags between them and tried to
stay with the flow of the foot traffic, but people wandered
aimlessly, gawking at this store and that, half of them on their
phones and the other half barely awake. Dion had tried to tell
her they should get to the Mall of America earlier, since it
opened at five a.m. on Black Friday, but Kesha wasn't about to
spend her only free weekend until Christmas bleary-eyed and
exhausted. By the time they got there and Dion found a place to
park, the mall was as full as she'd ever seen it. He grouched
about the lack of parking spaces and how far away they'd eventually had to park, and he complained about the parents dragging along little kids to get bored and bratty. The only thing he
hadn't complained about was the candy store and lunch.

Kesha adjusted her bag on her shoulder and kept an eye out
for the lingerie store. As if she was going to buy something
special to wear for Dion! And if she were, he definitely wasn't
going to get to see it tonight and maybe not even tomorrow
night.

"Pain in my ass." Trouble was, her anger was already
fading. Dion had his moments, but he'd been good to her, and
she knew he loathed shopping. Just being in the mall today was

a feat for him. Kesha knew she should be kinder and less snappy with him, especially with the clock ticking down to her high school graduation. Summer would fly by because she and Dion both worked as many hours as possible, trying to save money for school. Once she started at Mankato State, the two-plus hour drive meant she wouldn't see Dion very often. Her freshman year in college was going to be tough for both of them. Kesha could take care of herself just fine, but she worried about Dion.

When they started dating two years ago, he'd been trying to change his life before his juvenile misdemeanors became adult jail time. Dion always credited her for giving him the motivation to stay out of trouble, but what would he do when she wasn't around? Her mother told her that she was overreacting, that Dion would be fine, and if he wasn't, Kesha still had to live her life.

"You have your whole life in front of you," she'd told Kesha the other day. "Dion might end up being the right one, but you need to experience the world to know for sure. You're going to meet people in college who are totally different to you, who come from entirely different cultures and areas of the country. Who knows what amazing things might happen to you?"

Lost in thought, she didn't see the man until she accidentally shoulder checked him while weaving through people to get to Victoria's Secret.

"I'm so sorry," she said, rubbing her shoulder. The guy was a couple inches taller than her, but somehow his chest had connected right in the divot connecting her arm and shoulder.

"No problem," he said, barely pausing to see if she was all right.

Kesha rolled her eyes. Everyone was always in such a hurry even when they had nowhere to go. Like Ferris Bueller said, life moved pretty fast. If you didn't stop and look around once in a while, you could miss it.

Kesha sighed with relief when she spotted the store. Like

everywhere else, it was full of shoppers, but at least she could leave the herd in the aisle. She perused the store, inwardly kicking herself for not getting here earlier. Most things in her size had already been picked over. Why in the hell did so much marketing cater to girls smaller than size ten? It shouldn't be so damned hard to find a bra with DD cups in a lingerie store. Her mother said her sizes were always in short supply because they had the highest demand, but it didn't feel like it when she was surrounded by thin girls and their skinny mothers.

Kesha dug through the pile of clearance bras, looking for anything close to her size. She found a couple of bras and went into the dressing room to try them on. One was way too small in the cups despite the size of the tag, but the other fit okay, even though the band was tight. Kesha fanned her damp face as she put her own clothes back on. Why did they keep the stores so hot?

Twenty minutes later, she finally got her turn at the register. The overly cheery staff tried to push a store credit card on her, even though she wouldn't turn eighteen for a few more months. The chick in line behind Kesha was so close that her hot breath hit the back of Kesha's neck every time the woman huffed with impatience. Finally, she left the store, wondering why she'd stood in line so long for a bra and some perfumed spray that wouldn't last more than a couple of hours.

Kesha reached into her backpack for her phone to text Dion, even though he was probably so absorbed in his game he wouldn't even notice. Her fingers grazed the lipstick she carried in the bag, her compact, and some gum along with her wallet, but no phone.

Her anxiety ticked up. Kesha had put her phone in the bag, but had she accidentally put it in the outside pocket? Had it fallen out in the store? Kesha made a U-turn and headed back towards Victoria's Secret, her pulse starting to race. She needed her phone. She was naked without it.

"Excuse me," an unfamiliar voice whispered, the lips dangerously close to her ear. "I've been looking everywhere for you. You must have dropped this when we collided earlier."

Kesha stared at the man, wondering why he hadn't just called out to her when he'd noticed it fall.

"I'm afraid it might be broken," he said again, his dark eyes staring right through her as he motioned for her to follow him out of the crowd. Kesha followed him but kept her distance. Was he on something? He wasn't sweating, but his chest heaved like he had been racing for his life.

"Thank you," she mustered, leaning against the wall.

He smiled. "You don't recognize me, do you?"

"No, I don't. Except for our run-in earlier. How do you know me?"

"I'm an old colleague of your mother's, but it's been a couple of years since I've seen her. And my face is definitely forgettable." He leaned closer, his pupils dilated. "See what I'm holding?"

Sweat pooled at the bottom of her back. "Looks like a remote or something..."

"It is," the man said. "To something hidden in Nickelodeon Universe just over there, and if you don't come with me right now, it goes off, Kesha."

He said the words so pleasantly that their conversation probably looked normal to anyone paying attention, and most people weren't. Kesha's vision slowly tunneled until she saw only the man's face.

Was he really telling her he'd planted a bomb in the middle of the Mall of America? Where were the mall security guards? What happened to the increased presence on Black Friday? Why had he chosen her? What did he intend to do to her? Would he just use her to escape?

The look in his eyes suggested he had more than that planned.

Kesha's armpits dampened, sweat trickling down her spine and pooling in the small of her back. The self-defense training she'd taken two years ago urged her to scream and fight, but her brain froze on the image of all the little ones at Nickelodeon Universe, running and screaming and eating. "You're bluffing." She finally managed to speak.

"I never bluff," he said. "I've got enough explosives rigged that hundreds will die, and most of them little, helpless kids. You want that on your conscience?"

Tears brimmed in her eyes. "Why are you doing this?"

"Because I can."

TWENTY

"Expect temperatures to drop below zero tonight, with windchills as low as minus twenty. Tomorrow will barely reach zero, but strong winds will make it feel more like ten below."

"Fantastic." The dangerous cold made searching for Parker even more difficult. A night search would be out of the question, and they only had a couple of hours until the sun went down.

Nikki killed the engine and headed inside the sheriff's station to meet Liam and Miller. They'd both spent the afternoon re-interviewing Parker's friends and family. Nikki doubted they'd uncover any new information, but she also wanted the family to know that the sheriff's department and FBI were involved. She caught up with Miller outside conference room B. "Any luck with the interviews?"

"Nope," he said. "Parker lives in a basement apartment, nothing unusual occurred in the weeks leading up to his disappearance. The only person he complained about is Colton. You get the chance to talk to him?"

"I did, and it sounds like someone might have been watching Parker." She set her things on the table and sat down next to Liam. He didn't look up from his computer, and red splotches had spread over his cheeks when she'd entered the room. So, he was still pissed off at her.

Nikki ran through her conversations with Colton and Maria Lopez. "Two different occasions of someone possibly scouting the location, although Maria could be lying for Danny. Has anyone heard from Dover about the eyewitness who claimed she saw Parker in a white truck after he was taken?"

"Just spoke with her," Liam said, still without looking at Nikki. "The witness said that the photo of Stanton's truck definitely wasn't the one she saw."

"Danny's got an alibi for the night Parker disappeared, too. I think we can take him off our suspect list once we've verified it. He's a pothead and borderline creep, but he isn't our guy."

"Dover also sent a copy of the sales receipts from the co-op, starting about a week before Parker was taken. We've been looking through them and trying to cross-reference," Miller said. "They were slow on the seventeenth, which is why he closed early. Only about half the sales were paid by card, the rest were cash."

"Damn," Nikki said. "I assume no red flags on the card receipts?"

"All women," Liam answered, flipping through his notes. "There's a cash sale at 3:27 p.m. that day, for twelve bucks. A soy candle. I cross referenced it, along with the others in the days leading up to, with the security video. All but two customers were women, and the man who bought the candle is short and round, probably in his sixties, with a cane."

"So not our guy," Nikki said, disappointed.

"I called the Shakopee police liaison for the tribe down at Mystic Lake," Liam said. "He confirmed the missing woman wore a bracelet similar to the one we saw on the victim with the dark hair. I told him we'd let him handle things with her family once we have an ID."

"Forest Lake PD really screwed the pooch on this one,"

Miller said. "And Chief Peek can come up with any excuse he wants, but the truth is he's a racist who didn't want to ask a black sheriff for help. And no, I don't have proof of that. I just know."

"I'm sure you're right, and it's frustrating," Nikki said. "But all we can do now is move forward. Liam, did you get hold of the Anchorage guys?"

He turned his laptop so that she could see the photo on the screen. A petite, lighter-haired female appeared to be hanging from her shackled wrists, her head slack but eyes open, staring blankly at the camera. The killer had sent a photocopy of a Polaroid photo, making it impossible to trace and hard to decipher the details of her face. Parker's photo was clearer, but other than the body bag hanging next to him, the poses were nearly identical.

"The Anchorage guys said Monday sent this photo for a ransom, ten days after the girl disappeared. When they finally caught him, he admitted she was dead when he took it. He'd killed her within the first twenty-four hours of the kidnapping, but he had to leave for a business trip, so he stored her in his shed in the backyard, under a tarp. January in Alaska means the victim was frozen solid when Monday returned four days later. He had to use space heaters to thaw her out because he wanted to have sex with her again since she looked 'incorruptible after death.' If you're not familiar with that term, it's Catholic. Divine intervention keeps select saints and beati from decomposing, and the lack of decomp is a sign the individual may be a saint. He bought some cheap makeup at the store to make her look more alive."

"Jesus." Nikki couldn't imagine what Monday had put the girl's corpse through.

"We might have a copycat on our hands, then," Miller said. "Monday never disposed of his victims in the state where he took them, except for this girl, which is the murder that finally got him caught."

"Not a copycat," Nikki said. "Or where he buried his victims would only be about subterfuge. This is more than that. It's almost like they're his own private collection. I bet he visits the site frequently, especially during the summer. He wants to make sure it's not disturbed, but he also gets off on knowing what he put in the ground."

"The ultimate form of control," Liam muttered.

"When did the book about Monday come out?" Nikki asked.

"Two years ago," Liam said. "Monday killed his first victim when he was twelve, because she rejected him. And the guy definitely was the type of Millennial killer, or whatever Roth called them. He'd read all of the true crime books, downloaded tons of podcasts, and spent hours studying how killers got caught and how they didn't. He got so familiar with police tactics that that's one of the ways he avoided capture. He talked his way out of a ticket more than once."

Nikki drummed her fingers on the tabletop, fighting the exhaustion that was starting to wash over her. "So our killer's a fan of Monday's. Who killed himself before trial, so there's no chance we could check prison logs for visitors and letters."

"Doug Elwood wrote the foreword," Liam said. "He called Monday the scariest and smartest he'd dealt with, and that included Bundy and all the others he'd encountered."

Elwood had been Nikki's teacher and mentor at Quantico. In the late seventies, when Douglas and Ressler were interviewing murderers and getting the original Behavioral Science team together, Elwood had been one of a select few rookie agents chosen to be part of the team. During his tenure on the team, he'd worked the Atlanta child murders and helped to catch Bundy and the Green River Killer, along with dozens of other horrific cases. By the time Nikki arrived at the academy, fresh out of college with a master's degree in psychology and the naïve idea that she could handle any criminal because of her parents' murders, Elwood had retired as a full-time agent. He taught several classes and oversaw the curriculum for new applicants in their department, and he still traveled as an author and trained law enforcement officers on basic profiling. She hadn't done the best job of staying in touch, but she knew without a doubt that he'd never make that statement unless he meant it.

"Elwood had interviewed Richard Ramirez twice when I first started at Quantico," Nikki said. "He had nightmares for weeks after sitting down with Ramirez."

Liam leaned back in his chair, balancing it on its back legs. "He writes that Monday was worse than anyone else, more sadistic and calculating and a lot smarter. You think our guy's trying to one-up this Monday somehow?"

"I don't know," Nikki admitted. "But I think it's more about this killer's ego than being inspired by some other serial killer."

"Sounds about right," Liam said. "I checked traffic records looking for a white pickup similar to the one seen at the lake, but no luck. I also called the Mall of America's security office and asked for parking garage videos from Black Friday, specifically on the east end of the mall, where Kesha disappeared. I've got Kendra and Jim looking for the pickup."

Nikki's email dinged with a new message from the medical examiner's office. Her stomach plummeted. "Blanchard identified the missing couple. Dee and John Henderson of rural Duluth, missing since September twelfth. When John and Dee both missed work, Dee's cousin went to their lake house. Both cars in the garage, Dee's purse, John's wallet, car keys, phone—all left behind. The house looked normal, but the fish house down by the lake had been bleached clean. They searched the area for weeks with no results."

Liam rubbed his temples. "Monday took a couple from

Ohio and buried them in Pennsylvania. He bragged about having sex with the man while his wife was forced to watch."

"Yet another reason for our killer to feel some kind of connection with Monday," Miller said. "Monday loathed himself and his sexuality. Did Blanchard say anything else?"

"John Henderson was sexually assaulted so badly his perineum was torn, right up to the scrotum." Nikki barely managed to get the words out of her dry mouth. "Spermicide found with both victims, so he used a condom. Dee was raped vaginally and anally. Cause of death for both was asphyxiation, and their stomach contents suggested they were killed within hours of each other. She doesn't know who was killed first."

"We need to ID the oldest victim," Liam said. "We've compiled a list of every unsolved missing female in the state between the ages of twelve and thirty in the last decade, but we need more information to narrow it down."

Nikki unlocked her phone and scrolled through her contacts until she found the forensic anthropologist's phone number. She'd almost given up when the call finally connected.

"Doctor JoAnn Willard."

"Hi, Doctor Willard, it's Agent Nikki Hunt. You're on speaker with the sheriff and Agent Wilson. I know it's a tough process, but have you made any progress on the remains?"

"As a matter of fact, I was just putting together my notes to call you," Willard said. "I presume Doctor Blanchard contacted you about the couple buried together?"

"Yes," Nikki said. "We're hoping you've made some headway with the oldest set of remains."

"Victim A is still a bit of a mystery," Willard said. "My initial assessment was correct. The remains belong to a female. Her bone plates are fused, but there's no indication she's given birth. Her wisdom teeth are present but hadn't erupted, and they were still in the jaw. I also measured the one femur we were able to recover. Between the size and the lack of degenerative evidence in the bone, I don't think she was older than thirty, and she may have been as young as a teenager. Her hyoid bone was gone, so I can't tell you if she was strangled, but her ribs and wrist bones are broken in a way that suggests a physical altercation. It also looks like she suffered blunt force trauma before she died. I can't tell you if that was her cause of death, however."

"Can you tell how long the bones have been there?"

"Given their condition and the lack of insects, organic material, these bones are at least twenty years old, and that's a conservative number."

"What about the victim next to her and the Native American woman?"

"Victim B, buried next to the remains in the towel, is still unidentified. I can tell you her hyoid was crushed, and she was most likely strangled with something long and cylindrical, strong enough to really pulverize some of the bone. She was likely between eighteen and thirty when she was killed, based on the pelvic bones and wisdom teeth, but that's preliminary. I've nothing yet on Victim C. Dental records did come in this morning for Victim D, the Native American female. Her name is Elyssia Kaiser, aged twenty-six. Reported missing after leaving her job at Mystic Lake Casino just over a year ago. Cause of death appears to be similar to Victim B's. Since these remains are skeletonized, I can't tell you if the women were sexually assaulted. So we've identified three out of the six."

But not the first victim, whose identity might be our best shot at catching this guy. Nikki thanked Willard and switched gears, calling Courtney. "Hopefully Courtney has some more information on Victim A."

"Maybe I do, maybe I don't."

Nikki hadn't realized she'd answered the phone. "Don't tease us. We're all too tired."

"Fine," Courtney said. "We're still trying to figure out the pattern on the towel, but Blanchard was right about Neutro-lene. Each body bag had a significant amount inside."

"So Victim B was killed some time after mid-2012, when the product launched." Liam stood and walked over to the whiteboard. He drew two parallel lines several inches apart to represent the mass grave. "Victim A is prior to 2012, Victims B and C had to have been killed in late 2012 but before summer 2020 because Victim D—Elyssia Kaiser—disappeared in November of 2020. The Hendersons were killed in September of this year."

"Eight years is a lot of missing persons cases to go through," Miller said.

Courtney's exaggerated sigh came through the speaker-phone. "It would save you guys time if you'd let me get through all of my results before you started theorizing."

Liam rolled his eyes. "Why do you always save the most important information for last?"

"I like to build up the suspense. Plus, your hanging on my every word is kind of awesome."

Liam's face reddened enough to match his hair. Nikki held up her hand and took over before the bickering wasted more time. "Just tell us, Court."

"Fine," Courtney said. "We've been using the electron microscope on the towel the oldest set of remains were in. It's cotton, with a white background. It's also got stripes in different colors, most likely a rainbow, and what looks like an orange cat tail and the letters 'is' underneath it, as part of a name."

"*Garfield*," Liam said. "Written by Jim Davis. Still my favorite comic."

"We're going to be lucky if we can recover fifty percent of the towel's design," Courtney said. "But we searched online for 'vintage Garfield towel rainbow' and found one that looks very similar to what we've seen so far. According to the eBay listing, it's a collector's item from 1978."

"If the towel was already faded when Victim A was buried," Nikki asked, "would you still be able to see the design under the microscope?"

"Depends on how faded," Courtney said. "But given the type of soil in the area and the water table, it seems unlikely the towel was very old when the victim was wrapped in it."

Nikki's chest felt tight, but for the first time she thought they might have a real chance to catch the killer. "Liam, check Washington and surrounding counties for missing females between 1978 and 2012. Prioritize Washington County, the 1980s, and include the Garfield beach towel. It may have been Victim A's and she had it with her when our guy took her. ViCAP and AFIS, too, in case Courtney manages to get a fingerprint."

Courtney snorted. "Highly doubtful. I'll call you if we find anything else."

Nikki muttered goodbye, her mind already on the next step. "That victim is the key to his identity, I can feel it in my bones, no pun intended."

"Based on the towel?" Miller asked. "It could have been old when she was wrapped in it."

"But not older than 2012, because of the Neutrolene granules," Nikki reminded him. "Willard's pretty confident the remains are at least twenty-five years old, and we know there was a gap between killing Victim A and B—possibly a large one. Combine that with the towel, assuming Courtney's right—and she likely is, because she wouldn't tell us about it if she wasn't confident—the chances are strong that this guy first killed when he was fairly young."

Liam nodded, his eyes blazing with the adrenaline rush that only came from a major breakthrough in a case. "Chelsea said he looked like he was in his forties, right?"

"Eyewitness statements are so unreliable," Miller said.

"Entertain us for a second." Liam turned back to the whiteboard and added the new information Courtney had given them. "Blanchard said Henderson was a bigger guy. Moving dead weight is hard work. Willard dates Victim A's remains to at least the mid-nineties, so even if you take everything but the towel's manufacture date out, we've narrowed our window down to about twenty years instead of thirty-plus. The gap between Victim A's death and B's death also suggests the killer wasn't an adult when he murdered her."

"Because if he were an adult, he'd have murdered someone else sooner?" Miller asked.

"Most likely," Nikki said. "Some serial killers do cool off, like BTK. That's not as unusual as we once thought it was. But to cool off at the beginning, when you've gotten away with it once?" She shook her head. "I don't think so. I think we're looking for someone who started killing when he was a young teenager. It takes him a long time to get the guts to do it again, not to mention it's a lot harder to dispose of a body when you're a kid." Nikki stopped talking, an idea niggling at the corners of her mind. "He wouldn't have taken her body very far to bury her, especially if he wasn't old enough to drive. Big Marine Lake's always been there, but when I was a kid, there were more houses around it and the landscape looked totally different."

Mayberry Trail, the road that bordered Big Marine Lake and led to the St. Croix Scenic Byway, was part of the original road created by the first settlers on the west side of Big Marine Lake, leading to the town of Marine on St. Croix. The land and settlements on both sides of the road had changed since then, but Nikki wasn't familiar with the historical details.

"It was," Miller said. "The park reserve opened in 2008, but it was in development for twenty years before that. The big focus was getting the land back to the way it was before it was settled, to restore the natural resources. Work started in the late eighties."

Liam finally sat back down, deep creases between his

eyebrows forming as he typed something on his laptop. "I noticed on the plat map that the area the bodies were buried is about an acre-sized tract that's changed hands and zoning designations a few times, but interestingly enough, it's been zoned as protected forest land for the last decade, so right before the odor-neutralizing agent was made available to the mass market. Before that, it was zoned as agriculture, but the property changed hands several times."

Nikki tried to keep up with what he was telling them. "Basically, throughout the last couple of decades, the small tract where the bodies were found hasn't changed much, even though a lot of the area around Big Marine Lake has been part of the project to reclaim the land and its natural resources. Before the project started in 1989, there were several older homes through here?"

Miller nodded. "But this was still a lot of rural area, without houses built on top of each other."

"That's the area we have to focus on," Nikki said. "Liam, you run point on that. See if we can find out who lived within a five-mile radius of the burial area in the seventies and eighties. Miller and I have to focus on searching for Parker."

Miller turned on the smartboard mounted next to the dingy whiteboard that Liam had been writing on. Maps of Washington County and Forest Lake appeared. "Chief Peek sent me these with the locations they've already searched marked. I want to start outside of city limits and push east toward the St. Croix River." He pointed the cursor at Highway 97, which ran through the city of Forest Lake and the north to the river. "We'll use Highway 97 for the dividing line. Peek and his team are going to search north of the highway, we're focusing south." He used the pointer to circle the large swatch of land southeast of Forest Lake. "We've got a good-size area between Big Marine and Forest Lake that hasn't been checked, including the O'Brien State Park. The northern part of the park is in Chisago

County, and they have a couple of deputies who will search tomorrow too. Our assigned search grid"—Miller glanced at Nikki as he outlined the area on the smartboard, south of Highway 97—"is this rectangular-shaped area. There's a fair amount of development, but there are also open fields as well as a big section of the park that runs along the St. Croix. I talked to Reuben, and he's willing to bring the K9 out tomorrow for a couple of hours, once the temperature hits zero. I want to start at the river and work west. That's the area most similar to Big Marine."

"The temperature and wind's going to be a problem," Nikki said. "I checked the weather and the sun's supposed to come out mid-morning, but with twenty-mile-an-hour winds, that doesn't help. Volunteers need to layer up, and we need to have warm vehicles within walking distance. I don't want someone getting frostbite. How many people do we have?" She hadn't done a search in sub-zero weather since returning to the area, but she and Miller would be responsible for any injuries sustained from the cold, so making sure the searchers had everything they needed was crucial.

"Not many," Miller said. "You, me, Reuben and his dog will search together. Reynolds and another deputy will be searching west of us. Chief Peek said he's got two or three lined up for tomorrow, weather pending. Fields, drainage ditches, watershed areas that may be frozen and able to walk on—all of those will be searched."

"Parker might still be alive," Nikki said. "He's been gone a little over a week, and with the ground and water frozen, our guy's options are limited. We need to remember how long this guy has been killing and what we know he's capable of," she reminded them. "I agree about the state park, though, especially this time of year. Less foot traffic and staff right now."

Liam's phone vibrated on the table. He rubbed his eyes and then squinted at the screen. She could tell he hadn't gotten much sleep the last couple of days, and the doctors had harped on about how important sleep was to his recovery.

"Shit." Liam pushed his phone aside.

"You're just tired," Nikki said. "If you're not careful—"

"No, that's not it," he cut in. "Parker's family released a statement about the FBI and the Washington County Sheriff ignoring the police's request for help in the disappearance. 'The delay and ego of Special Agent Nicole Hunt may very well have cost Parker Jameson his life,' says the family's spokesperson." He looked up at Nikki. "Want me to keep reading?"

"No," she seethed. "Dover's behind this. I told her the family was her primary responsibility. She wasn't happy about not being in on the action."

Miller pushed away from the table, livid. "I'm going to the Jamesons' now."

"I'll come with you," Nikki said.

The sheriff shook his head. "Let me do it. The family's more likely to listen to me. I hope."

TWENTY-ONE

Nikki parked her jeep on the street that overlooked the frozen Mississippi River in downtown Stillwater. As pretty as the river was in the summer, it was desolate in the winter. The gusting winds tore across the ice, sweeping snow onto the shore like a wave. It practically blew Nikki across the street as she headed toward the Oasis Café, a small riverfront diner with decent food and coffee just a few minutes' drive from the sheriff's station. She'd tried to convince Sheriff Miller to let her go with him to talk with Parker's family, but he'd refused. Deep down, she knew that his decision was probably the right one. Nikki wasn't sure she could overcome her exhaustion well enough to keep from telling the family that Dover was only using them to cover her own ass.

She and Liam had spent the last hour going through information and trying to narrow down their search window for the first victim. She'd left the sheriff's office with the intention of heading home, but then remembered that Roth had said he'd be at Oak Park Heights Correctional all day. The prison was only three miles from downtown, so Nikki had arranged to meet with Roth before he headed back into the metro area.

She didn't see Roth when she arrived. The diner was mostly empty, save for a pair of retired couples having coffee together. Nikki asked for a table in the back corner. She sat down facing the door, her stomach reminding her that she hadn't eaten since the donuts this morning. Her stomach felt sour from too much coffee, but she needed to eat, so Nikki ordered a BLT and iced tea. While she waited for Roth, she went through her notes and plans for tomorrow. She had plenty of cold weather gear, including insulated facemasks, but hopefully the trees in the state park provided some sort of windbreak. She needed to have extra socks and gloves and make sure her thermal underwear was clean. Rory had some hand and feet warmers he used during the cold months; Nikki made a note to pack them. Since Miller and his family spent a lot of time outdoors year round, he kept necessities like extra clothes, blankets and ice shoes in his SUV. And the walking sticks, Nikki remembered. The second case she'd worked with Miller was the murder of a mother and her young son. They'd been left in a deep ravine and getting down to the bodies wouldn't have been possible without the titanium hiking sticks Miller kept in the SUV.

The sleigh bells hanging on the restaurant's front door jingled. Roth entered, looking windblown but still too chic to be a psychologist. Nikki waved from her corner table. He smiled and headed her way, smoothing his sandy blond hair. His already sunburned face looked a bit chapped from the wind.

"Good afternoon." He smiled and sank into the booth across from Nikki, his eyes missing some of this morning's luster. Talking to killers did that to a person. Roth asked for water and nothing else.

"I know it's early to eat—or late, depending how you look at it," Nikki said. "But those donuts this morning were my last meal."

"Please, you don't have to justify anything to me," he said.

"I'm just not hungry after today's interviews. The last one was... challenging to say the least."

"Anyone I know?" Nikki joked.

Roth looked down at the table. "Unfortunately, yes."

Her stomach bottomed out. "Which one?"

"We don't have to talk about it today, Agent Hunt. I'd like to some time, though."

"Call me Nicole, please. Which one?"

"Oliver, your brother."

"Frost," she corrected him. "He's a half-brother I didn't even know I had who murdered multiple women and my ex-husband. He traumatized my daughter."

"That's why I said we should talk about it another time."

"Did he tell you that he wrote me a letter? I got it on Christmas Eve."

Roth ran his fingers through his hair. "I'm actually the one who suggested he write to you."

Nikki stared at him. "Excuse me?"

"Let me explain," Roth said. "I first met with him in early November. I already knew the case file, so I was aware of his connection to you, of course." He shifted in his seat. "You know talking to these guys isn't easy. Sometimes you have to say things you don't mean to earn their trust. Like pretending to empathize with your brother over his childhood, acting as though I understood his pain, maybe even warranted it." He laughed nervously. "This is one of the only times a scientist doesn't have to be honest to get honest results."

As much as she hated to admit it, Nikki did understand. "I remember the first prison interview I went on when I was still in the academy. My mentor told me that I needed to learn to compartmentalize. I remember fighting not to laugh because compartmentalizing is the only way I survived after my parents died. But we needed to get information out of a man who'd raped and killed a thirteen-year-old girl. Listening to Agent

Elwood pretend to understand and even feel sorry for that bastard was excruciating. I can't count how many times I've had to do the same thing since then."

Roth sighed with relief. "I'm so glad you understand. He wanted to write to you, and I suggested it might be beneficial." He shook his head. "I must admit to you that I gave him that advice for selfish reasons. Now that I have to see the consequences of my actions, I feel terrible. I'm sorry if he sent you something upsetting."

"It's okay," Nikki said. "He would have probably done it anyway just to get to me."

"He is quite the manipulator," Roth said.

"Did you scan his brain?" Nikki asked. "For your study?"

"He's not sure he wants to," Roth said. "He's playing the cat and mouse game. He likes the attention of my coming back. But obviously, you didn't ask me here to talk about Oliver. This afternoon yielded results?"

"To an extent. Three of the bodies were identified. The male was severely sexually assaulted. We're getting closer to figuring out who Victim A is, I think. We've at least narrowed down our search window. I'm afraid it might be too late for Parker Jameson, though."

Roth sipped his water. "Yes, I heard the family's statement. You put Detective Dover in charge of them this morning, if I recall correctly."

Nikki was impressed he'd paid attention and remembered that detail. "Yes, and she's clearly trying to cover for their delay in notifying Miller and myself. We're heading out tomorrow to search."

"For his remains?"

Nikki nodded. "I'm hopeful that he might still be alive somewhere, that the killer is on his heels because we found his bodies, and he knows he's got to lay low."

"I pray you're right," Roth said. "But I sense you'll take on immense guilt if you're wrong."

"Very observant."

"That is part of my job," he said. "I won't waste your time telling you not to feel bad and that it isn't your fault. It's not going to help. That's a realization you have to come to on your own."

Nikki leaned back from the power of his gaze. She wasn't used to being read and analyzed, and she definitely didn't want to spend the short amount of time she had with Roth discussing her issues. "After what you told us about Monday in Alaska and everything else we've learned today, I think we're looking for a highly intelligent man who never felt recognized in his personal life, who knows how to mimic certain emotions to get what he wants, which is control over another's life. That's what gets him off. He also knows how far ahead of us he is, so he's cocky. Mistakes are coming, I'm certain of it."

"Interesting," Roth said. "How can you be certain?"

"Gut instinct, which usually doesn't fail me," Nikki said. "He didn't expect us to find Kesha and he definitely didn't expect the others to be found. But now he's also in the spotlight, so he preens a bit and sends the photo of Parker to the police."

"Peacocking," Roth said. "That's what my mother always called it. But you believe it's a false flag of sorts?"

"Absolutely. This prick has been in control for so long and in less than a week, his misdeeds are being exposed and the manhunt is on. Reaching out to police almost always suggests fear of getting caught, ego or both."

"I agree with you on the high intelligence," Roth said. "Let's hope you're right about his mental state. You mentioned identifying the couple. When were they murdered?"

"September. The Native American woman was a year before that."

"Now he's taken two people within the span of a few months. He's escalated, but why?"

"I don't know, but that's why we need to find Parker. This guy's pattern suggests he's going to take another person and probably soon." Nikki shook her head. "I can't have that on my conscience."

"When do you expect additional test results back?" Roth asked.

"Hopefully soon," she said. "We have people working around the clock. Are you able to come into the task force for a briefing in the morning?"

"I believe so," Roth said.

Her phone flashed with a text message from Liam:

Jim and Kendra went over mall security videos. Parker's boyfriend Colton was in the mall that day. He followed Kesha after she left Dion and approached her. Miller going to Forest Lake to ask him to come in and talk.

Colton? She'd bought his story about Parker. He'd told her that he didn't know Kesha. And what about the mass graves? If the first body was as old as they thought, Colton couldn't have killed her. But what if he'd been at the lake and somehow stumbled on remains and decided to use the spot for his own? She texted Liam to start looking for connections between Colton and the other identified victims.

"I'm sorry, we just got some new information and I need to get back to the sheriff's office." Nikki dug into her bag and found enough cash to pay the bill and leave a tip. "Thank you for coming, Doctor Roth. I'll touch base with you later."

Roth stood and shrugged into his coat. "I believe I may have parked behind you. Red jeep?"

"Yep, right across the street," Nikki said. They left the diner together. Nikki cursed when the wind struck her face. Her skin had already been dry, and her cheeks were getting chapped. "It's colder than it was when I got here."

"I'm seriously considering a permanent move to the tropics," Roth grumbled.

Nikki started to laugh, but her attention was on the jeep. "My damn tire is flat."

"I'll help you change it," Roth said. "You have a spare?"

"Yeah, in the garage at my boyfriend's place. It had a hole. I've been meaning to pick up another."

"No worries." Roth walked to his black Audi. "Hop in. I'll drive you to the sheriff's station."

Nikki liked to take care of things herself, but the cold and exhaustion made Roth's offer too inviting to pass up.

The inside of the Audi was as plush as the outside. The pristine leather gleamed, and Nikki couldn't see a speck of dust on the dash. She buckled her seat belt and thanked Roth again.

His gray eyes were the last thing she saw before the needle sank into her skin.

TWENTY-TWO

Nikki's amaretto sour smelled like burnt almonds with a dash of apricot oil. Except she'd never ordered an amaretto sour at the Oasis Café. She'd ordered iced tea and a sandwich, which was now fighting its way out of her stomach through her esophagus.

Vomit gurgled in her mouth. Nikki needed to turn over, but her body had been glued to the bed.

A bed? She didn't remember driving home.

A warm, strong hand cupped her shoulder and rolled Nikki on her side just in time for the vomit to breach her lips.

"Just relax," a man whispered near her ear. "I won't let you asphyxiate, Agent. Not yet, anyway."

Nikki's mind stilled, the merry-go-round of blurry memories becoming crystal clear. Roth had offered to drive her back to the sheriff's station since the jeep's tire had gone flat. He'd said something about false truths and...

Nikki peeled her eyes open. She blinked, her blurred vision slowly coming into focus.

Alex Roth's concerned face looked down at her. "Thank goodness. You were out longer than I anticipated."

She stared at him, trying to piece her memory together.

He'd injected her with something. How had she missed the menace in his gray eyes?

"Why do I smell bitter almond and apricot?" Her tongue felt coated with the taste.

Roth pointed to the plants lined up against the wall next to the rickety bed. "Oleander. Beautiful, strong-smelling, deadly. Animals won't bother a place it's been planted."

The grave. Courtney had talked about the possibility of a poisonous plant as a reason animals hadn't bothered with the area.

Nikki tried to sit up, but Roth shook his head. "I wouldn't advise that. You're going to be as wobbly as a newborn colt for a little while."

"Where are we?"

"In my secret place," he said. "My grandparents left it to me."

Nikki tried to take stock of her surroundings. They were in a bedroom, with a boarded-up window covered in black plastic. The space was barely big enough for a twin bed, small nightstand and half closet. The doors had been taken off the closet, with several shelves mounted on the walls. Nikki couldn't make out everything on the shelves, but she did see the restraints and a couple of very painful-looking sex toys.

"Don't worry, I changed the sheets before you came over."

She tried to control her breathing, but fear paralyzed her. No one knew she'd met with Roth. She didn't have a clue where they were.

Roth followed her gaze to the closet and then chuckled. "Don't worry, Agent. I don't intend on using those on you, not after the rapport we've established. I'm not a complete louse. I just need you for the final act of my story before I'm gone."

Nikki forced her dry mouth and cracked lips to move. "Where are you going?"

"Most people would say hell, but I'm holding out hope for a miracle."

Hell was too good for him. "I don't understand." Nikki's head was pounding. "What the hell did you give me?"

"Ketamine," he said. "I normally don't result to such barbaric tactics, but this is the first time I've kidnapped a cop, so I brought in reinforcements. For what it's worth, I'm truly sorry it's come to this. But I fear that without you, my story will be covered up much like Monday's."

Nikki struggled to keep her vision clear. Her body still felt weak and heavy, like she'd been drinking in the hot tub and stepped out before realizing she was too tipsy to walk straight. "No cover-up..." she mumbled.

"Sure there is," Roth said. "Detective Dover and Forest Lake are already doing it. Your boss expected it to happen, which is why he brought me in. That's when I knew how all of this was supposed to play out. It's our destiny."

"No," Nikki said. "Hernandez brought you in because of the media. We didn't need you to solve the case."

Roth threw his head back and laughed, the sound sending chills down Nikki's spine. "Of course you did, Agent. You never would have realized it was me if I hadn't taken you."

"It can't be you," she said. "I trusted you." How could she have missed him? Her instincts were better than that. Yet Roth had blindsided her. He'd looked through the crime scene photos without any sort of reaction, something most serial killers would be unable to do.

Roth smiled. "I have that effect on people. But don't feel badly, Agent Hunt. I've been doing this a very long time."

"The girl in the *Garfield* towel," Nikki croaked. "Who was she?"

"*Garfield*?" Roth clapped his hands. "Your forensic people could still see that pattern? Very impressive. Isn't technology wonderful?"

Nikki moved her hands and feet. Roth hadn't restrained her. Not that she had an ounce of strength right now. Her limbs still felt like jelly, and her memories from earlier in the day were a big, tangled mess of neurons.

"Do you know why I chose ketamine?" he asked. "Its effect is similar to GHB, you know." Roth smiled pleasantly, but she could see the meanness in his gray eyes. In the diner, Roth had told her that he'd only spoken with Oliver at the prison, but he'd clearly made nice with someone else responsible for destroying Nikki's life.

"You're a bastard."

He laughed. "I'm much more than that, but talking with your parents' killer today inspired me."

On the night her parents were murdered, Nikki had been drugged with GHB by the same man who'd killed her parents. Mark Todd had saved Nikki from being raped, but his heroic actions set off a chain of events that resulted in her parents' murders and Mark's wrongful imprisonment.

"You said you spoke to Frost today."

"I did, but I spoke to others as well."

Hate rolled through Nikki. She needed to get to her gun and...

Her gun was locked in the jeep, and Roth would have taken her purse and phone. He was probably smart enough to ditch the phone too.

"Don't you want answers?" Roth asked.

"I want you in prison for life."

Roth grinned. "That's the spirit, Agent. You're one of the best. The criminals you've caught were some of the most dangerous of our generation. That's why it had to be you. No one's going to sweep my legacy under the rug if my final victim is Nikki Hunt."

"Sure I am. You'll pack up here and move somewhere else and start over."

"I wish that were true, but an enemy I believed I had beaten has returned with a vengeance. I don't have much time left."

"Cancer? That's what you're going with?"

He shrugged. "I've already endured chemo and radiation once. Doctors assure me this time they won't do any more than give me a few more weeks of misery."

"Then why aren't you on a beach somewhere?"

"I intend to live out my final days on the beach, actually. I'm not spending them in a filthy cell. My story will be told because of your sacrifice. Think of the contribution you'll be making to your peers."

Nikki couldn't tell if her strength was coming back or if anger and adrenaline had propelled her to a sitting position. "Why didn't you just write it down before you went to die on the beach?"

"Because I should be studied, but no one will do that if I'm forgotten or hidden away like a dirty family secret." Roth offered her a glass of water, but Nikki refused. "By the way, everything I've told you about Monday and my impressions of the killer are true."

"You were talking about yourself," Nikki said.

"Exactly. But I am a big fan of Monday's. His suicide was a complete failure by law enforcement. His mind should have been protected." Roth shifted on the bed, his hand on his crotch. "If only I could have got to him before that happened."

Nikki swallowed the bile in her throat. "Is Parker Jameson alive?"

"What do you think?"

"I think you wanted to be remembered as even more deranged than Isaac Monday, and Parker was dead in that photo."

"Ding, ding." Roth tapped his index finger on his nose. "Parker was an unfortunate choice, however. I hadn't intended to take any action until the results of my scans came back. I'd already chosen him—he was quite beautiful in life, like an androgynous model—and that day I couldn't wait any longer."

"You're a sexual sadist who enjoys both men and women," Nikki said through gritted teeth. "Are you as forthright in your professional life?"

Roth snorted. "Of course not. It raises too many questions. My colleagues think I'm too focused on my research to date."

"You don't want a relationship, you want power and control," Nikki said.

"That's it." Roth stood up and paced the small bedroom. "That's why you're the only choice. We have history, you know."

"I swear to God, if you're going to tell me you're another long-lost relative—"

"No, no." Roth sat back down again, his heel bouncing against the floor. "April 1992. The misery of my freshman year at Stillwater High School was coming to an end. The teacher didn't like my drawings. While I waited to talk to the principal, one of the most popular girls in our class was getting chewed out for skipping that morning."

Nikki could nearly feel the color leaving her face. "That was... are you..."

"Manny the dirty Greek. At least, that's what everyone called me. Except you."

"No, it wasn't because you were Greek," Nikki said. "Back then, people called your family gypsies. They'd peddle stuff during town carnivals and other events. People said they were grifters." Had his last name been Roth back then? Nikki only remembered the nasty names kids used to call him.

"Do you know that in addition to being offensive, the word 'gypsy' is a misnomer?" Roth asked. "When my ancestors originally came from the Punjab region of India to Greece, people assumed they were from Egypt. But we are not. We're Roma. But the Greeks persecuted us, and so many decided to try their luck in this new world. As you know, it wasn't much different. Roma were transient groups, ushered out by the police, never accepted. My maternal grandparents were Swedish immigrants who loathed my father. His choice to run off after my sister's death only proved them right about Roma, at least to their eyes. That's all I was, despite my Swedish heritage they'd passed on."

"Your sister's remains are in the towel." At least Nikki had been right about that.

"They loved her because she looked like she'd stepped off the proverbial boat from Sweden. White-blonde hair, blue eyes, fair skin. Even though I had fairer skin, too, I'm able to tan. So I was always, compared to my father, the dirty gypsy Greek. She was the only one who accepted me for who I was, though."

"Why did you kill her?" Nikki asked.

"She was going to leave, run off with her dumb boyfriend. I didn't matter anymore."

"What about the next victim?"

"You'll have to narrow it down, Agent Hunt."

"There are others besides the ones who were buried in the grave?"

"Oh yes, I didn't go back there until I returned to the area several years ago." Roth smiled at her. "You know, that's one of the reasons I agreed to consult with Hernandez. I needed to confirm you were the right one to bare my soul to, as it were." He reached into his pocket and Nikki froze. "I want you to take this, keep it in your pocket." Roth handed her a flash drive. "I filled out the same questionnaire I give to convicted killers. I also included a victims list. I don't know most of their names, but I know where I took them from and where I left them. That way, when they find you, your colleagues will still give you credit for cracking the case."

Nikki felt frozen with fear, but her mind raced. She had to buy time until she could figure a way out of this mess. "Tell me your story, then. Before you kill me. Let me understand you before I die. Please give me that small mercy."

Roth seemed to debate the idea, his fingers too close to her legs. "Agent Hunt, you realize I know you're stalling."

"I also deserve answers." She glared back at him. She wasn't going down without a fight. He wanted to kill her and escape with infamy.

"Very well," he said, enjoying the spotlight. "After my sister's death, I was satisfied for a while, and then the desire just built and built until I couldn't handle it anymore." Roth leaned closer. "That day in the principal's office, you asked me about my drawings, but I let you assume they were only sexual. I'm sure you can deduce they were much more than that. In fact, I acted on the drawing that got me in trouble just a few days later. I believe that case is still unsolved to this day. But don't worry, it's in the flash drive. Have you met John Douglas, the great FBI profiler?"

Nikki stared at him, her still cloudy brain trying to keep up with his subject changes. "A couple of times. My mentor worked with him. Why?"

"I'm a fan," Roth said. "When I first started, I didn't understand my urges or that there were others like me. *Mindhunter* by Douglas opened my life to a new world. I'd found my people."

It had done the same for Nikki. The book inspired her to major in behavioral psychology instead of criminal justice, which she'd minored in. Her psychology training had opened the door for her at the FBI, just as it had done with Douglas. When Nikki had learned her mentor had worked with the legendary profiler, she'd literally shouted with joy.

"After your death, I will become enemy *numero uno*," Roth said. "I hope Douglas is the one who ultimately tells my story. Talk about a cherry on top."

Narcissism. She could work with that. Narcissists could talk about themselves for hours. "Why did you become a neuro-scientist?"

"I wanted to understand my own brain better, and I knew about the research in New Mexico. I thought it a perfect way to sharpen my skills." Roth checked his watch. "If you'll excuse me, I have a short conference call with my assistant at the institute. He'll be handling things during my leave of absence."

"I thought you said you were dying?" Nikki asked.

"They don't need to know that," he said. "I don't want their looks of pity. Now, I'm not going to restrain you, Nicole. The window doesn't open, it's almost twenty degrees below zero with the wind chill, and we're a long way from any neighbors. I trust you're smart enough not to go on a suicide mission. I will bring you a humane end. Mother Nature won't."

He left the room, locking the door behind him. Nikki heard three clicks, including the sliding sound made by a deadbolt. She scanned the room again, her vision finally clear enough to search for hidden cameras. She didn't see any, but she assumed Roth would be keeping an eye on her. The door appeared not to lock from the inside.

Slowly, she swung her legs off the bed. He'd taken off her boots, and she could feel the cold floor through her socks. Fake wooden paneling had been peeled from part of the wall, revealing insulation. Nikki gingerly stood, making sure her legs could hold her weight, and shuffled to the wall. Rory had shown her the difference between fiberglass and foam insulation when she'd helped him in the garage a few weeks ago. Nikki was confident this was a batt of fiberglass insulation that had been rolled out to fit into the damaged piece of wall. Fiberglass insulation irritated the skin and eyes if it made contact. If she could find something to protect her own skin and eyes, she could ambush Roth and make a run for it.

Into the dangerous cold and wind, without shoes. Nikki went to the closet and tried not to pay attention to the various bondage devices and other torture mechanisms. She crouched down and inspected the shoes lined neatly across the floor. Some were men's, some were women's, with a variety of sizes.

Roth's victims' shoes. He'd probably kept them as trophies. Nikki hated to disrespect the dead, but she had to get out of here. She grabbed the tennis shoes that looked closer to her size and slipped them on. Her heart pounded against her chest. How was she going to do this? Roth could see the whole room when he opened the door. His laugh drifted through the cheap paneling. She couldn't count on his being gone very long.

Think, Nicole.

Her gaze fell on the insulation again. She shuffled back to the exposed section and took her socks off. Nikki slipped them on her hands to protect her skin and then peeled off a long, thick layer of insulation. She took the shoestring out of one of the Nikes and used it to secure the insulation to the bottom of the shoe, and then did the same with the other foot. She put the socks back on and then the shoes. Footsteps came from somewhere in the next room. Nikki crawled back into bed. She grabbed the blanket at the edge of the bed and pulled it over her, shifting her weight so that her knees touched her chest, her feet together. When Roth got close enough, she'd yank back the blanket and kick him in the face.

Her heart pounded as she waited for him to return. She heard the sound of the deadbolt being pulled back, followed by the two other locks. Nikki pulled the blanket to her chin and hoped she looked cold enough to fool him.

TWENTY-THREE

"Now, where were we?" Roth asked, closing the door behind him. "I apologize for the chilly room. This was my grandparents' old trailer. I only come here when I'm... well, you know."

"Your Roma grandparents?"

"Yes," Roth said. "They were fortune tellers. Well, my grandmother. Grandpa just put on a show. But my grandmother predicted some oddly accurate things."

"I know," Nikki said. The memory she'd been fighting since she realized who Roth was might be the only thing that would buy her enough time to escape. "I saw her a couple of months before my parents' murder. During some town festival. The gypsies... sorry, Roma, had a couple of tents, selling crafts and stuff. My best friend and I thought it would be funny to have our fortunes told."

"I know. I watched through the gap in the door. I recognized you from school, the popular girl who'd been nice to me. I always wondered what Ya-Ya told you."

"Ya-Ya? That's what you called her?" Nikki tried not to wonder how many other times he'd spied on her back then.

"It's Greek for 'grandmother,'" Roth said. "That's where my

family originally migrated to before eventually coming here. The Romani word is *puri mai*, but I couldn't say it when I was little. What did she tell you?"

Nikki's muscles tensed as she spoke. She hadn't told this to anyone, including Rory. "Your grandmother said death was coming to my house. And that it would follow me all of my life."

"Did you believe her?"

"No, but she scared us. When my parents were killed, I tried to find her, but I didn't know where she lived. Not that she could have done anything, but I wanted to know what she saw."

Roth looked genuinely sad. "I wish I'd known you needed her. I would have made sure she spoke to you."

Was he serious? Even now, Roth sounded like a distinguished professor rather than someone who could rape a man so violently he'd ripped his skin. He'd fooled her completely.

Roth walked toward the bed. Beneath the blanket, Nikki flexed her toes, making sure her feet hadn't gone numb again. Her heart beat so loud against her chest it hurt. She felt breathless from trying to be still and act normal. Roth started to sit down on the edge of the bed as he'd done before. Nikki yanked the dirty quilt back and kicked him in the face as hard as she could. Roth shouted in surprise, his arms moving to his face. She kicked him in the side and jumped to her feet. Nikki grabbed the door handle. Roth's hand closed around her ankle.

"You bitch. I trusted you."

His fair skin was already irritated from the insulation, his eyes watering. Blood trickled from his nose. Before he could grab her other ankle, Nikki lifted her foot and brought it down on his hand, grinding the fiberglass insulation into his skin. Roth shouted and loosened his grip enough for her to pull her ankle free.

Nikki sloughed off the insulation from her shoes and ran down the short hallway, slamming into an old recliner. She barely noticed, desperately searching for the trailer's front door.

Roth had gotten to his feet in the bedroom. He shouted at her. Nikki reached the front door and fought with the lock.

Roth stormed down the hall. She finally wrenched the door open and sprinted outside.

It was dark, the full moon illuminating the snow-covered trees. Bitter cold air chapped her face and stung her lungs, but Nikki didn't stop running.

She ran down the narrow, plowed driveway with no idea how long it was or where she was headed. The moon's position might help her figure out which direction she needed to go, but Nikki couldn't stop to think. She had to keep running until her legs gave out or...

Headlights suddenly shined from behind her. She glanced over her shoulder and saw Roth bearing down in his Audi. The ill-fitting shoes slowed her pace, but Nikki tried to dive out of the car's way. Pain exploded in her hip as the vehicle made contact. Her body flew through the air and landed in an ice-covered snowbank.

Nikki tried to stand, but the pain in her leg was excruciating. Her head hurt from the impact, and fresh vomit boiled in her stomach. She managed to roll over on her back. She wanted to see Roth's face when he attacked.

She stared at the clear night sky. Was it clear in Florida too? A sob started deep in her stomach at the thought of her daughter. Lacey would be raised by Tyler's parents. Nikki had barely survived losing her own at sixteen, and Lacey was so young. How could her baby get through life without her?

Roth still hadn't come. Nikki couldn't just lie here and wait, but her leg was definitely broken. She twisted her neck to get a better look and nearly screamed. Her tibia stuck out of her leg, blood pooling on the snow.

At least the bitter cold would buy her time from bleeding out. Her tears had frozen on her cheeks. Every time she tried to sit up, vertigo dragged her back down.

Nikki worked to roll back over and used her good leg to try to crawl, but her body seemed rooted to the spot. Roth was probably watching and enjoying the show. If he did have cancer, Nikki prayed his end was excruciating.

An engine rumbled. Nikki heard shouts. And then a gunshot. Half delirious from pain, Nikki wondered if Roth had decided to shoot her and be done with it.

"Her bag's in his damn car!" a familiar voice shouted. "She's here somewhere."

Nikki almost cried at the sound of Rory's voice. How had he found her? How far from the driveway had she been thrown? What if she lay here in the snow and froze to death while they were searching? Between the wind and cold, it wouldn't take long for snow to cover her entire body.

"Nikki!" Rory's voice carried through the air.

"Here," she tried to say. The words caught in her dry throat. Nikki gulped snow down like water and tried again.

This time, she screamed.

EPILOGUE

Nikki must have frozen to death. Her fingers and toes were stiff. Yet the air around her felt warm against her face. Someone had slathered her chapped cheeks with petroleum jelly or something as equally messy. Her right arm seemed much heavier than the other.

Nikki groaned. "Get this off me." She tried to lift the splinted arm, but a woman shushed her.

"You dislocated your shoulder, honey. It needs to stay immobile." A gentle hand smoothed her hair back.

For one glorious moment, Nikki thought her mother had come to her bedside like she'd done when Nikki was little. Her mom would sit next to her when she had a fever or felt bad, stroking her hair and telling silly stories. Then she'd bring Nikki 7 Up and chocolate-chip cookies.

Nikki willed her eyes to open. "Ruth?"

"Rory's just gone to the bathroom," Ruth said. "He'll be right back." She put a fresh straw in the pink, plastic cup sitting on the small table next to the bed. "Water. Drink."

Nikki slowly sipped the water while Ruth fussed with the

stiff hospital blanket, tucking it around Nikki's chin with shaking hands. "It's good to hear your voice, honey."

"How did I get here?"

Ruth turned around. "Mark, why don't you tell her?"

Nikki heard the sound of a chair moving against the tile floor, and Mark lumbered into her still-fuzzy vision. "You know, Walsh, this is twice I've saved your ass." His tone was light, but he looked pale and tired. Only Mark would still call her by her maiden name Walsh, just as he'd done when they were kids.

"What?"

"I'll try to keep it short," Mark said. "That doctor—Roth—interviewed John Banks this afternoon. I guess he's interviewed him for his research before, but today the guy asked John a lot of weird questions about you and mentioned you were working together. They talked about how long John had gotten away with killing your mom and dad, and how you were so strong now." Mark adjusted his baseball cap, bouncing on the balls of his feet the way he always did when he told a story. "Roth said something about you being the greatest catch. He gave John a really bad vibe. Word got around last night that an FBI agent was missing, and he put it together. He knew the FBI and police wouldn't take him seriously, so he called me."

Nikki struggled to process what Mark was saying. "I don't understand. Why would he have your number?"

"I spent a long time in that prison," Mark said. "I have friends. I go back and see them. A couple have my cell number. John used the rest of his phone minutes for this month to call me. Rory and I were already out searching, and so were Miller and Liam and every other cop. They ran Roth's information, and that trailer was registered to him. Liam told us to wait for backup, but Rory wasn't going to wait."

Nikki needed a few seconds to process what he'd said. Of all the people she'd have expected to come to her aid, John Banks was at the bottom of the list.

"Are you telling me that if John Banks hadn't called you, I would be dead right now?" Nikki asked. She should be grateful, and deep down, she was, but the idea of being beholden to the bastard who'd ruined her life and Mark's made her sick to her stomach.

"Basically," Mark said. "For what it's worth, he apologized. I forgave him."

His mother shook her head. "You're a saint. I pray for that man to rot in hell every night." She sighed. "I suppose I should stop that now."

"Did Roth get away? He said he was dying from cancer. I was his final victim, so he'd never be forgotten." Nikki's head had started to clear, and the ringing in her ears had stopped.

"He kept driving after he clipped you with the car," Mark said. "Good thing because Rory had his damned rifle loaded and ready. Idiot. I told him you'd be mad as hell if he got arrested for murder, even if the guy was Roth."

"Still would have done it." Rory had returned from the bathroom. He hurried over to the other side of the bed and rested his forehead against Nikki's. Tears brimmed in his eyes. "I was so scared, Nik. Please don't put me through that again."

Nikki's throat was too tight with emotion to speak. She touched Rory's chapped lips and then the angry-looking skin on his cheek. "What happened?"

"Dumbass remembered his gun, but not winter gear," Mark said. "I think it makes him look more manly and less like a pretty boy, you know?"

Rory flipped Mark off.

"Both of you stop that right now," Ruth hissed. "We're in a hospital, for Pete's sake."

"They caught him, though, right?"

"Yep," Mark said. "Miller had roadblocks set up everywhere. Roth tried to outrun them and wound up in the ditch. I think they stitched him up and took him to jail."

"Did Miller and Liam get the flash drive he gave me? It was in my pocket." Nikki's throat felt raw from the cold, but she needed to make sure the flash drive had been recovered.

Rory nodded. "You don't remember the ambulance ride?"

"The last thing I remember is flying through the air," she said.

"You were in and out of it on the way to the hospital," he said. "You kept trying to get something out of your pocket and mumbling that Liam needed it. You told me to give it to him, and I did."

"Roth claimed his victims' locations were on it."

"They were," Rory said. "He texted me earlier and told me to tell you there were at least thirty more victims in New Mexico, Nebraska, Kansas and Arizona. He and Miller are coordinating with the other agencies to sort it out. I'm supposed to tell you that it's your turn to be the invalid. Oh, and that Roth had receipts for a tanning salon in his wallet. He made a big deal about his vacation, but Liam said he was in town the whole time. The sun burn was part of his alibi. Bastard thought ahead."

"Did Roth lie about the cancer?" Nikki asked. She didn't want him to have the satisfaction of dying instead of rotting in prison.

"We don't know," Mark said. "I hope not, because if he isn't dying, he's going to end up in Oak Park with John and Oliver. They're bad dudes, but they both care about you in really twisted ways. He'll be dealt with."

"I told Lacey you had the flu," Rory said, worry lines between his eyes. "I didn't want to lie to her, but I wasn't sure what you would want me to say, and she's been through so much. If she knew how close she came to losing you..."

"You did the right thing." Nikki wrapped her arm around Rory's neck and took Mark's hand with the other. "Thank you. You guys risked your lives for me. I owe you everything."

Ruth patted Nikki's arm. "Sweetheart, we're family. We stick together."

A LETTER FROM STACY

Thank you so much for reading the Nikki Hunt series. It's still hard to believe how much readers have bonded with her! I have so much fun writing the books and I hope you enjoy reading them just as much. If you want to be notified about new releases in the series, just sign up at the link below. Your email address will never be shared, and you can unsubscribe at any time.

www.bookouture.com/stacy-green

One of the best parts about storytelling is hearing from the readers. If you loved the book, please take a moment to leave a review.

I love hearing from readers, and you can reach me on Facebook, Twitter, or Instagram.

Stay safe and healthy,

Stacy

facebook.com/StacyGreenAuthor

twitter.com/StacyGreen26

instagram.com/authorstacygreen

ACKNOWLEDGMENTS

Writing a book really is a group effort, and I want to make sure I thank everyone who helped with *Her Frozen Heart*. It was a big idea that was tough to execute, and I'm so grateful for the fantastic editors at Bookouture and their patience with my always-changing schedule.

To John Kelly, thank you so much for the time you spent telling me about Big Marine Lake and Washington County. I wouldn't have the small details without you, and those are what brings the book to life.

To Kristine, thanks for your faith in me and the push to write. Thank you to Jan for being a second mom and grandma to Grace. Thanks to Rob and Grace for being so supportive and encouraging.

Many thanks to Jill Olivia at the Minnesota Bureau of Investigation for her help with warrants and legal procedures.

Finally, thank you to my readers for embracing the Nikki Hunt series. I can't wait to share the next chapter with you!

Printed in Great Britain
by Amazon

87708530R00150